Who

Who Goes There?

JOHN W. CAMPBELL

The right of John W. Campbell to be identified as the author
of this work has been asserted by him in accordance with the
Copyright, Designs and Patents Act 1988.

This edition first published in Great Britain in 2011 by
Gollancz
An imprint of the Orion Publishing Group
Orion House, 5 Upper St Martin's Lane,
London WC2H 9EA
An Hachette UK Company

9 10 8

A CIP catalogue record for this book is
available from the British Library

ISBN 978 0 575 09103 0

Typeset by Deltatype Ltd, Birkenhead, Merseyside

Printed in Great Britain by
Clays Ltd, Elcograf S.p.A.

The Orion Publishing Group's policy is to use papers that
are natural, renewable and recyclable products and made
from wood grown in sustainable forests. The logging
and manufacturing processes are expected to conform
to the environmental regulations of the country of origin.

www.orionbooks.co.uk

To

Dona S.

For

More help than supplying a pen name

Contents

Introduction

Basically, science-fiction is an effort to predict the future on the basis of known facts, culled largely from present-day science laboratories. Within that broad field – and it is exceedingly broad, indeed, far more so, in fact, than even modern science-fiction readers fully realize – there are many species, types, and families of story material. The dividing up of the field of science-fiction into classes and groups is a task literary dissectors are only starting on. I'm not an expert in that field – my division is purely the rule-of-thumb method of the story-teller, not the analytical method of the critic.

To me, there are three broad types – the gadget story, the concept story, and the character story. In those broad groups, there will of course be more or less cross-over between types, but those classifications serve to help an author get started building. In this volume, the gadget story and the concept story predominate. *Elimination* is perhaps the nearest to the pure-gadget story, but it is a study of the effect of a device upon the human character of the inventor; the unstated proposition being that the one and only way for the discoverers to attain their goal is to ignore – to destroy and forget – their invention. Which is, of course, the one thing that they, as human scientists, couldn't possibly do. To a large extent too, *Frictional Losses* is a gadget story, as is *Blindness*. But in *Blindness* there is much more cross-over with the character-type story than there is in *Frictional Losses*.

The other stories in the book are concept-stories. Where *Elimination* starts, for instance, with the author's consideration of 'What if a man invented a time-viewer which—' and proceeds from the interaction of the gadget and the man, *Twilight* – and its sequel, *Night* – originated with the concept of men who had forgotten their greatness, lonely and puzzled and unimportant in the immense majesty of the past accomplishments of their race. It is almost purely an effort to put across to the reader the mood and the feeling of that concept. It predicts no particular scientific advance, nor does it study a character as an individual – it's simply an effort to share a conception, a pure feeling. It's an effort to do, with words, what certain melodies and songs can do in evoking pure emotions. 'Stardust' or 'Memories' do it for some; 'Finlandia' has the same emotion-stirring power on a different order, for others. *Twilight* was the first Don A. Stuart story, and it was done in an effort to determine three things: 1. Could it be done in science-fiction? 2. Could I do it? 3. Would it be liked and accepted if I did?

Incidentally, *Twilight* had a unique record; it was submitted to and immediately bounced by every science-fiction and fantasy magazine in the business when it was first written. Only after Astounding had changed hands and been re-issued by Street & Smith was the story accepted and published. Usually editors do a fair job of guessing their reader's reactions; that time they did miss, because despite the fact that it was entirely different from any science-fiction that had appeared before, it was immediately liked. It led to the development of the Don A. Stuart stories, and thus to the modern Astounding.

Who Goes There? is a quite different mood-concept story. In a sense, the Alien of *Who Goes There?* could be considered a gadget – a non-mechanical gadget. But the emphasis of the story is on putting over to the reader a feeling of the inescapable tension and fear brooding in the Antarctic camp. If *Twilight's* mood is in the direction of 'Stardust,' *Who Goes There?* heads off toward 'Night On Bald Mountain.' Yet they have the fundamental similarity that each is an effort to provoke a certain special mood-reaction in the reader.

One of the real problems of the science-fiction author is to select the method of application of a gadget idea; a basically good idea can, many times, give you more trouble in working out a story than a weak idea. The weak idea *has* to have a strong story to get anywhere at all; the strong idea may tempt the author into using it as a crutch to carry a weak story.

The story *Blindness*, as a matter of fact, was such a problem – the real idea of the story being the one finally used as the snapper. Although the yarn was developed through 95% of its length as a straight character story so far as its telling goes, its inception was, nevertheless, that of a gadget story. In mulling over the basic idea of the wonderful heat-to-electric power alloy, stories ranging from domes on the burning hot deserts of Mercury to how to build an atomic engine with the alloy as the energy-converter were considered, tried, and died dismally on my hands. *Frictional Losses* was another one that I couldn't get anywhere with; I tried at least fifteen different plots all of which went incredibly flat about Page 25.

But that's the fun of science-fiction writing; the plotting is as nearly 100% uninhibited as anything imaginable. If the idea doesn't fit in with conditions of Earth, you're free to invent a planet where it will fit – so long as you don't defy some obvious law of Nature. A planet with an atmosphere of hydrogen and chlorine lit by a blue-white star, for instance, isn't simply another fantastic world somewhere in space – it's a non-existent nightmare. Hydrogen and chlorine combine explosively when illuminated by blue and blue-violet light; that atmosphere couldn't possibly exist.

But don't pull any boners of that nature – and you can set up a world to play with as you like. You can consider any social structure you like, carried to any extreme you need, to bring out your points. One thing, and one thing only, is properly demanded of the story, once its reasonable premise is set forth: the story must be self-consistent from there on. Then, science-fiction is the freest, least formularized of any literary medium. In this field, the reader can never be sure just how the author may wind up – and because the author feels that freedom, he can let the story have its head, let it develop in any direction that the logic of the developing situations may dictate. Many times a story actually winds up entirely different from the idea with which the author started. And, very rarely, an author can simply start a story, and let it work its own way out to a conclusion!

I tried that trick many times – but once and only once did it work out into a satisfactory yarn for me. And that one time I had one definite, basic plan in mind. You see, in science-fiction, the ordinary detective story is impossible; it can't be fair to the reader because of the very freedom of science-fiction that allows the author to invent new devices, even new cultural patterns, during the course of the story. To an extent that few detective story readers realize, the modern murder mystery is bound by a very rigid code. At one time, the murder 'by an unidentifiable South American jungle poison he had picked up somewhere in his wanderings' was considered legitimate; today, even that small amount of freedom isn't permitted. Now in science-fiction, the murder in the locked room may have been committed by entering the room via time-machine before it was locked, or after the corpse was found, and time-travelling back to the fatal hour. Or the murderer may have invented invisibility, or a fourth-dimensional snickersnee that can reach into a three-dimensional room and do its dirty work.

Nevertheless, a mystery story can be written for science-fiction. Logically, to be fair, the conclusions should be drawn from the material supplied in the first parts of the story. So *Dead Knowledge* was written as a mystery story. It was, in full truth, a mystery to me when I wrote the first three-quarters!

But no matter what the type – science-fiction is fun!

JOHN W. CAMPBELL

New York, N.Y.
2 February, 1948

Who Goes There?

The place stank. A queer, mingled stench that only the ice-buried cabins of an Antarctic camp know, compounded of reeking human sweat, and the heavy, fish-oil stench of melted seal blubber. An overtone of liniment combated the musty smell of sweat-and-snow-drenched furs. The acrid odor of burnt cooking fat, and the animal, not-unpleasant smell of dogs, diluted by time, hung in the air.

Lingering odors of machine oil contrasted sharply with the taint of harness dressing and leather. Yet, somehow, through all that reek of human beings and their associates – dogs, machines, and cooking – came another taint. It was a queer, neck-ruffling thing, a faintest suggestion of an odor alien among the smells of industry and life. And it was a life-smell. But it came from the thing that lay bound with cord and tarpaulin on the table, dripping slowly, methodically onto the heavy planks, dank and gaunt under the unshielded glare of the electric light.

Blair, the little bald-pated biologist of the expedition, twitched nervously at the wrappings, exposing clear, dark ice beneath and then pulling the tarpaulin back into place restlessly. His little birdlike motions of suppressed eagerness danced his shadow across the fringe of dingy gray underwear hanging from the low ceiling, the equatorial fringe of stiff, graying hair around his naked skull a comical halo about the shadow's head.

Commander Garry brushed aside the lax legs of a suit of underwear, and stepped toward the table. Slowly his eyes traced around the rings of men sardined into the Administration Building. His tall, stiff body straightened finally, and he nodded. 'Thirty-seven. All here.' His voice was low, yet carried the clear authority of the commander by nature, as well as by title.

'You know the outline of the story back of that find of the Secondary Pole Expedition. I have been conferring with Second-in-Command McReady, and Norris, as well as Blair and Dr Copper. There is a difference of opinion, and because it involves the entire group, it is only just that the entire Expedition personnel act on it.

'I am going to ask McReady to give you the details of the story, because each of you has been too busy with his own work to follow closely the endeavors of the others. McReady?'

Moving from the smoke-blued background, McReady was a figure from some forgotten myth, a looming, bronze statue that held life, and walked. Six feet four inches he stood as he halted beside the table, and with a characteristic glance upward to assure himself of room under the low ceiling beams, straightened. His rough, clashingly orange windproof jacket he still had on, yet on his huge frame it did not seem misplaced. Even here, four feet beneath the drift-wind that droned across the Antarctic waste above the ceiling, the cold of the frozen continent leaked in, and gave meaning to the harshness of the man. And he was bronze – his great red-bronze beard, the heavy hair that matched it. The gnarled, corded hands gripping, relaxing, gripping and relaxing on the table planks were bronze. Even the deep-sunken eyes beneath heavy brows were bronzed.

Age-resisting endurance of the metal spoke in the cragged

heavy outlines of his face, and the mellow tones of the heavy voice. 'Norris and Blair agree on one thing; that animal we found was not – terrestrial in origin. Norris fears there may be danger in that; Blair says there is none.

'But I'll go back to how, and why we found it. To all that was known before we came here, it appeared that this point was exactly over the South Magnetic Pole of Earth. The compass does point straight down here, as you all know. The more delicate instruments of the physicists, instruments especially designed for this expedition and its study of the magnetic pole, detected a secondary effect, a secondary, less powerful magnetic influence about eighty miles southwest of here.

'The Secondary Magnetic Expedition went out to investigate it. There is no need for details. We found it, but it was not the huge meteorite or magnetic mountain Norris had expected to find. Iron ore is magnetic, of course; iron more so – and certain special steels even more magnetic. From the surface indications, the secondary pole we found was small, so small that the magnetic effect it had was preposterous. No magnetic material conceivable could have that effect. Soundings through the ice indicated it was within one hundred feet of the glacier surface.

'I think you should know the structure of the place. There is a broad plateau, a level sweep that runs more than 150 miles due south from the Secondary Station, Van Wall says. He didn't have time or fuel to fly farther, but it was running smoothly due south then. Right there, where that buried thing was, there is an ice-drowned mountain ridge, a granite wall of unshakable strength that has dammed back the ice creeping from the south.

'And four hundred miles due south is the South Polar

Plateau. You have asked me at various times why it gets warmer here when the wind rises, and most of you know. As a meteorologist I'd have staked my word that no wind could blow at -70 degrees; that no more than a five-mile wind could blow at -50; without causing warming due to friction with ground, snow and ice and the air itself.

'We camped there on the lip of that ice-drowned mountain range for twelve days. We dug our camp into the blue ice that formed the surface, and escaped most of it. But for twelve consecutive days the wind blew at 45 miles an hour. It went as high as 48, and fell to 41 at times. The temperature was -63 degrees. It rose to -60 and fell to -68. It was meteorologically impossible, and it went on uninterruptedly for twelve days and twelve nights.

'Somewhere to the south, the frozen air of the South Polar Plateau slides down from that 18,000-foot bowl, down a mountain pass, over a glacier, and starts north. There must be a funneling mountain chain that directs it, and sweeps it away for 400 miles to hit that bald plateau where we found the secondary pole, and 350 miles farther north reaches the Antarctic Ocean.

'It's been frozen there since Antarctica froze twenty million years ago. There never has been a thaw there.

'Twenty million years ago Antarctica was beginning to freeze. We've investigated, though, and built speculations. What we believe happened was about like this.

'Something came down out of space, a ship. We saw it there in the blue ice, a thing like a submarine without a conning tower or directive vanes, 280 feet long and 45 feet in diameter at its thickest.

'Eh, Van Wall? Space? Yes, but I'll explain that better later.' McReady's steady voice went on.

'It came down from space, driven and lifted by forces men haven't discovered yet, and somehow – perhaps something went wrong then – it tangled with Earth's magnetic field. It came south here, out of control probably, circling the magnetic pole. That's a savage country there; but when Antarctica was still freezing, it must have been a thousand times more savage. There must have been blizzard snow, as well as drift, new snow falling as the continent glaciated. The swirl there must have been particularly bad, the wind hurling a solid blanket of white over the lip of that now-buried mountain.

'The ship struck solid granite head-on, and cracked up. Not every one of the passengers in it was killed, but the ship must have been ruined, her driving mechanism locked. It tangled with Earth's field, Norris believes. No thing made by intelligent beings can tangle with the dead immensity of a planet's natural forces and survive.

'One of its passengers stepped out. The wind we saw there never fell below 41, and the temperature never rose above -60. Then – the wind must have been stronger. And there was drift falling in a solid sheet. The *thing* was lost completely in ten paces.' He paused for a moment, the deep, steady voice giving way to the drone of wind overhead and the uneasy, malicious gurgling in the pipe of the galley stove.

Drift – a drift-wind was sweeping by overhead. Right now the snow picked up by the mumbling wind fled in level, blinding lines across the face of the buried camp. If a man stepped out of the tunnels that connected each of the camp buildings beneath the surface, he'd be lost in ten paces. Out there, the slim, black finger of the radio mast lifted 300 feet into the air, and at its peak was the clear night sky. A sky of thin, whining wind rushing steadily from beyond to another beyond under the licking, curling mantle of the aurora. And off north, the horizon flamed with queer, angry colors of the midnight twilight. That was Spring 300 feet above Antarctica.

At the surface – it was white death. Death of a needle-fingered cold driven before the wind, sucking heat from any warm thing. Cold – and white mist of endless, everlasting drift, the fine, fine particles of licking snow that obscured all things.

Kinner, the little, scar-faced cook, winced. Five days ago he had stepped out to the surface to reach a cache of frozen beef. He had reached it, started back – and the drift-wind leapt out of the south. Cold, white death that streamed across the ground blinded him in twenty seconds. He stumbled on wildly in circles. It was half an hour before rope-guided men from below found him in the impenetrable murk.

It was easy for man – or *thing* – to get lost in ten paces.

'And the drift-wind then was probably more impenetrable than we know.' McReady's voice snapped Kinner's mind back. Back to the welcome, dank warmth of the Ad Building. 'The passenger of the ship wasn't prepared either, it appears. It froze within ten feet of the ship.

'We dug down to find the ship, and our tunnel happened to find the frozen – animal. Barclay's ice-ax struck its skull.

'When we saw what it was, Barclay went back to the tractor, started the fire up and when the steam pressure built, sent a call for Blair and Dr Copper. Barclay himself was sick then. Stayed sick for three days, as a matter of fact.

'When Blair and Copper came, we cut out the animal in a block of ice, as you see, wrapped it and loaded it on the tractor for return here. We wanted to get into that ship.

6

'We reached the side and found the metal was something we didn't know. Our beryllium-bronze, non-magnetic tools wouldn't touch it. Barclay had some tool-steel on the tractor, and that wouldn't scratch it either. We made reasonable tests – even tried some acid from the batteries with no results.

'They must have had a passivating process to make magnesium metal resist acid that way, and the alloy must have been at least 95 per cent magnesium. But we had no way of guessing that, so when we spotted the barely opened lock door, we cut around it. There was clear, hard ice inside the lock, where we couldn't reach it. Through the little crack we could look in and see that only metal and tools were in there, so we decided to loosen the ice with a bomb.

'We had decanite bombs and thermite. Thermite is the ice-softener; decanite might have shattered valuable things, where the thermite's heat would just loosen the ice. Dr. Copper, Norris and I placed a 25-pound thermite bomb, wired it, and took the connector up the tunnel to the surface, where Blair had the steam tractor waiting. A hundred yards the other side of that granite wall we set off the thermite bomb.

'The magnesium metal of the ship caught of course. The glow of the bomb flared and died, then it began to flare again. We ran back to the tractor, and gradually the glare built up. From where we were we could see the whole ice-field illuminated from beneath with an unbearable light; the ship's shadow was a great, dark cone reaching off toward the north, where the twilight was just about gone. For a moment it lasted, and we counted three other shadow-things that might have been other – passengers – frozen there. Then the ice was crashing down and against the ship.

'That's why I told you about that place. The wind sweeping down from the Pole was at our backs. Steam and hydrogen flame were torn away in white ice-fog; the flaming heat under the ice there was yanked away toward the Antarctic Ocean before it touched us. Otherwise we wouldn't have come back, even with the shelter of that granite ridge that stopped the light.

'Somehow in the blinding inferno we could see great hunched things – black bulks. They shed even the furious incandescence of the magnesium for a time. Those must have been the engines, we knew. Secrets going in blazing glory – secrets that might have given Man the planets. Mysterious things that could lift and hurl that ship – and had soaked in the force of the Earth's magnetic field. I saw Norris' mouth move, and ducked. I couldn't hear him.

'Insulation – something – gave way. All Earth's field they'd soaked up twenty million years before broke loose. The aurora in the sky above licked down, and the whole plateau there was bathed in cold fire that blanketed vision. The ice-ax in my hand got red hot, and hissed on the ice. Metal buttons on my clothes burned into me. And a flash of electric blue seared upward from beyond the granite wall.

'Then the walls of ice crashed down on it. For an instant it squealed the way dry ice does when it's pressed between metal.

'We were blind and groping in the dark for hours while our eyes recovered. We found every coil within a mile was fused rubbish, the dynamo and every radio set, the earphones and speakers. If we hadn't had the steam tractor, we wouldn't have gotten over to the Secondary Camp.

'Van Wall flew in from Big Magnet at sun-up, as you know. We came home as soon as possible. That is the history of – that.' McReady's great bronze beard gestured toward the thing on the table.

II

Blair stirred uneasily, his little, bony fingers wriggling under the harsh light. Little brown freckles on his knuckles slid back and forth as the tendons under the skin twitched. He pulled aside a bit of the tarpaulin and looked impatiently at the dark ice-bound thing inside.

McReady's big body straightened somewhat. He'd ridden the rocking, jarring steam tractor forty miles that day, pushing on to Big Magnet here. Even his calm will had been pressed by the anxiety to mix again with humans. It was lone and quiet out there in Secondary Camp, where a wolf-wind howled down from the Pole. Wolf-wind howling in his sleep – winds droning and the evil, unspeakable face of that monster leering up as he'd first seen it through clear, blue ice, with a bronze ice-ax buried in its skull.

The giant meteorologist spoke again. 'The problem is this. Blair wants to examine the thing. Thaw it out and make micro slides of its tissues and so forth. Norris doesn't believe that is safe, and Blair does. Dr Copper agrees pretty much with Blair. Norris is a physicist, of course, not a biologist. But he makes a point I think we should all hear. Blair has described the microscopic life-forms biologists find living, even in this cold and inhospitable place. They freeze every winter, and thaw every summer – for three months – and live.

'The point Norris makes is – they thaw, and live again. There must have been microscopic life associated with this creature. There is with every living thing we know. And Norris is afraid that we may release a plague – some germ

9

disease unknown to Earth – if we thaw those microscopic things that have been frozen there for twenty million years.

'Blair admits that such micro-life might retain the power of living. Such unorganized things as individual cells can retain life for unknown periods, when solidly frozen. The beast itself is as dead as those frozen mammoths they find in Siberia. Organized, highly developed life-forms can't stand that treatment.

'But micro-life could. Norris suggests that we may release some disease-form that man, never having met it before, will be utterly defenseless against.

'Blair's answer is that there may be such still-living germs, but that Norris has the case reversed. They are utterly non-immune to man. Our life-chemistry probably—'

'Probably!' The little biologist's head lifted in a quick, birdlike motion. The halo of gray hair about his bald head ruffled as though angry. 'Heh, one look—'

'I know,' McReady acknowledged. 'The thing is not Earthly. It does not seem likely that it can have a life-chemistry sufficiently like ours to make cross-infection remotely possible. I would say that there is no danger.'

McReady looked toward Dr Copper. The physician shook his head slowly. 'None whatever,' he asserted confidently. 'Man cannot infect or be infected by germs that live in such comparatively close relatives as the snakes. And they are, I assure you,' his clean-shaven face grimaced uneasily, '*much nearer to us than – that.*'

Vance Norris moved angrily. He was comparatively short in this gathering of big men, some five feet eight, and his stocky, powerful build tended to make him seem shorter. His black hair was crisp and hard, like short, steel wires, and his eyes were the gray of fractured steel. If McReady was a man of bronze, Norris was all steel. His movements, his thoughts, his whole bearing had the quick, hard impulse of a steel spring. His nerves were steel – hard, quick acting – swift corroding.

He was decided on his point now, and he lashed out in its defense with a characteristic quick, clipped flow of words. 'Different chemistry be damned. That thing may be dead – or, by God, it may not – but I don't like it. Damn it, Blair, let them see the monstrosity you are petting over there. Let them see the foul thing and decide for themselves whether they want that thing thawed out in this camp.

'Thawed out, by the way. That's got to be thawed out in one of the shacks tonight, if it is thawed out. Somebody – who's watchman tonight? Magnetic – oh, Connant. Cosmic rays tonight. Well, you get to sit up with that twenty-million-year-old mummy of his. Unwrap it, Blair. How the hell can they tell what they are buying, if they can't see it? It may have a different chemistry. I don't care what else it has, but I know it has something I don't want. If you can judge by the look on its face – it isn't human so maybe you can't – it was annoyed when it froze. Annoyed, in fact, is just about as close an approximation of the way it felt, as crazy, mad, insane hatred. Neither one touches the subject.

'How the hell can these birds tell what they are voting on? They haven't seen those three red eyes and that blue hair like crawling worms. Crawling – damn, it's crawling there in the ice right now!

'Nothing Earth ever spawned had the unutterable sublimation of devastating wrath that thing let loose in its face when it looked around its frozen desolation twenty million years ago. Mad? It was mad clear through – searing, blistering mad!

'Hell, I've had bad dreams ever since I looked at those three red eyes. Nightmares. Dreaming the thing thawed out and came to life – that it wasn't dead, or even wholly unconscious all those twenty million years, but just slowed, waiting – waiting. You'll dream, too, while that damned thing that Earth wouldn't own is dripping, dripping in the Cosmos House tonight.

'And, Connant,' Norris whipped toward the cosmic ray specialist, 'won't you have fun sitting up all night in the quiet. Wind whining above – and that thing dripping—' he stopped for a moment, and looked around.

'I know. That's not science. But this is, it's psychology. You'll have nightmares for a year to come. Every night since I looked at that thing I've had 'em. That's why I hate it – sure I do – and don't want it around. Put it back where it came from and let it freeze for another twenty million years. I had some swell nightmares – that it wasn't made like we are – which is obvious – but of a different kind of flesh that it can really control. That it can change its shape, and look like a man – and wait to kill and eat—

'That's not a logical argument. I know it isn't. The thing isn't Earth-logic anyway.

'Maybe it has an alien body-chemistry, and maybe its bugs do have a different body-chemistry. A germ might not stand that, but, Blair and Copper, how about a virus? That's just an enzyme molecule, you've said. That wouldn't need anything but a protein molecule of any body to work on.

'And how are you so sure that, of the million varieties of microscopic life it may have, *none* of them are dangerous. How about diseases like hydrophobia – rabies – that attack any warm-blooded creature, whatever its body-chemistry may be? And parrot fever? Have you a body like a parrot,

12

Blair? And plain rot – gangrene – necrosis if you want? *That* isn't choosy about body chemistry!'

Blair looked up from his puttering long enough to meet Norris' angry, gray eyes for an instant. 'So far the only thing you have said this thing gave off that was catching was dreams. I'll go so far as to admit that.' An impish, slightly malignant grin crossed the little man's seamed face. 'I had some, too. So. It's dream-infectious. No doubt an exceedingly dangerous malady.

'So far as your other things go, you have a badly mistaken idea about viruses. In the first place, nobody has shown that the enzyme-molecule theory, and that alone, explains them. And in the second place, when you catch tobacco mosaic or wheat rust, let me know. A wheat plant is a lot nearer your body-chemistry than this other-world creature is.

'And your rabies is limited, strictly limited. You can't get it from, nor give it to, a wheat plant or a fish – which is a collateral descendant of a common ancestor of yours. Which this, Norris, is not.' Blair nodded pleasantly toward the tarpaulined bulk on the table.

'Well, thaw the damned thing in a tub of formalin if you must. I've suggested that—'

'And I've said there would be no sense in it. You can't compromise. Why did you and Commander Garry come down here to study magnetism? Why weren't you content to stay at home? There's magnetic force enough in New York. I could no more study the life this thing once had from a formalin-pickled sample than you could get the information you wanted back in New York. And – if this one is so treated, *never in all time to come can there be a duplicate!* The race it came from must have passed away in the twenty million years it lay frozen, so that even if it came from Mars

13

then, we'd never find its like. And – the ship is gone.

'There's only one way to do this – and that is the best possible way. It must be thawed slowly, carefully, and not in formalin.'

Commander Garry stood forward again, and Norris stepped back muttering angrily. 'I think Blair is right, gentlemen. What do you say?'

Connant grunted. 'It sounds right to us, I think – only perhaps he ought to stand watch over it while it's thawing.' He grinned ruefully, brushing a stray lock of ripe-cherry hair back from his forehead. 'Swell idea, in fact – if he sits up with his jolly little corpse.'

Garry smiled slightly. A general chuckle of agreement rippled over the group. 'I should think any ghost it may have had would have starved to death if it hung around here that long, Connant,' Garry suggested. 'And you look capable of taking care of it. 'Ironman' Connant ought to be able to take out any opposing players, still.'

Connant shook himself uneasily. 'I'm not worrying about ghosts. Let's see that thing. I—'

Eagerly Blair was stripping back the ropes. A single throw of the tarpaulin revealed the thing. The ice had melted somewhat in the heat of the room, and it was clear and blue as thick, good glass. It shone wet and sleek under the harsh light of the unshielded globe above.

The room stiffened abruptly. It was face-up there on the plain, greasy planks of the table. The broken haft of the bronze ice-ax was still buried in the queer skull. Three mad, hate-filled eyes blazed up with a living fire, bright as fresh-spilled blood, from a face ringed with a writhing, loathsome nest of worms, blue, mobile worms that crawled where hair should grow—

Van Wall, six feet and 200 pounds of ice-nerved pilot, gave a queer, strangled gasp, and butted, stumbled his way out to the corridor. Half the company broke for the doors. The others stumbled away from the table.

McReady stood at one end of the table watching them, his great body planted solid on his powerful legs. Norris from the opposite end glowered at the thing with smouldering hate. Outside the door, Garry was talking with half a dozen of the men at once.

Blair had a tack hammer. The ice that cased the thing *schluffed* crisply under its steel claw as it peeled from the thing it had cased for twenty thousand thousand years—

III

'I know you don't like the thing, Connant, but it just has to be thawed out right. You say leave it as it is till we get back to civilization. All right, I'll admit your argument that we could do a better and more complete job there is sound. But – how are we going to get this across the Line? We have to take this through one temperate zone, the equatorial zone, and halfway through the other temperate zone before we get it to New York. You don't want to sit with it one night, but you suggest, then, that I hang its corpse in the freezer with the beef?' Blair looked up from his cautious chipping, his bald freckled skull nodding triumphantly.

Kinner, the stocky, scar-faced cook, saved Connant the trouble of answering. 'Hey, you listen, mister. You put that thing in the box with the meat, and by all the gods there ever were, I'll put you in to keep it company. You birds have brought everything movable in this camp in onto my mess tables here already, and I had to stand for that. But you go putting things like that in my meat box, or even my meat cache here, and you cook your own damn grub.'

'But, Kinner, this is the only table in Big Magnet that's big enough to work on,' Blair objected. 'Everybody's explained that.'

'Yeah, and everybody's brought everything in here. Clark brings his dogs every time there's a fight and sews them up on that table. Ralsen brings in his sledges. Hell, the only thing you haven't had on that table is the Boeing. And you'd 'a' had that in if you coulda figured a way to get it through the tunnels.'

Commander Garry chuckled and grinned at Van Wall, the huge Chief Pilot. Van Wall's great blond beard twitched suspiciously as he nodded gravely to Kinner. 'You're right, Kinner. The aviation department is the only one that treats you right.'

'It does get crowded, Kinner,' Garry acknowledged. 'But I'm afraid we all find it that way at times. Not much privacy in an Antarctic camp.'

'Privacy? What the hell's that? You know, the thing that really made me weep, was when I saw Barclay marchin' through here chantin' 'The last lumber in the camp! The last lumber in the camp!' and carryin' it out to build that house on his tractor. Damn it, I missed that moon cut in the door he carried out more'n I missed the sun when it set. That wasn't just the last lumber Barclay was walkin' off with. He was carryin' off the last bit of privacy in this blasted place.'

A grin rode even Connant's heavy face as Kinner's perennial, good-natured grouch came up again. But it died away quickly as his dark, deep-set eyes turned again to the red-eyed thing Blair was chipping from its cocoon of ice. A big hand ruffed his shoulder-length hair, and tugged at a twisted lock that fell behind his ear in a familiar gesture. 'I know that cosmic ray shack's going to be too crowded if I have to sit up with that thing,' he growled. 'Why can't you go on chipping the ice away from around it – you can do that without anybody butting in, I assure you – and then hang the thing up over the power-plant boiler? That's warm enough. It'll thaw out a chicken, even a whole side of beef, in a few hours.'

'I know,' Blair protested, dropping the tack hammer to gesture more effectively with his bony, freckled fingers, his small body tense with eagerness, 'but this is too important to take any chances. There never was a find like this; there never can be again. It's the only chance men will ever have, and it has to be done exactly right.

'Look, you know how the fish we caught down near the Ross Sea would freeze almost as soon as we got them on deck, and come to life again if we thawed them gently? Low forms of life aren't killed by quick freezing and slow thawing. We have—'

'Hey, for the love of Heaven – you mean that damned thing will come to life!' Connant yelled. 'You get the damned thing – Let me at it! That's going to be in so many pieces—'

'No! *No*, you fool—' Blair jumped in front of Connant to protect his precious find. 'No. Just low forms of life. For Pete's sake let me finish. You can't thaw higher forms of life and have them come to. Wait a moment now – hold it! A fish can come to after freezing because it's so low a form of life that the individual cells of its body can revive, and that alone is enough to reestablish life. Any higher forms thawed out that way are dead. Though the individual cells revive, they die because there must be organization and cooperative effort to live. That cooperation cannot be reestablished.

There is a sort of potential life in any uninjured, quick-frozen animal. But it can't – can't under any circumstances – become active life in higher animals. The higher animals are too complex, too delicate. This is an intelligent creature as high in its evolution as we are in ours. Perhaps higher. It is as dead as a frozen man would be.'

'How do you know?' demanded Connant, hefting the ice-ax he had seized a moment before.

Commander Garry laid a restraining hand on his heavy shoulder. 'Wait a minute, Connant. I want to get this straight. I agree that there is going to be no thawing of this thing if there is the remotest chance of its revival. I quite agree it is much too unpleasant to have alive, but I had no idea there was the remotest possibility.'

Dr Copper pulled his pipe from between his teeth and heaved his stocky, dark body from the bunk he had been sitting in. 'Blair's being technical. That's dead. As dead as the mammoths they find frozen in Siberia. We have all sorts of proof that things don't live after being frozen – not even fish, generally speaking – and no proof that higher animal life can under any circumstances. What's the point, Blair?'

The little biologist shook himself. The little ruff of hair standing out around his bald pate waved in righteous anger. 'The point is,' he said in an injured tone, 'that the individual cells might show the characteristics they had in life if it is properly thawed. A man's muscle cells live many hours after he has died. Just because they live, and a few things like hair and fingernail cells still live, you wouldn't accuse a corpse of being a zombie, or something.

'Now if I thaw this right, I may have a chance to determine what sort of world it's native to. We don't, and can't

18

know by any other means, whether it came from Earth or Mars or Venus or from beyond the stars.

'And just because it looks unlike men, you don't have to accuse it of being evil, or vicious or something. Maybe that expression on its face is its equivalent to a resignation to fate. White is the color of mourning to the Chinese. If men can have different customs, why can't a so-different race have different understandings of facial expressions?'

Connant laughed softly, mirthlessly. 'Peaceful resignation! If that is the best it could do in the way of resignation, I should exceedingly dislike seeing it when it was looking mad. That face was never designed to express peace. It just didn't have any philosophical thoughts like peace in its make-up.

'I know it's your pet – but be sane about it. That thing grew up on evil, adolesced slowly roasting alive the local equivalent of kittens, and amused itself through maturity on new and ingenious torture.'

'You haven't the slightest right to say that,' snapped Blair. 'How do you know the first thing about the meaning of a facial expression inherently inhuman? It may well have no human equivalent whatever. That is just a different development of Nature, another example of Nature's wonderful adaptability. Growing on another, perhaps harsher world, it has different form and features. But it is just as much a legitimate child of Nature as you are. You are displaying that childish human weakness of hating the different. On its own world it would probably class you as a fish-belly, white monstrosity with an insufficient number of eyes and a fungoid body pale and bloated with gas.

'Just because its nature is different, you haven't any right to say it's necessarily evil.'

Norris burst out a single, explosive, 'Haw!' He looked down at the thing. 'May be that things from other worlds don't *have* to be evil just because they're different. But that thing *was*! Child of Nature, eh? Well, it was a hell of an evil Nature.'

'Aw, will you mugs cut crabbing at each other and get the damned thing off my table?' Kinner growled. 'And put a canvas over it. It looks indecent.'

'Kinner's gone modest,' jeered Connant.

Kinner slanted his eyes up to the big physicist. The scarred cheek twisted to join the line of his tight lips in a twisted grin. 'All right, big boy, and what were you grousing about a minute ago? We can set the thing in a chair next to you tonight, if you want.'

'I'm not afraid of its face,' Connant snapped. 'I don't like keeping a wake over its corpse particularly, but I'm going to do it.'

Kinner's grin spread. 'Uh-huh.' He went off to the galley stove and shook down ashes vigorously, drowning the brittle chipping of the ice as Blair fell to work again.

IV

'Cluck,' reported the cosmic-ray counter, '*cluck-burrrp-cluck*.'

Connant started and dropped his pencil.

'Damnation.' The physicist looked toward the far corner, back at the Geiger counter on the table near that corner. And crawled under the desk at which he had been working to retrieve the pencil. He sat down at his work again, trying to make his writing more even. It tended to have jerks and quavers in it, in time with the abrupt proud-hen noises of the Geiger counter. The muted whoosh of the pressure lamp he was using for illumination, the mingled gargles and bugle calls of a dozen men sleeping down the corridor in Paradise House formed the background sounds for the irregular, clucking noises of the counter, the occasional rustle of falling coal in the copper-bellied stove. And a soft, steady *drip-drip-drip* from the thing in the corner.

Connant jerked a pack of cigarettes from his pocket, snapped it so that a cigarette protruded, and jabbed the cylinder into his mouth. The lighter failed to function, and he pawed angrily through the pile of papers in search of a match. He scratched the wheel of the lighter several times, dropped it with a curse and got up to pluck a hot coat from the stove with the coal tongs.

The lighter functioned instantly when he tried it on returning to the desk. The counter ripped out a series of chuckling guffaws as a burst of cosmic rays struck through to it. Connant turned to glower at it, and tried to concentrate on the interpretation of data collected during the past week. The weekly summary—

He gave up and yielded to curiosity, or nervousness. He lifted the pressure lamp from the desk and carried it over to the table in the corner. Then he returned to the stove and picked up the coal tongs. The beast had been thawing for nearly 18 hours now. He poked at it with an unconscious caution; the flesh was no longer hard as armor plate, but had assumed a rubbery texture. It looked like wet, blue rubber glistening under droplets of water like little round jewels in the glare of the gasoline pressure lantern. Connant felt an unreasoning desire to pour the contents of the lamp's reservoir over the thing in its box and drop the cigarette into it. The three red eyes glared up at him sightlessly, the ruby eyeballs reflecting murky, smoky rays of light.

He realized vaguely that he had been looking at them for a very long time, even vaguely understood that they were no longer sightless. But it did not seem of importance, of no more importance than the labored, slow motion of the tentacular things that sprouted from the base of the scrawny, slowly pulsing neck.

Connant picked up the pressure lamp and returned to his chair. He sat down, staring at the pages of mathematics before him. The clucking of the counter was strangely less disturbing, the rustle of the coals in the stove no longer distracting.

The creak of the floorboards behind him didn't interrupt his thoughts as he went about his weekly report in an automatic manner, filling in columns of data and making brief, summarizing notes.

The creak of the floorboards sounded nearer.

V

Blair came up from the nightmare-haunted depths of sleep abruptly. Connant's face floated vaguely above him; for a moment it seemed a continuance of the wild horror of the dream. But Connant's face was angry, and a little frightened. 'Blair – Blair you damned log, wake up.'

'Uh-eh?' the little biologist rubbed his eyes, his bony, freckled fingers crooked to a mutilated child-fist. From surrounding bunks other faces lifted to stare down at them.

Connant straightened up. 'Get up – and get a lift on. Your damned animal's escaped.'

'Escaped – what!' Chief Pilot Van Wall's bull voice roared out with a volume that shook the walls. Down the communication tunnels other voices yelled suddenly. The dozen inhabitants of Paradise House tumbled in abruptly, Barclay, stocky and bulbous in long woolen underwear, carrying a fire extinguisher.

'What the hell's the matter?' Barclay demanded.

'Your damned beast got loose. I fell asleep about twenty minutes ago, and when I woke up, the thing was gone. Hey, Doc, the hell you say those things can't come to life. Blair's blasted potential life developed a hell of a lot of potential and walked out on us.'

Copper stared blankly. 'It wasn't – Earthly,' he sighed suddenly. 'I – I guess Earthly laws don't apply.'

'Well, it applied for leave of absence and took it. We've got to find it and capture it somehow.' Connant swore bitterly, his deep-set black eyes sullen and angry. 'It's a wonder the hellish creature didn't eat me in my sleep.'

Blair started back, his pale eyes suddenly fear-struck. 'Maybe it di – er – uh – we'll have to find it.'

'You find it. It's your pet. I've had all I want to do with it, sitting there for seven hours with the counter clucking every few seconds, and you birds in here singing night-music. It's a wonder I got to sleep. I'm going through to the Ad Building.'

Commander Garry ducked through the doorway, pulling his belt tight. 'You won't have to. Van's roar sounded like the Boeing taking off downwind. So it wasn't dead?'

'I didn't carry it off in my arms, I assure you,' Connant snapped. 'The last I saw, the split skull was oozing green goo, like a squashed caterpillar. Doc just said our laws don't work – it's unearthly. Well, it's an unearthly monster, with an unearthly disposition, judging by the face, wandering around with a split skull and brains oozing out.' Norris and McReady appeared in the doorway, a doorway filling with other shivering men. 'Has anybody seen it coming over here?' Norris asked innocently. 'About four feet tall – three red eyes – brains oozing out – Hey, has anybody checked to make sure this isn't a cracked idea of humor? If it is, I think we'll unite in tying Blair's pet around Connant's neck like the Ancient Mariner's albatross.'

'It's no humor,' Connant shivered. 'Lord, I wish it were. I'd rather wear—' He stopped. A wild, weird howl shrieked through the corridors. The men stiffened abruptly, and half turned.

'I think it's been located,' Connant finished. His dark eyes shifted with a queer unease. He darted back to his bunk in Paradise House, to return almost immediately with a heavy .45 revolver and an ice-ax. He hefted both gently as he started for the corridor toward Dogtown.

'It blundered down the wrong corridor – and landed among the huskies. Listen – the dogs have broken their chains—'

The half-terrorized howl of the dog pack had changed to a wild hunting melee. The voices of the dogs thundered in the narrow corridors, and through them came a low rippling snarl of distilled hate. A shrill of pain, a dozen snarling yelps.

Connant broke for the door. Close behind him, McReady, then Barclay and Commander Garry came. Other men broke for the Ad Building, and weapons – the sledge house. Pomroy, in charge of Big Magnet's five cows, started down the corridor in the opposite direction – he had a six-foot-handled, long-tined pitchfork in mind.

Barclay slid to a halt, as McReady's giant bulk turned abruptly away from the tunnel leading to Dogtown, and vanished off at an angle. Uncertainly, the mechanician wavered a moment, the fire extinguisher in his hands, hesitating from one side to the other. Then he was racing after Connant's broad back. Whatever McReady had in mind, he could be trusted to make it work.

Connant stopped at the bend in the corridor. His breath hissed suddenly through his throat. 'Great God—' The revolver exploded thunderously; three numbing, palpable waves of sound crashed through the confined corridors. Two more. The revolver dropped to the hard-packed snow of the trail, and Barclay saw the ice-ax shift into defensive position. Connant's powerful body blocked his vision, but beyond he heard something mewing, and, insanely, chuckling. The dogs were quieter; there was a deadly seriousness in their low snarls. Taloned feet scratched at hard-packed snow, broken chains were clinking and tangling.

Connant shifted abruptly, and Barclay could see what lay beyond. For a second he stood frozen, then his breath went out in a gusty curse. The Thing launched itself at Connant, the powerful arms of the man swung the ice-ax flat-side first at what might have been a head. It scrunched horribly, and the tattered flesh, ripped by a half-dozen savage huskies, leapt to its feet again. The red eyes blazed with an unearthly hatred, an unearthly, unkillable vitality.

Barclay turned the fire extinguisher on it; the blinding, blistering stream of chemical spray confused it, baffled it, together with the savage attacks of the huskies, not for long afraid of anything that did, or could live, and held it at bay.

McReady wedged men out of his way and drove down the narrow corridor packed with men unable to reach the scene. There was a sure foreplanned drive to McReady's attack. One of the giant blowtorches used in warming the plane's engines was in his bronzed hands. It roared gustily as he turned the corner and opened the valve. The mad

25

mewing hissed louder. The dogs scrambled back from the three-foot lance of blue-hot flame.

'Bar, get a power cable, run it in somehow. And a handle. We can electrocute this – monster, if I don't incinerate it.' McReady spoke with an authority of planned action. Barclay turned down the long corridor to the power plant, but already before him Norris and Van Wall were racing down.

Barclay found the cable in the electrical cache in the tunnel wall. In a half minute he was hacking at it, walking back. Van Wall's voice rang out in warning shout of 'Power!' as the emergency gasoline-powered dynamo thudded into action. Half a dozen other men were down there now; the coal, kindling were going into the firebox of the steam power plant. Norris, cursing in a low, deadly monotone, was working with quick, sure fingers on the other end of Barclay's cable, splicing a contractor into one of the power leads.

The dogs had fallen back when Barclay reached the corridor bend, fallen back before a furious monstrosity that glared from baleful red eyes, mewing in trapped hatred. The dogs were a semi-circle of red-dipped muzzles with a fringe of glistening white teeth, whining with a vicious eagerness that near matched the fury of the red eyes. McReady stood confidently alert at the corridor bend, the gustily muttering torch held loose and ready for action in his hands. He stepped aside without moving his eyes from the beast as Barclay came up. There was a slight, tight smile on his lean, bronzed face.

Norris' voice called down the corridor, and Barclay stepped forward. The cable was taped to the long handle of a snow shovel, the two conductors split and held eighteen inches apart by a scrap of lumber lashed at right angles across the far end of the handle. Bare copper conductors, charged with 220 volts, glinted in the light of pressure lamps. The Thing mewed and hated and dodged. McReady advanced to Barclay's side. The dogs beyond sensed the plan with the almost telepathic intelligence of trained huskies. Their whining grew shriller, softer, their mincing steps carried them nearer. Abruptly a huge night-black Alaskan leapt onto the trapped thing. It turned squalling, saber-clawed feet slashing.

Barclay leapt forward and jabbed. A weird, shrill scream rose and choked out. The smell of burnt flesh in the corridor intensified; greasy smoke curled up. The echoing pound of the gas-electric dynamo down the corridor became a slogging thud.

The red eyes clouded over in a stiffening, jerking travesty of a face. Armlike, leglike members quivered and jerked. The dogs leapt forward, and Barclay yanked back his shovel-handled weapon. The thing on the snow did not move as gleaming teeth ripped it open.

VI

Garry looked about the crowded room. Thirty-two men, some tensed nervously standing against the wall, some uneasily relaxed, some sitting, most perforce standing as intimate as sardines. Thirty-two, plus the five engaged in sewing up wounded dogs, made thirty-seven, the total personnel.

Garry started speaking. 'All right, I guess we're here. Some of you – three or four at most – saw what happened. All of you have seen that thing on the table, and can get a general idea. Anyone hasn't, I'll lift—' His hand strayed to the tarpaulin bulking over the thing on the table. There was an acrid odor of singed flesh seeping out of it. The men stirred restlessly, hasty denials.

'It looks rather as though Charnauk isn't going to lead any more teams,' Garry went on. 'Blair wants to get at this thing, and make some more detailed examination. We want to know what happened, and make sure right now that this is permanently, totally dead. Right?'

Connant grinned. 'Anybody that doesn't can sit up with it tonight.'

'All right then, Blair, what can you say about it? What was it?' Garry turned to the little biologist.

'I wonder if we ever saw its natural form,' Blair looked at the covered mass. 'It may have been imitating the beings that built that ship – but I don't think it was. I think that was its true form. Those of us who were up near the bend saw the thing in action; the thing on the table is the result. When it got loose, apparently, it started looking around. Antarctica still frozen as it was ages ago when the creature first saw it – and froze. From my observations while it was thawing out, and the bits of tissue I cut and hardened then, I think it was native to a hotter planet than Earth. It couldn't, in its natural form, stand the temperature. There is no life-form on Earth that can live in Antarctica during the winter, but the best compromise is the dog. It found the dogs, and somehow got near enough to Charnauk to get him. The others smelled it – heard it – I don't know – anyway they went wild, and broke chains, and attacked it before it was finished. The thing we found was part Charnauk, queerly only half-dead, part Charnauk half-digested by the jellylike protoplasm of that creature, and part the remains of the thing we originally found, sort of melted down to the basic protoplasm.

28

'When the dogs attacked it, it turned into the best fighting thing it could think of. Some other-world beast apparently.'

'Turned,' snapped Garry. 'How?'

'Every living thing is made up of jelly – protoplasm and minute, submicroscopic things called nuclei, which control the bulk, the protoplasm. This thing was just a modification of that same world-wide plan of Nature; cells made up of protoplasm, controlled by infinitely tinier nuclei. You physicists might compare it – an individual cell of any living thing – with an atom; the bulk of the atom, the space-filling part, is made up of the electron orbits, but the character of the thing is determined by the atomic nucleus.

'This isn't wildly beyond what we already know. It's just a modification we haven't seen before. It's as natural, as logical, as any other manifestation of life. It obeys exactly the same laws. The cells are made of protoplasm, their character determined by the nucleus.

'Only, in this creature, the cell nuclei can control those cells *at will*. It digested Charnauk, and as it digested, studied every cell of his tissue, and shaped its own cells to imitate them exactly. Parts of it – parts that had time to finish changing – are dog-cells. But they don't have dog-cell nuclei.' Blair lifted a fraction of the tarpaulin. A torn dog's leg, with stiff gray fur protruded. 'That, for instance, isn't dog at all; it's imitation. Some parts I'm uncertain about; the nucleus was hiding itself, covering up with dog-cell imitation nucleus. In time, not even a microscope would have shown the difference.'

'Suppose,' asked Norris bitterly, 'it had had lots of time?'

'Then it would have been a dog. The other dogs would have accepted it. We would have accepted it. I don't think anything would have distinguished it, not microscope, nor

X-ray, nor any other means. This is a member of a supremely intelligent race, a race that has learned the deepest secrets of biology, and turned them to its use.'

'What was it planning to do?' Barclay looked at the humped tarpaulin.

Blair grinned unpleasantly. The wavering halo of thin hair round his bald pate wavered in a stir of air. 'Take over the world, I imagine.'

'Take over the world! Just it, all by itself?' Connant gasped. 'Set itself up as a lone dictator?'

'No,' Blair shook his head. The scalpel he had been fumbling in his bony fingers dropped; he bent to pick it up, so that his face was hidden as he spoke. 'It would become the population of the world.'

'Become – populate the world? Does it reproduce asexually?'

Blair shook his head and gulped. 'It's – it doesn't have to. It weighed 85 pounds. Charnauk weighed about 90. It would have become Charnauk, and had 85 pounds left, to become – oh, Jack, for instance, or Chinook. It can imitate anything – that is, become anything. If it had reached the Antarctic Sea, it would have become a seal, maybe two seals. They might have attacked a killer whale, and become either killers, or a herd of seals. Or maybe it would have caught an albatross, or a skua gull, and flown to South America.'

Norris cursed softly. 'And every time it digested something, and imitated it—'

'It would have had its original bulk left, to start again,' Blair finished. 'Nothing would kill it. It has no natural enemies, because it becomes whatever it wants to. If a killer whale attacked it, it would become a killer whale. If it was an albatross, and an eagle attacked it, it would become an eagle.

30

Lord, it might become a female eagle. Go back – build a nest and lay eggs!'

'Are you sure that thing from hell is dead?' Dr. Copper asked softly.

'Yes, thank Heaven,' the little biologist gasped. 'After they drove the dogs off, I stood there poking Bar's electrocution thing into it for five minutes. It's dead and – cooked.'

'Then we can only give thanks that this is Antarctica, where there is not one, single, solitary, living thing for it to imitate, except these animals in camp.'

'Us,' Blair giggled. 'It can imitate us. Dogs can't make 400 miles to the sea; there's no food. There aren't any skua gulls to imitate at this season. There aren't any penguins this far inland. There's nothing that can reach the sea from this point – except us. We've got brains. We can do it. Don't you see – *it's got to imitate us – it's got to be one of us – that's the only way it can fly an airplane – fly a plane for two hours, and rule – be – all Earth's inhabitants.* A world for the taking – *if it imitates us!*

'It didn't know yet. It hadn't had a chance to learn. It was rushed – hurried – took the thing nearest its own size. Look – I'm Pandora! I opened the box! And the only hope that can come out is – that nothing can come out. You didn't see me. I did it. I fixed it. I smashed every magneto. Not a plane can fly. Nothing can fly.' Blair giggled and lay down on the floor crying.

Chief Pilot Van Wall made for the door. His feet were fading echoes in the corridors as Dr Copper bent unhurriedly over the little man on the floor. From his office at the end of the room he brought something and injected a solution into Blair's arm. 'He might come out of it when he wakes up,' he sighed, rising. McReady helped him lift the biologist onto

31

a nearby bunk. 'It all depends on whether we can convince him that thing is dead.'

Van Wall ducked into the shack, brushing his heavy blond beard absently. 'I didn't think a biologist would do a thing like that up thoroughly. He missed the spares in the second cache. It's all right. I smashed them.'

Commander Garry nodded. 'I was wondering about the radio.'

Dr Copper snorted. 'You don't think it can leak out on a radio wave, do you? You'd have five rescue attempts in the next three months if you stop the broadcasts. The thing to do is talk loud and not make a sound. Now I wonder—'

McReady looked speculatively at the doctor. 'It might be like an infectious disease. Everything that drank any of its blood—'

Copper shook his head. 'Blair missed something. Imitate it may, but it has, to a certain extent, its own body chemistry, its own metabolism. If it didn't, it would become a dog – and be a dog and nothing more. It has to be an imitation dog. Therefore you can detect it by serum tests. And its chemistry, since it comes from another world, must be so wholly, radically different that a few cells, such as gained by drops of blood, would be treated as disease germs by the dog, or human body.'

'Blood – would one of those imitations bleed?' Norris demanded.

'Surely. Nothing mystic about blood. Muscle is about 90 per cent water; blood differs only in having a couple percent more water, and less connective tissue. They'd bleed all right,' Copper assured him.

Blair sat up in his bunk suddenly. 'Connant – where's Connant?'

The physicist moved over toward the little biologist. 'Here I am. What do you want?'

'Are you?' giggled Blair. He lapsed back into the bunk contorted with silent laughter.

Connant looked at him blankly. 'Huh? Am I what?'

'*Are* you there?' Blair burst into gales of laughter. '*Are* you Connant? The beast wanted to be man – not a dog—'

VII

Dr Copper rose wearily from the bunk, and washed the hypodermic carefully. The little tinkles it made seemed loud in the packed room, now that Blair's gurgling laughter had finally quieted. Copper looked toward Garry and shook his head slowly. 'Hopeless, I'm afraid. I don't think we can ever convince him the thing is dead now.'

Norris laughed uncertainly. 'I'm not sure you can convince me. Oh, damn you, McReady.'

'McReady?' Commander Garry turned to look from Norris to McReady curiously.

'The nightmares,' Norris explained. 'He had a theory about the nightmares we had at the Secondary Station after finding that thing.'

'And that was?' Garry looked at McReady levelly.

Norris answered for him, jerkily, uneasily. 'That the creature wasn't dead, had a sort of enormously slowed existence, an existence that permitted it, nonetheless, to be vaguely aware of the passing of time, of our coming, after endless years. I had a dream it could imitate things.'

'Well,' Copper grunted, 'it can.'

'Don't be an ass,' Norris snapped. 'That's not what's

bothering me. In the dream it could read minds, read thoughts and ideas and mannerisms.'

'What's so bad about that? It seems to be worrying you more than the thought of the joy we're going to have with a madman in an Antarctic camp.' Copper nodded toward Blair's sleeping form.

McReady shook his great head slowly. 'You know that Connant is Connant, because he not merely looks like Connant – which we're beginning to believe that beast might be able to do – but he thinks like Connant, moves himself around as Connant does. That takes more than merely a body that looks like him; that takes Connant's own mind, and thoughts and mannerisms. Therefore, though you know that the thing might make itself *look* like Connant, you aren't much bothered, because you know it has a mind from another world, a totally unhuman mind, that couldn't possibly react and think and talk like a man we know, and do it so well as to fool us for a moment. The idea of the creature imitating one of us is fascinating, but unreal, because it is too completely unhuman to deceive us. It doesn't have a human mind.'

'As I said before,' Norris repeated, looking steadily at McReady, 'you can say the damnedest things at the damnedest times. Will you be so good as to finish that thought – one way or the other?'

Kinner, the scar-faced expedition cook, had been standing near Connant. Suddenly he moved down the length of the crowded room toward his familiar galley. He shook the ashes from the galley stove noisily.

'It would do it no good,' said Dr Copper, softly as though thinking out loud, 'to merely look like something it was trying to imitate; it would have to understand its feelings, its reactions. It is unhuman; it has powers of imitation beyond any conception of man. A good actor, by training himself, can imitate another man, another man's mannerisms, well enough to fool most people. Of course no actor could imitate so perfectly as to deceive men who had been living with the imitated one in the complete lack of privacy of an Antarctic camp. That would take a superhuman skill.'

'Oh, you've got the bug, too?' Norris cursed softly.

Connant, standing alone at one end of the room, looked about him wildly, his face white. A gentle eddying of the men had crowded them slowly down toward the other end of the room, so that he stood quite alone. 'My God, will you two Jeremiahs shut up?' Connant's voice shook. 'What am I? Some kind of microscopic specimen you're dissecting? Some unpleasant worm you're discussing in the third person?'

McReady looked up at him; his slowly twisting hands stopped for a moment. 'Having a lovely time. Wish you were here. Signed: Everybody.

'Connant, if you think you're having a hell of a time, just move over on the other end for a while. You've got one thing we haven't; you know what the answer is. I'll tell you this, right now you're the most feared and respected man in Big Magnet.'

'Lord, I wish you could see your eyes,' Connant gasped. 'Stop staring, will you! What the hell are you going to do?'

'Have you any suggestions, Dr Copper?' Commander Garry asked steadily. 'The present situation is impossible.'

'Oh, is it?' Connant snapped. 'Come over here and look at that crowd. By Heaven, they look exactly like that gang of huskies around the corridor bend. Benning, will you stop hefting that damned ice-ax?'

The coppery blade rang on the floor as the aviation

mechanic nervously dropped it. He bent over and picked it up instantly, hefting it slowly, turning it in his hands, his brown eyes moving jerkily about the room.

Copper sat down on the bunk beside Blair. The wood creaked noisily in the room. Far down a corridor, a dog yelped in pain, and the dog-drivers' tense voices floated softly back. 'Microscopic examination,' said the doctor thoughtfully, 'would be useless, as Blair pointed out. Considerable time has passed. However, serum tests would be definitive.'

'Serum tests? What do you mean exactly?' Commander Garry asked.

'If I had a rabbit that had been injected with human blood – a poison to rabbits, of course, as is the blood of any animal save that of another rabbit – and the injections continued in increasing doses for some time, the rabbit would be human-immune. If a small quantity of its blood were drawn off, allowed to separate in a test tube, and to the clear serum, a bit of human blood were added, there would be a visible reaction, proving the blood was human. If cow, or dog blood were added – or any protein material other than that one thing – human blood – no reaction would take place. That would prove definitely.'

'Can you suggest where I might catch a rabbit for you, Doc?' Norris asked. 'That is, nearer than Australia; we don't want to waste time going that far.'

'I know there aren't any rabbits in Antarctica,' Copper nodded, 'but that is simply the usual animal. Any animal except man will do. A dog for instance. But it will take several days, and due to the greater size of the animal, considerable blood. Two of us will have to contribute.'

'Would I do?' Garry asked.

'That will make two,' Copper nodded. 'I'll get to work on it right away.'

'What about Connant in the meantime,' Kinner demanded. 'I'm going out that door and head off for the Ross Sea before I cook for him.'

'He may be human—' Copper started.

Connant burst out in a flood of curses. 'Human! *May* be human, you damned sawbones! What in hell do you think I am?'

'A monster,' Copper snapped sharply. 'Now shut up and listen.' Connant's face drained of color and he sat down heavily as the indictment was put in words. 'Until we know – you know as well as we do that we have reason to question the fact, and only you know how that question is to be answered – we may reasonably be expected to lock you up. If you are – unhuman – you're a lot more dangerous than poor Blair there, and I'm going to see that he's locked up thoroughly. I expect that his next stage will be a violent desire to kill you, all the dogs, and probably all of us. When he wakes, he will be convinced we're all unhuman, and nothing on the planet will ever change his conviction. It would be kinder to let him die, but we can't do that, of course. He's going in one shack, and you can stay in Cosmos House with your cosmic ray apparatus. Which is about what you'd do anyway. I've got to fix up a couple of dogs.'

Connant nodded bitterly. 'I'm human. Hurry that test. Your eyes – Lord, I wish you could see your eyes staring—'

Commander Garry watched anxiously as Clark, the dog-handler, held the big brown Alaskan husky, while Copper began the injection treatment. The dog was not anxious to cooperate; the needle was painful, and already he'd experienced considerable needle work that morning. Five stitches

37

held closed a slash that ran from his shoulder, across the ribs, halfway down his body. One long fang was broken off short; the missing part was to be found half buried in the shoulder bone of the monstrous thing on the table in the Ad Building.

'How long will that take?' Garry asked, pressing his arm gently. It was sore from the prick of the needle Dr Copper had used to withdraw blood.

Copper shrugged. 'I don't know, to be frank. I know the general method. I've used it on rabbits. But I haven't experimented with dogs. They're big, clumsy animals to work with; naturally rabbits are preferable, and serve ordinarily. In civilized places you can buy a stock of human-immune rabbits from suppliers, and not many investigators take the trouble to prepare their own.'

'What do they want with them back there?' Clark asked.

'Criminology is one large field. A says he didn't murder B, but that the blood on his shirt came from killing a chicken. The State makes a test, then it's up to A to explain how it is the blood reacts on human-immune rabbits, but not on chicken-immunes.'

'What are we going to do with Blair in the meantime?' Garry asked wearily. 'It's all right to let him sleep where he is for a while, but when he wakes up—'

'Barclay and Benning are fitting some bolts on the door of Cosmos House,' Copper replied grimly. 'Connant's acting like a gentleman. I think perhaps the way the other men look at him makes him rather want privacy. Lord knows, heretofore we've all of us individually prayed for a little privacy.'

Clark laughed brittlely. 'Not any more, thank you. The more the merrier.'

38

'Blair,' Copper went on, 'will also have to have privacy – and locks. He's going to have a pretty definite plan in mind when he wakes up. Ever hear the old story of how to stop hoof-and-mouth disease in cattle?'

Clark and Garry shook their heads silently.

'If there isn't any hoof-and-mouth disease, there won't be any hoof-and-mouth disease,' Copper explained. 'You get rid of it by killing every animal that exhibits it, and every animal that's been near the diseased animal. Blair's a biologist, and knows that story. He's afraid of this thing we loosed. The answer is probably pretty clear in his mind now. Kill everybody and everything in this camp before a skua gull or a wandering albatross coming in with the spring chances out this way and – catches the disease.'

Clark's lips curled in a twisted grin. 'Sounds logical to me. If things get too bad – maybe we'd better let Blair get loose. It would save us committing suicide. We might also make something of a vow that if things get bad, we see that that does happen.'

Copper laughed softly. 'The last man alive in Big Magnet – wouldn't be a man,' he pointed out. 'Somebody's got to kill those – creatures that don't desire to kill themselves, you know. We don't have enough thermite to do it all at once, and the decanite explosive wouldn't help much. I have an idea that even small pieces of one of those beings would be self-sufficient.'

'If,' said Garry thoughtfully, 'they can modify their proto-plasm at will, won't they simply modify themselves to birds and fly away? They can read all about birds, and imitate their structure without even meeting them. Or imitate, perhaps, birds of their home planet.'

Copper shook his head, and helped Clark to free the dog.

'Man studied birds for centuries, trying to learn how to make a machine to fly like them. He never did do the trick; his final success came when he broke away entirely and tried new methods. Knowing the general idea, and knowing the detailed structure of wing and bone and nerve-tissue is something far, far different. And as for other-world birds, perhaps, in fact very probably, the atmospheric conditions here are so vastly different that their birds couldn't fly. Perhaps, even, the being came from a planet like Mars with such a thin atmosphere that there were no birds.'

Barclay came into the building, trailing a length of airplane control cable. 'It's finished, Doc. Cosmos House can't be opened from the inside. Now where do we put Blair?'

Copper looked toward Garry. 'There wasn't any biology building. I don't know where we can isolate him.'

'How about East Cache?' Garry said after a moment's thought. 'Will Blair be able to look after himself – or need attention?'

'He'll be capable enough. We'll be the ones to watch out,' Copper assured him grimly. 'Take a stove, a couple of bags of coal, necessary supplies and a few tools to fix it up. Nobody's been out there since last fall, have they?'

Garry shook his head. 'If he gets noisy – I thought that might be a good idea.'

Barclay hefted the tools he was carrying and looked up at Garry. 'If the muttering he's doing now is any sign, he's going to sing away the night hours. And we won't like his song.'

'What's he saying?' Copper asked.

Barclay shook his head. 'I didn't care to listen much. You can if you want to. But I gathered that the blasted idiot had all the dreams McReady had, and a few more. He slept beside the thing when we stopped on the trail coming in from Secondary Magnetic, remember. He dreamt the thing was alive, and dreamt more details. And – damn his soul – knew it wasn't all dream, or had reason to. He knew it had telepathic powers that were stirring vaguely, and that it could not only read minds, but project thoughts. They weren't dreams, you see. They were stray thoughts that thing was broadcasting, the way Blair's broadcasting his thoughts now – a sort of telepathic muttering in its sleep. That's why he knew so much about its powers. I guess you and I, Doc, weren't so sensitive – if you want to believe in telepathy.'

'I have to,' Copper sighed. 'Dr Rhine of Duke University has shown that it exists, shown that some are much more sensitive than others.'

'Well, if you want to learn a lot of details, go listen in on Blair's broadcast. He's driven most of the boys out of the Ad Building; Kinner's rattling pans like coal going down a chute. When he can't rattle a pan, he shakes ashes.

'By the way, Commander, what are we going to do this spring, now the planes are out of it?'

Garry sighed. 'I'm afraid our expedition is going to be a loss. We cannot divide our strength now.'

'It won't be a loss – if we continue to live, and come out of this,' Copper promised him. 'The find we've made, if we can get it under control, is important enough. The cosmic ray data, magnetic work, and atmospheric work won't be greatly hindered.'

Garry laughed mirthlessly. 'I was just thinking of the radio broadcasts. Telling half the world about the wonderful results of our exploration flights, trying to fool men like Byrd and Ellsworth back home there that we're doing something.'

Copper nodded gravely. 'They'll know something's

wrong. But men like that have judgment enough to know we wouldn't do tricks without some sort of reason, and will wait for our return to judge us. I think it comes to this: men who know enough to recognize our deception will wait for our return. Men who haven't discretion and faith enough to wait will not have the experience to detect any fraud. We know enough of the conditions here to put through a good bluff.'

'Just so they don't send 'rescue' expeditions,' Garry prayed. 'When – if – we're ever ready to come out, we'll have to send word to Captain Forsythe to bring a stock of magnetos with him when he comes down. But – never mind that.'

'You mean if we don't come out?' asked Barclay. 'I was wondering if a nice running account of an eruption or an earthquake via radio – with a swell windup by using a stick of decanite under the microphone – would help. Nothing, of course, will entirely keep people out. One of those swell, melodramatic 'last-man-alive-scenes' might make 'em go easy though.'

Garry smiled with genuine humor. 'Is everybody in camp trying to figure that out, too?'

Copper laughed. 'What do you think, Garry? We're confident we can win out. But not too easy about it, I guess.'

Clark grinned up from the dog he was petting into calmness. 'Confident, did you say, Doc?'

VIII

Blair moved restlessly around the small shack. His eyes jerked and quivered in vague, fleeting glances at the four men with him; Barclay, six feet tall and weighing over 190 pounds; McReady, a bronze giant of a man; Dr Copper, short, squatly powerful; and Benning, five feet ten of wiry strength.

Blair was huddled up against the far wall of the East Cache cabin, his gear piled in the middle of the floor beside the heating stove, forming an island between him and the four men. His bony hands clenched and fluttered, terrified. His pale eyes wavered uneasily as his bald, freckled head darted about in birdlike motion.

'I don't want anybody coming here. I'll cook my own food,' he snapped nervously. 'Kinner may be human now, but I don't believe it. I'm going to get out of here, but I'm not going to eat any food you send me. I want cans. Sealed cans.'

'OK, Blair, we'll bring 'em tonight,' Barclay promised. 'You've got coal, and the fire's started. I'll make a last—' Barclay started forward.

Blair instantly scurried to the farthest corner. 'Get out! Keep away from me, you monster!' the little biologist shrieked, and tried to claw his way through the wall of the shack. 'Keep away from me – keep away – I won't be absorbed – I won't be—'

Barclay relaxed and moved back. Dr Copper shook his head. 'Leave him alone, Bar. It's easier for him to fix the thing himself. We'll have to fix the door, I think—'

The four men let themselves out. Efficiently, Benning and Barclay fell to work. There were no locks in Antarctica; there wasn't enough privacy to make them needed. But powerful screws had been driven in each side of the door frame, and the spare aviation control cable, immensely strong, woven steel wire, was rapidly caught between them and drawn taut. Barclay went to work with a drill and a key-hole saw.

43

Presently he had a trap cut in the door through which goods could be passed without unlashing the entrance. Three powerful hinges made from a stock crate, two hasps and a pair of three-inch cotter pins made it proof against opening from the other side.

Blair moved about restlessly inside. He was dragging something over to the door with panting gasps, and muttering frantic curses. Barclay opened the hatch and glanced in, Dr Copper peering over his shoulder. Blair had moved the heavy bunk against the door. It could not be opened without his cooperation now.

'Don't know but what the poor man's right at that,' McReady sighed. 'If he gets loose, it is his avowed intention to kill each and all of us as quickly as possible, which is something we don't agree with. But we've something on our side of that door that is worse than a homicidal maniac. If one or the other has to get loose, I think I'll come up and undo these lashings here.'

Barclay grinned. 'You let me know, and I'll show you how to get these off fast. Let's go back.'

The sun was painting the northern horizon in multi-colored rainbows still, though it was two hours below the horizon. The field of drift swept off to the north, sparkling under its flaming colors in a million reflected glories. Low mounds of rounded white on the northern horizon showed the Magnet Range was barely awash above the sweeping drift. Little eddies of wind-lifted snow swirled away from their skis as they set out toward the main encampment two miles away. The spidery finger of the broadcast radiator lifted a gaunt black needle against the white of the Antarctic continent. The snow under their skis was like fine sand, hard and gritty.

'Spring,' said Benning bitterly, 'is come. Ain't we got fun! And I've been looking forward to getting away from this blasted hole in the ice.'

'I wouldn't try it now, if I were you.' Barclay grunted. 'Guys that set out from here in the next few days are going to be marvelously unpopular.'

'How is your dog getting along, Dr Copper?' McReady asked. 'Any results yet?'

'In 30 hours? I wish there were. I gave him an injection of my blood today. But I imagine another five days will be needed. I don't know certainly enough to stop sooner.'

'I've been wondering – if Connant were – changed, would he have warned us so soon after the animal escaped? Wouldn't he have waited long enough for it to have a real chance to fix itself? Until we woke up naturally?' McReady asked slowly.

'The thing is selfish. You didn't think it looked as though it were possessed of a store of the higher justices, did you?' Dr Copper pointed out. 'Every part of it is all of it, every part of it is all for itself, I imagine. If Connant were changed, to save his skin, he'd have to – but Connant's feelings aren't changed; they're imitated perfectly, or they're his own. Naturally, the imitation, imitating perfectly Connant's feelings, would do exactly what Connant would do.'

'Say, couldn't Norris or Vane give Connant some kind of a test? If the thing is brighter than men, it might know more physics than Connant should, and they'd catch it out,' Barclay suggested.

Copper shook his head wearily. 'Not if it reads minds. You can't plan a trap for it. Vane suggested that last night. He hoped it would answer some of the questions of physics he'd like to know answers to.'

'This expedition-of-four idea is going to make life happy.' Benning looked at his companions. 'Each of us with an eye on the other to make sure he doesn't do something – peculiar. Man – aren't we going to be a trusting bunch! Each man eyeing his neighbors with the grandest exhibition of faith and truth – I'm beginning to know what Connant meant by 'I wish you could see your eyes.' Every now and then we all have it, I guess. One of you looks around with a sort of 'I-wonder-if-the-other-*three*-are look.' Incidentally, I'm not excepting myself.'

'So far as we know, the animal is dead, with a slight question as to Connant. No other is suspected,' McReady stated slowly. 'The 'always-four' order is merely a precautionary measure.'

'I'm waiting for Garry to make it four-in-a-bunk,' Barclay sighed. 'I thought I didn't have any privacy before, but since that order—'

IX

None watched more tensely than Connant. A little sterile glass test tube, half filled with straw-colored fluid. One – two – three – four – five drops of the clear solution Dr Copper had prepared from the drops of blood from Connant's arm. The tube was shaken carefully, then set in a beaker of clear, warm water. The thermometer read blood heat, a little thermostat clicked noisily, and the electric hotplate began to glow as the lights flickered slightly. Then – little white flecks of precipitation were forming, snowing down in the clear straw-colored fluid. 'Lord,' said Connant. He dropped heavily into a bunk, crying like a baby. 'Six days—' Connant sobbed, 'six days in there – wondering if that damned test would lie—'

Garry moved over silently, and slipped his arm across the physicist's back.

'It couldn't lie,' Dr. Copper said. 'The dog was human-immune – and the serum reacted.'

'He's – all right?' Norris gasped. 'Then – the animal is dead – dead forever?'

'He is human,' Copper spoke definitely, 'and the animal is dead.'

Kinner burst out laughing, laughing hysterically. McReady turned toward him and slapped his face with a methodical one-two, one-two action. The cook laughed, gulped, cried a moment, and sat up rubbing his cheeks, mumbling his thanks vaguely. 'I was scared. Lord, I was scared—'

Norris laughed brittlely. 'You think we weren't, you ape? You think maybe Connant wasn't?'

The Ad Building stirred with a sudden rejuvenation. Voices laughed, the men clustering around Connant spoke with unnecessarily loud voices, jittery, nervous voices relievedly friendly again. Somebody called out a suggestion, and a dozen started for their skis. Blair, Blair might recover – Dr Copper fussed with his test tubes in nervous relief, trying solutions. The party of relief for Blair's shack started out the door, skis clapping noisily. Down the corridor, the dogs set up a quick yelping howl as the air of excited relief reached them.

Dr Copper fussed with his tubes. McReady noticed him first, sitting on the edge of the bunk, with two precipitin-whitened test-tubes of straw-colored fluid, his face whiter than the stuff in the tubes, silent tears slipping down from horror-widened eyes.

McReady felt a cold knife of fear pierce through his heart and freeze in his breast. Dr Copper looked up. 'Garry,' he called hoarsely. 'Garry, for God's sake, come here.'

Commander Garry walked toward him sharply. Silence clapped down on the Ad Building. Connant looked up, rose stiffly from his seat.

'Garry – tissue from the monster – precipitates, too. It proves nothing. Nothing – but the dog was monster-immune too. That *one of the two contributing blood – one of us two*, you and I, Garry – *one of us is a monster.*'

X

'Bar, call back those men before they tell Blair,' McReady said quietly. Barclay went to the door; faintly his shouts came back to the tensely silent men in the room. Then he was back.

'They're coming,' he said. 'I didn't tell them why. Just that Dr Copper said not to go.'

'McReady,' Garry sighed, 'you're in command now. May God help you. I cannot.'

The bronzed giant nodded slowly, his deep eyes on Commander Garry.

'I may be the one,' Garry added. 'I know I'm not, but I cannot prove it to you in any way. Dr Copper's test has broken down. The fact that he showed it was useless, when it was to the advantage of the monster to have that useless-ness not known, would seem to prove he was human.'

Copper rocked back and forth slowly on the bunk. 'I know I'm human. I can't prove it either. One of us two is a liar, for that test cannot lie, and it says one of us is. I gave proof that the test was wrong, which seems to prove

I'm human, and now Garry has given that argument which proves me human – which he, as the monster, should not do. Round and round and round and round and—'

Dr Copper's head, then his neck and shoulders began circling slowly in time to the words. Suddenly he was lying back on the bunk, roaring with laughter. 'It doesn't have to prove *one* of us is a monster! It doesn't have to prove that at all! Ho-ho. If we're *all* monsters it works the same – we're all monsters – all of us – Connant and Garry and I – and all of you.'

'McReady,' Van Wall, the blond-bearded Chief Pilot, called softly, 'you were on the way to an MD when you took up meteorology, weren't you? Can you make some kind of test?'

McReady went over to Copper slowly, took the hypodermic from his hand, and washed it carefully in 95 per cent alcohol. Garry sat on the bunk edge with wooden face, watching Copper and McReady expressionlessly. 'What Copper said is possible,' McReady sighed. 'Van, will you help me here? Thanks.' The filled needle jabbed into Copper's thigh. The man's laughter did not stop, but slowly faded into sobs, then sound sleep as the morphia took hold.

McReady turned again. The men who had started for Blair stood at the far end of the room, skis dripping snow, their faces as white as their skis. Connant had a lighted cigarette in each hand; one he was puffing absently, and staring at the floor. The heat of the one in his left hand attracted him and he stared at it and the one in the other hand stupidly for a moment. He dropped one and crushed it under his heel slowly.

'Dr Copper,' McReady repeated, 'could be right. I know I'm human – but of course can't prove it. I'll repeat the test for my own information. Any of you others who wish may do the same.'

Two minutes later, McReady held a test tube with white precipitin settling slowly from straw-colored serum. 'It reacts to human blood too, so they aren't both monsters.'

'I didn't think they were,' Van Wall sighed. 'That wouldn't suit the monster either; we could have destroyed them if we knew. Why hasn't the monster destroyed us, do you suppose? It seems to be loose.'

McReady snorted. Then laughed softly. 'Elementary, my dear Watson. The monster wants to have life-forms available. It cannot animate a dead body, apparently. It is just waiting – waiting until the best opportunities come. We who remain human, it is holding in reserve.'

Kinner shuddered violently. 'Hey. Hey, Mac. Mac, would I know if I was a monster? Would I know if the monster had already got me? Oh Lord, I may be a monster already.'

'You'd know,' McReady answered.

'But we wouldn't,' Norris laughed shortly, half hysterically.

McReady looked at the vial of serum remaining. 'There's one thing this damned stuff is good for, at that,' he said thoughtfully. 'Clark, will you and Van help me? The rest of the gang better stick together here. Keep an eye on each other,' he said bitterly. 'See that you don't get into mischief, shall we say?'

McReady started down the tunnel toward Dogtown, with Clark and Van Wall behind him. 'You need more serum?' Clark asked.

McReady shook his head. 'Tests. There's four cows and a bull, and nearly seventy dogs down there. This stuff reacts only to human blood and – monsters.'

XI

McReady came back to the Ad Building and went silently to the wash stand. Clark and Van Wall joined him a moment later. Clark's lips had developed a tic, jerking into sudden, unexpected sneers.

'What did you do?' Connant exploded suddenly. 'More immunizing?'

Clark snickered, and stopped with a hiccough. 'Immunizing. Haw! Immune all right.'

'That monster,' said Van Wall steadily, 'is quite logical. Our immune dog was quite all right, and we drew a little more serum for the tests. But we won't make any more.'

'Can't – can't you use one man's blood on another dog—' Norris began.

'There aren't,' said McReady softly, 'any more dogs. Nor cattle, I might add.'

'No more dogs?' Benning sat down slowly.

'They're very nasty when they start changing,' Van Wall said precisely. 'But slow. That electrocution iron you made up, Barclay, is very fast. There is only one dog left – our immune. The monster left that for us, so we could play with our little test. The rest—' He shrugged and dried his hands.

'The cattle—' gulped Kinner.

'Also. Reacted very nicely. They look funny as hell when they start melting. The beast hasn't any quick escape, when it's tied in dog chains, or halters, and it had to be to imitate.'

Kinner stood up slowly. His eyes darted around the room, and came to rest horribly quivering on a tin bucket in the galley. Slowly, step by step, he retreated toward the door, his mouth opening and closing silently, like a fish out of water.

'The milk—' he gasped. 'I milked 'em an hour ago—' His

voice broke into a scream as he dived through the door. He was out on the ice cap without windproof or heavy clothing.

Van Wall looked after him for a moment thoughtfully. 'He's probably hopelessly mad,' he said at length, 'but he might be a monster escaping. He hasn't skis. Take a blow torch – in case.'

The physical motion of the chased helped them; something that needed doing. Three of the men were quietly being sick. Norris was lying flat on his back, his face greenish, looking steadily at the bottom of the bunk above him.

'Mac, how long have the – cows been not-cows—'

McReady shrugged his shoulders hopelessly. He went over to the milk bucket, and with his little tube of serum set to work on it. The milk clouded it, making certainty difficult. Finally he dropped the test tube in the stand, and shook his head. 'It tests negatively. Which means either they were cows then, or that, being perfect imitations, they gave perfectly good milk.'

Copper stirred restlessly in his sleep and gave a gurgling cross between a snore and a laugh. Silent eyes fastened on him. 'Would morphia – a monster—' somebody started to ask.

'Lord knows,' McReady shrugged. 'It affects every Earthly animal I know of.'

Connant suddenly raised his head. 'Mac! The dogs must have swallowed pieces of the monster, and the pieces destroyed them! The dogs were where the monster resided. I was locked up. Doesn't that prove—'

Van Wall shook his head. 'Sorry. Proves nothing about what you are, only proves what you didn't do.'

'It doesn't do that,' McReady sighed. 'We are helpless because we don't know enough, and so jittery we don't think straight. Locked up! Ever watch a white corpuscle of the blood go through the wall of a blood vessel? No? It sticks out a pseudopod. And there it is – on the far side of the wall.'

'Oh,' said Van Wall unhappily. 'The cattle tried to melt down, didn't they? They could have melted down – become just a thread of stuff and leaked under a door to re-collect on the other side. Ropes – no – no, that wouldn't do it. They couldn't live in a sealed tank or—'

'If,' said McReady, 'you shoot it through the heart, and it doesn't die, it's a monster. That's the best test I can think of, offhand.'

'No dogs,' said Garry quietly, 'and no cattle. It has to imitate men now. And locking up doesn't do any good. Your test might work, Mac, but I'm afraid it would be hard on the men.'

XII

Clark looked up from the galley stove as Van Wall, Barclay, McReady, and Benning came in, brushing the drift from their clothes. The other men jammed into the Ad Building continued studiously to do as they were doing, playing chess, poker, reading. Ralsen was fixing a sledge on the table; Vane and Norris had their heads together over magnetic data, while Harvey read tables in a low voice.

Dr Copper snored softly on the bunk. Garry was working with Dutton over a sheaf of radio messages on the corner of Dutton's bunk and a small fraction of the radio table. Connant was using most of the table for cosmic ray sheets.

Quite plainly through the corridor, despite two closed doors, they could hear Kinner's voice. Clark banged a kettle onto the galley stove and beckoned McReady silently. The meteorologist went over to him.

'I don't mind the cooking so damn much,' Clark said nervously, 'but isn't there some way to stop that bird? We all agreed that it would be safe to move him into Cosmos House.'

'Kinner?' McReady nodded toward the door. 'I'm afraid not. I can dope him, I suppose, but we don't have an unlimited supply of morphia, and he's not in danger of losing his mind. Just hysterical.'

'Well, we're in danger of losing ours. You've been out for an hour and a half. That's been going on steadily ever since, and it was going for two hours before. There's a limit, you know.'

Garry wandered over slowly, apologetically. For an instant, McReady caught the feral spark of fear – horror – in Clark's eyes, and knew at the same instant it was in his own. Garry – Garry or Copper – was certainly a monster.

'If you could stop that, I think it would be a sound policy, Mac,' Garry spoke quietly. 'There are – tensions enough in this room. We agreed that it would be safe for Kinner in there, because everyone else in camp is under constant eyeing.' Garry shivered slightly. 'And try, try in God's name, to find some test that will work.' McReady sighed. 'Watched or unwatched, everyone's tense. Blair's jammed the trap so it won't open now. Says he's got food enough, and keeps screaming 'Go away, go away – you're monsters. I won't be absorbed. I won't. I'll tell men when they come. Go away.' So – we went away.'

'There's no other test?' Garry pleaded.

McReady shrugged his shoulders. 'Copper was perfectly right. The serum test could be absolutely definitive if

54

it hadn't been – contaminated. But that's the only dog left, and he's fixed now.'

'Chemicals? Chemical tests?'

McReady shook his head. 'Our chemistry isn't that good. I tried the microscope you know.'

Garry nodded. 'Monster-dog and real dog were identical. But – you've got to go on. What are you going to do after dinner?'

Van Wall had joined them quietly. 'Rotation sleeping. Half the crowd sleep; half stay awake. I wonder how many of us are monsters? All the dogs were. We thought we were safe, but somehow it got Copper – or you.' Van Wall's eyes flashed uneasily. 'It may have gotten every one of you – all of you but myself may be wondering, looking. No, that's not possible. You'd just spring then, I'd be helpless. We humans must somehow have the greater numbers now. But—' he stopped.

McReady laughed shortly. 'You're doing what Norris complained of in me. Leaving it hanging. 'But if one more is changed – that may shift the balance of power.' It doesn't fight. I don't think it ever fights. It must be a peaceable thing, in its own – inimitable – way. It never had to, because it always gained its end otherwise.'

Van Wall's mouth twisted in a sickly grin. 'You're suggesting then, that perhaps it already *has* the greater numbers, but is just waiting – waiting, all of them – all of you, for all I know – waiting till I, the last human, drop my wariness in sleep. Mac, did you notice their eyes, all looking at us.'

Garry sighed. 'You haven't been sitting here for four straight hours, while all their eyes silently weighed the information that one of us two, Copper or I, is a monster certainly – perhaps both of us.'

55

Clark repeated his request. 'Will you stop that bird's noise? He's driving me nuts. Make him tone down, anyway.'

'Still praying?' McReady asked.

'Still praying,' Clark groaned. 'He hasn't stopped for a second. I don't mind his praying if it relieves him, but he yells, he sings psalms and hymns and shouts prayers. He thinks God can't hear well way down here.'

'Maybe he can't,' Barclay grunted. 'Or he'd have done something about this thing loosed from hell.'

'Somebody's going to try that test you mentioned, if you don't stop him,' Clark stated grimly. 'I think a cleaver in the head would be as positive a test as a bullet in the heart.'

'Go ahead with the food. I'll see what I can do. There may be something in the cabinets.' McReady moved wearily toward the corner Copper had used as his dispensary. Three tall cabinets of rough boards, two locked, were the repositories of the camp's medical supplies. Twelve years ago, McReady had graduated, had started for an internship, and been diverted to meteorology. Copper was a picked man, a man who knew his profession thoroughly and modernly. More than half the drugs available were totally unfamiliar to McReady; many of the others he had forgotten. There was no huge medical library here, no series of journals available to learn the things he had forgotten, the elementary, simple things to Copper, things that did not merit inclusion in the small library he had been forced to content himself with. Books are heavy, and every ounce of supplies had been freighted in by air.

McReady picked a barbiturate hopefully. Barclay and Van Wall went with him. One man never went anywhere alone in Big Magnet.

Ralsen had his sledge put away, and the physicists had

moved off the table, the poker game broken up when they got back. Clark was putting out the food. The clicks of spoons and the muffled sounds of eating were the only sign of life in the room. There were no words spoken as the three returned; simply all eyes focused on them questioningly while the jaws moved methodically.

McReady stiffened suddenly. Kinner was screeching out a hymn in a hoarse, cracked voice. He looked wearily at Van Wall with a twisted grin and shook his head. 'Uh-uh.'

Van Wall cursed bitterly, and sat down at the table. 'We'll just plumb have to take that till his voice wears out. He can't yell like that forever.'

'He's got a brass throat and a cast-iron larynx,' Norris declared savagely. 'Then we could be hopeful, and suggest he's one of our friends. In that case he could go on renewing his throat till doomsday.'

Silence clamped down. For twenty minutes they ate without a word. Then Connant jumped up with an angry violence. 'You sit as still as a bunch of graven images. You don't say a word, but oh, Lord, what expressive eyes you've got. They roll around like a bunch of glass marbles spilling down a table. They wink and blink and stare – and whisper things. Can you guys look somewhere else for a change, please?

'Listen, Mac, you're in charge here. Let's run movies for the rest of the night. We've been saving those reels to make 'em last. Last for what? Who is it's going to see those last reels, eh? Let's see 'em while we can, and look at something other than each other.'

'Sound idea, Connant. I, for one, am quite willing to change this in any way I can.'

'Turn the sound up loud, Dutton. Maybe you can drown out the hymns,' Clark suggested.

'But don't,' Norris said softly, 'turn off the lights altogether.'

'The lights will be out.' McReady shook his head. 'We'll show all the cartoon movies we have. You won't mind seeing the old cartoons will you?'

'Goody, goody – a moom-pitcher show. I'm just in the mood.' McReady turned to look at the speaker, a lean, lanky New Englander, by the name of Caldwell. Caldwell was stuffing his pipe slowly, a sour eye cocked up to McReady.

The bronze giant was forced to laugh. 'OK, Bart, you win. Maybe we aren't quite in the mood for Popeye and trick ducks, but it's something.'

'Let's play Classifications,' Caldwell suggested slowly. 'Or maybe you call it Guggenheim. You draw lines on a piece of paper, and put down classes of things – like animals, you know. One for 'H' and one for 'U' and so on. Like 'Human' and 'Unknown' for instance. I think that would be a hell of a lot better game. Classification, I sort of figure, is what we need right now a lot more than movies. Maybe somebody's got a pencil that he can draw lines with, draw lines between the 'U' animals and the 'H' animals for instance.'

'McReady's trying to find that kind of a pencil,' Van Wall answered quietly, 'but, we've got three kinds of animals here, you know. One that begins with 'M.' We don't want any more.'

'Mad ones, you mean. Uh-huh. Clark, I'll help you with those pots so we can get our little peep show going.' Caldwell got up slowly.

Dutton and Barclay and Benning, in charge of the projector and sound mechanism arrangements, went about their job silently, while the Ad Building was cleared and the dishes and pans disposed of. McReady drifted over toward Van Wall slowly, and leaned back in the bunk beside him. 'I've been wondering, Van,' he said with a wry grin, 'whether or not to report my ideas in advance. I forgot the 'U animal' as Caldwell named it, could read minds. I've a vague idea of something that might work. It's too vague to bother with, though. Go ahead with your show, while I try to figure out the logic of the thing. I'll take this bunk.'

Van Wall glanced up, and nodded. The movie screen would be practically on a line with this bunk, hence making the pictures least distracting here, because least intelligible. 'Perhaps you should tell us what you have in mind. As it is, only the unknowns know what you plan. You might be – unknown before you got it into operation.'

'Won't take long, if I get it figured out right. But I don't want any more all-but-the-test-dog-monsters things. We better move Copper into this bunk directly above me. He won't be watching the screen either.' McReady nodded toward Copper's gently snoring bulk. Garry helped them lift and move the doctor.

McReady leaned back against the bunk, and sank into a trance, almost, of concentration, trying to calculate chances, operations, methods. He was scarcely aware as the others distributed themselves silently, and the screen lit up. Vaguely Kinner's hectic, shouted prayers and his rasping hymn-singing annoyed him till the sound accompaniment started. The lights were turned out, but the large, light-colored areas of the screen reflected enough light for ready visibility. Kinner was still praying, shouting, his voice a raucous accompaniment to the mechanical sound. Dutton stepped up the amplification.

So long had the voice been going on, that only vaguely at first was McReady aware that something seemed missing. Lying as he was, just across the narrow room from the corridor leading to Cosmos House, Kinner's voice had reached him fairly clearly, despite the sound accompaniment of the pictures. It struck him abruptly that it had stopped.

'Dutton, cut that sound,' McReady called as he sat up abruptly. The pictures flickered a moment, soundless and strangely futile in the sudden, deep silence. The rising wind on the surface above bubbled melancholy tears of sound down the stove pipes. 'Kinner's stopped,' McReady said softly.

'For God's sake start that sound then; he may have stopped to listen,' Norris snapped.

McReady rose and went down the corridor. Barclay and Van Wall left their places at the far end of the room to follow him. The flickers bulged and twisted on the back of Barclay's gray underwear as he crossed the still-functioning beam of the projector. Dutton snapped on the lights, and the pictures vanished.

Norris stood at the door as McReady had asked. Garry sat down quietly in the bunk nearest the door, forcing Clark to make room for him. Most of the others had stayed exactly where they were. Only Connant walked slowly up and down the room, in steady, unvarying rhythm.

'If you're going to do that, Connant,' Clark spat, 'we can get along without you altogether, whether you're human or not. Will you stop that damned rhythm?'

'Sorry.' The physicist sat down in a bunk, and watched his toes thoughtfully. It was almost five minutes, five ages, while the wind made the only sound, before McReady appeared at the door.

'Well,' he announced, 'haven't got enough grief here already. Somebody's tried to help us out. Kinner has a knife in his throat, which was why he stopped singing, probably. We've got monsters, madmen and murderers. Any more 'M's' you can think of, Caldwell? If there are, we'll probably have 'em before long.'

XIII

'Is Blair loose?' someone asked.

'Blair is not loose. Or he flew in. If there's any doubt about where our gentle helper came from – this may clear it up.' Van Wall held a foot-long, thin-bladed knife in a cloth. The wooden handle was half burnt, charred with the peculiar pattern of the top of the galley stove.

Clark stared at it. 'I did that this afternoon. I forgot the damn thing and left it on the stove.'

Van Wall nodded. 'I smelled it, if you remember. I knew the knife came from the galley.'

'I wonder,' said Benning, looking around at the party warily, 'how many more monsters have we? If somebody could slip out of his place, go back of the screen to the galley and then down to the Cosmos House and back – he did come back, didn't he? Yes – everybody's here. Well, if one of the gang could do all that—'

'Maybe a monster did it,' Garry suggested quietly.

'There's that possibility.'

'The monster, as you pointed out today, has only men left to imitate. Would he decrease his – supply, shall we say?' Van Wall pointed out. 'No, we just have a plain, ordinary louse, a murderer to deal with. Ordinarily we'd call him an 'inhuman murderer' I suppose, but we have to distinguish now. We have inhuman murderers, and now we have human murderers. Or one at least.'

'There's one less human,' Norris said softly. 'Maybe the monsters have the balance of power now.'

'Never mind that,' McReady sighed and turned to Barclay. 'Bar, will you get your electric gadget? I'm going to make certain—'

Barclay turned down the corridor to get the pronged electrocuter, while McReady and Van Wall went back toward Cosmos House. Barclay followed them in some thirty seconds.

The corridor to Cosmos House twisted, as did nearly all corridors in Big Magnet, and Norris stood at the entrance again. But they heard, rather muffled, McReady's sudden shout. There was a savage flurry of blows, dull *ch-thunk, shluff* sounds. 'Bar – Bar—' And a curious, savage mewing scream, silenced before even quick-moving Norris had reached the bend.

Kinner – or what had been Kinner – lay on the floor, cut half in two by the great knife McReady had had. The meteorologist stood against the wall, the knife dripping red in his hand. Van Wall was stirring vaguely on the floor, moaning, his hand half-consciously rubbing at his jaw. Barclay, an unutterably savage gleam in his eyes, was methodically leaning on the pronged weapon in his hand, jabbing – jabbing, jabbing.

Kinner's arms had developed a queer, scaly fur, and the flesh had twisted. The fingers had shortened, the hand rounded, the fingernails become three-inch long things of dull red horn, keened to steel-hard, razor-sharp talons.

McReady raised his head, looked at the knife in his hand and dropped it. 'Well, whoever did it can speak up now. He

62

was an inhuman murderer at that – in that he murdered an inhuman. I swear by all that's holy, Kinner was a lifeless corpse on the floor here when we arrived. But when It found we were going to jab It with the power – It changed.'

Norris stared unsteadily. 'Oh, Lord, those things can act. Ye gods – sitting in here for hours, mouthing prayers to a God it hated! Shouting hymns in a cracked voice – hymns about a Church it never knew. Driving us mad with its ceaseless howling –

'Well. Speak up, whoever did it. You didn't know it, but you did the camp a favor. And I want to know how in blazes you got out of the room without anyone seeing you. It might help in guarding ourselves.'

'His screaming – his singing. Even the sound projector couldn't drown it.' Clark shivered. 'It was a monster.'

'Oh,' said Van Wall in sudden comprehension. 'You were sitting right next to the door, weren't you? And almost behind the projection screen already.'

Clark nodded dumbly. 'He – it's quiet now. It's a dead – Mac, your test's no damn good. It was dead anyway, monster or man, it was dead.'

McReady chuckled softly. 'Boys, meet Clark, the only one we know is human! Meet Clark, the one who proves he's human by trying to commit murder – and failing. Will the rest of you please refrain from trying to prove you're human for a while? I think we may have another test.'

'A test!' Connant snapped joyfully, then his face sagged in disappointment. 'I suppose it's another either-way-you-want-it.'

'No,' said McReady steadily. 'Look sharp and be careful. Come into the Ad Building. Barclay, bring your electrocuter. And somebody – Dutton – stand with Barclay to make sure he does it. Watch every neighbor, for by the Hell these monsters came from, I've got something, and they know it. They're going to get dangerous!'

The group tensed abruptly. An air of crushing menace entered into every man's body, sharply they looked at each other. More keenly than ever before – *is that man next to me an inhuman monster?*

'What is it?' Garry asked, as they stood again in the main room. 'How long will it take?'

'I don't know, exactly,' said McReady, his voice brittle with angry determination. 'But I *know* it will work, and no two ways about it. It depends on a basic quality of the *monsters*, not on us. *'Kinner'* just convinced me.' He stood heavy and solid in bronzed immobility, completely sure of himself again at last.

'This,' said Barclay, hefting the wooden-handled weapon tipped with its two sharp-pointed, charged conductors, 'is going to be rather necessary, I take it. Is the power plant assured?'

Dutton nodded sharply. 'The automatic stoker bin is full. The gas power plant is on standby. Van Wall and I set it for the movie operation – and we've checked it over rather carefully several times, you know. Anything those wires touch, dies,' he assured them grimly. 'I know that.'

Dr Copper stirred vaguely in his bunk, rubbed his eyes with fumbling hand. He sat up slowly, blinked his eyes blurred with sleep and drugs, widened with an unutterable horror of drug-ridden nightmares. 'Garry,' he mumbled, 'Garry – listen. Selfish – from hell they came, and hellish shellfish – I mean self – Do I? What do I mean?' He sank back in his bunk, and snored softly.

McReady looked at him thoughtfully. 'We'll know

presently,' he nodded slowly. 'But selfish is what you mean, all right. You may have thought of that, half sleeping, dreaming there. I didn't stop to think what dreams you might be having. But that's all right. Selfish is the word. They must be, you see.' He turned to the men in the cabin, tense, silent men staring with wolfish eyes each at his neighbor. 'Selfish, and as Dr Copper said – *every part is a whole.* Every piece is self-sufficient, an animal in itself.

'That, and one other thing, tell the story. There's nothing mysterious about blood; it's just as normal a body tissue as a piece of muscle, or a piece of liver. But it hasn't so much connective tissue, though it has millions, billions of life-cells.'

McReady's great bronze beard ruffled in a grim smile. 'This is satisfying, in a way. I'm pretty sure we humans still outnumber you – others. Others standing here. And we have what you, your other-world race, evidently doesn't. Not an imitated, but a bred-in-the-bone instinct, a driving, unquenchable fire that's genuine. We'll fight, fight with a ferocity you may attempt to imitate, but you'll never equal! We're human. We're real. You're imitations, false to the core of your every cell.'

'All right. It's a showdown now. *You* know. You, with your mind reading. You've lifted the idea from my brain. You can't do a thing about it.

'Standing here—

'Let it pass. Blood is tissue. They have to bleed; if they bleed when cut, then by Heaven, they're phoney from hell! If they don't bleed – then that blood, separated from them, is an individual – *a newly formed individual in its own right, just as they – split, all of them, from one original – are individuals!*

'Get it, Van? See the answer, Bar?'

Van Wall laughed very softly. 'The blood – the blood will not obey. It's a new individual, with all the desire to protect its own life that the original – the main mass from which it was split – has. The *blood* will live – and try to crawl away from a hot needle, say!'

McReady picked up the scalpel from the table. From the cabinet, he took a rack of test tubes, a tiny alcohol lamp, and a length of platinum wire set in a little glass rod. A smile of grim satisfaction rode his lips. For a moment he glanced up at those around him. Barclay and Dutton moved toward him slowly, the wooden-handled electric instrument alert.

'Dutton,' said McReady, 'suppose you stand over by the splice there where you've connected that in. Just make sure no – thing pulls it loose.'

Dutton moved away. 'Now, Van, suppose you be first on this.'

White-faced, Van Wall stepped forward. With a delicate precision, McReady cut a vein in the base of his thumb. Van Wall winced slightly, then held steady as a half inch of bright blood collected in the tube. McReady put the tube in the rack, gave Van Wall a bit of alum, and indicated the iodine bottle.

Van Wall stood motionlessly watching. McReady heated the platinum wire in the alcohol lamp flame, then dipped it into the tube. It hissed softly. Five times he repeated the test. 'Human, I'd say,' McReady sighed, and straightened. 'As yet, my theory hasn't been actually proven – but I have hopes. I have hopes.

'Don't, by the way, get too interested in this. We have with us some unwelcome ones, no doubt. Van, will you relieve Barclay at the switch? Thanks. OK, Barclay, and may I say I hope you stay with us? You're a damned good guy.'

Barclay grinned uncertainly; winced under the keen edge of the scalpel. Presently, smiling widely, he retrieved his long-handled weapon.

'Mr. Samuel Dutt – *Bar!*'

The tensity was released in that second. Whatever of hell the monsters may have had within them, the men in that instant matched it. Barclay had no chance to move his weapon, as a score of men poured down on the thing that had seemed Dutton. It mewed, and spat, and tried to grow fangs – and was a hundred broken, torn pieces. Without knives, or any weapon save the brute-given strength of a staff of picked men, the thing was crushed, rent.

Slowly they picked themselves up, their eyes smouldering, very quiet in their motions. A curious wrinkling of their lips betrayed a species of nervousness.

Barclay went over with the electric weapon. Things smouldered and stank. The caustic acid Van Wall dropped on each spilled drop of blood gave off tickling, cough-provoking fumes.

McReady grinned, his deep-set eyes alight and dancing. 'Maybe,' he said softly, 'I underrated man's abilities when I said nothing human could have the ferocity in the eyes of that thing we found. I wish we could have the opportunity to treat in a more befitting manner these things. Something with boiling oil, or melted lead in it, or maybe slow roasting in the power boiler. When I think what a man Dutton was—

'Never mind. My theory is confirmed by – by one who knew? Well, Van Wall and Barclay are proven. I think, then, that I'll try to show you what I already know. That I, too, am human.' McReady swished the scalpel in absolute alcohol, burned it off the metal blade, and cut the base of his thumb expertly.

Twenty seconds later he looked up from the desk at the waiting men. There were more grins out there now, friendly grins, yet withal, something else in the eyes.

'Connant,' McReady laughed softly, 'was right. The huskies watching that thing in the corridor bend had nothing on you. Wonder why we think only the wolf blood has the right to ferocity? Maybe on spontaneous viciousness a wolf takes tops, but after these seven days – abandon all hope, ye wolves who enter here!

'Maybe we can save time. Connant, would you step for—'

Again Barclay was too slow. There were more grins, less tensity still, when Barclay and Van Wall finished their work.

Garry spoke in a low, bitter voice. 'Connant was one of the finest men we had here – and five minutes ago I'd have sworn he was a man. Those damnable things are more than imitation.' Garry shuddered and sat back in his bunk.

And thirty seconds later, Garry's blood shrank from the hot platinum wire, and struggled to escape the tube, struggled as frantically as a suddenly feral, red-eyed, dissolving imitation of Garry struggled to dodge the snake-tongue weapon Barclay advanced at him, white-faced and sweating. The Thing in the test tube screamed with a tiny, tinny voice as McReady dropped it into the glowing coal of the galley stove.

XIV

'The last of it?' Dr Copper looked down from his bunk with bloodshot, saddened eyes. 'Fourteen of them—'

McReady nodded shortly. 'In some ways – if only we could have permanently prevented their spreading – I'd like to have even the imitations back. Commander Garry – Connant – Dutton – Clark—'

'Where are they taking those things?' Copper nodded to the stretcher Barclay and Norris were carrying out.

'Outside. Outside on the ice, where they've got fifteen smashed crates, half a ton of coal, and presently will add 10 gallons of kerosene. We've dumped acid on every spilled drop, every torn fragment. We're going to incinerate those.'

'Sounds like a good plan.' Copper nodded wearily. 'I wonder, you haven't said whether Blair—'

McReady started. 'We forgot him? We had so much else! I wonder – do you suppose we can cure him now?'

'If—' began Dr Copper, and stopped meaningly.

McReady started a second time. 'Even a madman. It imitated Kinner and his praying hysteria—' McReady turned toward Van Wall at the long table. 'Van, we've got to make an expedition to Blair's shack.'

Van looked up sharply, the frown of worry faded for an instant in surprised remembrance. Then he rose, nodded. 'Barclay better go along. He applied the lashings, and may figure how to get in without frightening Blair too much.'

Three quarters of an hour, through -37 degrees cold, while the aurora curtain bellied overhead. The twilight was nearly twelve hours long, flaming in the north on snow like white, crystalline sand under their skis. A five-mile wind piled it in drift-lines pointing off to the northwest. Three quarters of an hour to reach the snow-buried shack. No smoke came from the little shack, and the men hastened.

'Blair!' Barclay roared into the wind and when he was still a hundred yards away. 'Blair!'

'Shut up,' said McReady softly. 'And hurry. He may be trying a lone hike. If we have to go after him – no planes, the tractors disabled—'

'Would a monster have the stamina a man has?'

'A broken leg wouldn't stop it for more than a minute,' McReady pointed out.

Barclay gasped suddenly and pointed aloft. Dim in the twilit sky, a winged thing circled in curves of indescribable grace and ease. Great white wings tipped gently, and the bird swept over them in silent curiosity. 'Albatross—' Barclay said softly. 'First of the season, and wandering way inland for some reason. If a monster's loose—'

Norris bent down on the ice, and tore hurriedly at his heavy, windproof clothing. He straightened, his coat flapping open, a grim blue-metaled weapon in his hand. It roared a challenge to the white silence of Antarctica.

The thing in the air screamed hoarsely. Its great wings worked frantically as a dozen feathers floated down from its tail. Norris fired again. The bird was moving swiftly now, but in an almost straight line of retreat. It screamed again, more feathers dropped, and with beating wings it soared behind a ridge of pressure ice, to vanish.

Norris hurried after the others. 'It won't come back,' he panted.

Barclay cautioned him to silence, pointing. A curiously, fiercely blue light beat out from the cracks of the shack's door. A very low, soft humming sounded inside, a low, soft humming and a clink and clink of tools, the very sounds somehow bearing a message of frantic haste.

McReady's face paled. 'Lord help us if that thing has—' He grabbed Barclay's shoulder, and made snipping motions with his fingers, pointing toward the lacing of control cables that held the door.

Barclay drew the wire cutters from his pocket, and kneeled soundlessly at the door. The snap and twang of cut wires made an unbearable racket in the utter quiet of the Antarctic hush. There was only that strange, sweetly soft hum from within the shack, and the queerly, hecticly clipped clicking and rattling of tools to drown their noises.

McReady peered through a crack in the door. His breath sucked in huskily and his great fingers clamped cruelly on Barclay's shoulder. The meteorologist backed down. 'It isn't,' he explained very softly, 'Blair. It's kneeling on something on the bunk – something that keeps lifting. Whatever it's working on is a thing like a knapsack – and it lifts.'

'All at once,' Barclay said grimly. 'No. Norris, hang back, and get that iron of yours out. It may have – weapons.'

Together, Barclay's powerful body and McReady's giant strength struck the door. Inside, the bunk jammed against the door screeched madly and crackled into kindling. The door flung down from broken hinges, the patched lumber of the doorpost dropping inward.

Like a blue rubber ball, a Thing bounced up. One of its four tentacle-like arms looped out like a striking snake. In a seven-tentacled hand a six-inch pencil of winking, shining metal glinted and swung upward to face them. Its line-thin lips twitched back from snake-fangs in a grin of hate, red eyes blazing.

Norris' revolver thundered in the confined space. The hate-washed face twitched in agony, the looping tentacle snatched back. The silvery thing in its hand a smashed ruin of metal, the seven-tentacled hand became a mass of mangled flesh oozing greenish-yellow ichor. The revolver thundered three times more. Dark holes drilled each of the three eyes before Norris hurled the empty weapon against its face.

The Thing screamed in feral hate, a lashing tentacle wiping at blinded eyes. For a moment it crawled on the floor, savage tentacles lashing out, the body twitching. Then it struggled up again, blinded eyes working, boiling hideously, the crushed flesh sloughing away in sodden gobbets.

Barclay lurched to his feet and dove forward with an ice-ax. The flat of the weighty thing crushed against the side of the head. Again the unkillable monster went down. The tentacles lashed out, and suddenly Barclay fell to his feet in the grip of a living, livid rope. The thing dissolved as he held it, a white-hot band that ate into the flesh of his hands like living fire. Frantically he tore the stuff from him, held his hands where they could not be reached. The blind Thing felt and ripped at the tough, heavy, windproof cloth, seeking flesh – flesh it could convert –

The huge blowtorch McReady had brought coughed solemnly. Abruptly it rumbled disapproval throatily. Then it laughed gurglingly, and thrust out a blue-white, three-foot tongue. The Thing on the floor shrieked, flailed out blindly with tentacles that writhed and withered in the bubbling wrath of the blowtorch. It crawled and turned on the floor, it shrieked and hobbled madly, but always McReady held the blowtorch on the face, the dead eyes burning and bubbling uselessly. Frantically the Thing crawled and howled.

A tentacle sprouted a savage talon – and crisped in the flame. Steadily McReady moved with a planned, grim campaign. Helpless, maddened, the Thing retreated from the grunting torch, the caressing, licking tongue. For a moment it rebelled, squalling in inhuman hatred at the touch of the icy snow. Then it fell back before the charring breath of the torch, the stench of its flesh bathing it. Hopelessly it retreated – on and on across the Antarctic snow. The bitter wind swept over it, twisting the torch-tongue; vainly it flopped, a trail of oily, stinking smoke bubbling away from it—

McReady walked back toward the shack silently. Barclay met him at the door. 'No more?' the giant meteorologist asked grimly.

Barclay shook his head. 'No more. It didn't split?'

'It had other things to think about,' McReady assured him. 'When I left it, it was a glowing coal. What was it doing?'

Norris laughed shortly. 'Wise boys, we are. Smash magnetos, so planes won't work. Rip the boiler tubing out of the tractors. And leave that Thing alone for a week in this shack. Alone and undisturbed.'

McReady looked in at the shack more carefully. The air, despite the ripped door, was hot and humid. On a table at the far end of the room rested a thing of coiled wires and small magnets, glass tubing and radio tubes. At the center a block of rough stone rested. From the center of the block came the light that flooded the place, the fiercely blue light bluer than the glare of an electric arc, and from it came the sweetly soft hum. Off to one side was another mechanism of crystal glass, blown with an incredible neatness and delicacy, metal plates and a queer, shimmery sphere of insubstantiality.

'What is that?' McReady moved nearer.

Norris grunted. 'Leave it for investigation. But I can guess pretty well. That's atomic power. That stuff to the left – that's a neat little thing for doing what men have been trying to do with 100-ton cyclotrons and so forth. It separates neutrons from heavy water, which he was getting from the surrounding ice.

'Where did he get all – oh. Of course. A monster couldn't be locked in – or out. He's been through the apparatus caches.' McReady stared at the apparatus. 'Lord, what minds that race must have—'

'The shimmery sphere – I think it's a sphere of pure force. Neutrons can pass through any matter, and he wanted a supply reservoir of neutrons. Just project neutrons against silica – calcium – beryllium – almost anything, and the atomic energy is released. That thing is the atomic generator.'

McReady plucked a thermometer from his coat. 'It's 120 degrees in here, despite the open door. Our clothes have kept the heat out to an extent, but I'm sweating now.'

Norris nodded. 'The light's cold. I found that. But it gives off heat to warm the place through that coil. He had all the power in the world. He could keep it warm and pleasant, as his race thought of warmth and pleasantness. Did you notice the light, the color of it?'

McReady nodded. 'Beyond the stars is the answer. From beyond the stars. From a hotter planet that circled a brighter, bluer sun they came.'

McReady glanced out the door toward the blasted, smoke-stained trail that flopped and wandered blindly off across the drift. 'There won't be any more coming. I guess. Sheer accident it landed here, and that was twenty million years ago. What did it do all that for?' He nodded toward the apparatus.

Barclay laughed softly. 'Did you notice what it was working on when we came? Look.' He pointed toward the ceiling of the shack.

Like a knapsack made of flattened coffee tins, with dangling cloth straps and leather belts, the mechanism clung to the ceiling. A tiny, glaring heart of supernal flame burned in it, yet burned through the ceiling's wood without scorching it. Barclay walked over to it, grasped two of the dangling straps in his hands, and pulled it down with an effort. He strapped it about his body. A slight jump carried him in a weirdly slow arc across the room.

'Antigravity,' said McReady softly.

'Antigravity,' Norris nodded. 'Yes, we had 'em stopped, with no planes, and no birds. The birds hadn't come – but it had coffee tins and radio parts, and glass and the machine shop at night. And a week – a whole week – all to itself. America in a single jump – with antigravity powered by the atomic energy of matter.

'We had 'em stopped. Another half hour – it was just tightening these straps on the device so it could wear it – and we'd have stayed in Antarctica, and shot down any moving thing that came from the rest of the world.'

'The albatross—' McReady said softly. 'Do you suppose—'

'With this thing almost finished? With that death weapon it held in its hand?

'No, by the grace of God, who evidently does hear very well, even down here, and the margin of half an hour, we keep our world, and the planets of the system, too. Antigravity, you know, and atomic power. Because They came from another sun, a star beyond the stars. *They* came from a world with a bluer sun.'

Blindness

Old Dr Malcolm Mackay is dead, and, with more than usual truth, one may say he is at last at peace. His life was hard and bitter, those last few years. He was blind, of course, blinded as everyone knew by the three-year-long exposure to the intolerable light of the Sun.

And he was bitter, of course, as everyone knew. But somehow they could not understand that; a man so great, so loved by the population of three worlds, it seemed there could be nothing in his life to embitter him, nor in the respect and love of the worlds for him.

Some, rather unkindly, I feel, put it down to his blindness, and his age – he was eighty-seven when he died – and in this they were unjust. The acclaim his great discovery brought him was the thing which embittered him. You see, he didn't *want* acclaim for that; it was for the lesser invention he really wanted praise.

That the 'Grand Old Man' may be better understood, I genuinely want people to understand better the story of his work. And his blindness, but not as most people speak of it. The blindness struck him long before the exposure to the Sun ruined his eyes. Perhaps I had better explain.

Malcolm Mackay was born in 1974, just one year after Cartwright finally succeeded in committing suicide as he had always wanted to – by dying of asphyxiation on the surface of the Moon, when his air gave out. He was three when

Garnall was drowned in Lake Erie, after returning from Luna, the first man to reach Earth again, alive. He didn't go on living, of course, but he was alive when he reached Earth. That we knew.

Mackay was eleven, and interested, when Randolph's expedition returned with mineralogtcal specimens, and the records of a year's stay on the Moon.

Mackay went to Massachusetts Institute of Technology at seventeen, and was graduated a member of the class of 1995. But he took physics – atomic physics.

Mackay had seen that on atomic power rested the only real hope of really commercial, economically sound, interplanetary travel. He was sure of that at seventeen when he entered MIT. He was convinced when he was graduated, and went back for more, because about that same time old Douglas A. Mackay died, and left him three quarters of a million.

Malcolm Mackay saw that the hand of Providence was stretched out to aid him. Money was the thing that he'd needed. Douglas Mackay always claimed that money was a higher form of life; that it answered the three tests of life. It was sensitive to stimulation. It was able to grow by accretion. And finally – the most important, in Mackay's estimation – the old Scot pointed out it was capable of reproduction. So Malcolm Mackay put his in an incubator, a large trust company, and left it to reproduce as rapidly as possible.

He lived in shabby quarters, and in shabby clothes most of the time, so he'd have money later on when he started his work. And he studied. Obviously, there is no question but that Mackay was one of the most highly intelligent human beings that ever lived. He started with the basis of atomic knowledge of that day, and he learned it all, too, and then he was ready to go ahead. He spent seventeen years at MIT learning and teaching, till he felt that he had learned enough to make the teaching more of a nuisance than a worthwhile use of his time.

By that time, the money had followed the laws of money, and life, and had reproduced itself, not once, but twice, for the Scot had picked a good company. He had two and a quarter millions.

There is no need to retell his early experiments. The story of the loss of three fingers on his left hand is an old one. The countless minor and semi-major explosions he had, the radiation burns he collected. But, perhaps those burns weren't so wholly injurious as was thought, for thirty-five years after he left MIT he was still working at an age when most men are resting – either in coffins or wheelchairs. The Grand Old Man didn't put his final determination into action until he was seventy-three.

John Burns was his laboratory assistant and mechanician then. Mackay's loss of his fingers had been serious, because it made delicate instrument work difficult, and John Burns, thirty-two at the time, was his mechanician, his hand, and his highly trained technical assistant. In May, 2047, the latest experiment having revealed only highly interesting but negative results, Malcolm Mackay looked at Burns.

'John, that settled it,' he said slowly. 'Something is missing, and we won't get it here in a pair of lifetimes, even long ones. You know the only place we can find it.'

'I suppose you mean the Sun,' replied Burns sadly. 'But since we can't get near enough to that, it doesn't do us a bit of good. Houston's the only man who has come back alive, and his nearest approach was 41,743,560 miles. And it didn't do any good, anyway. The automatic rockets get nearer, but not very much nearer; the heat beats them – all of them. And you, yourself, said we'd have to get within four millions, not four tens of millions of miles. And that's utterly hopeless. Nothing could stand it that close to old Sol.'

'We're going,' said Mackay grimly. 'I've spent close to three quarters of a century working on the problem of atomic energy, and we're going.' He paused for a moment, then looked up at Burns with a kindly smile. 'No; I guess it's not we who are going, but I. I'm more than willing to go, and lose perhaps two years off the tail end of my overlong life if need be, if I can send back the word to the world that will set it free of that age-old problem of power.

'Power. Maybe we can use Sun power, after all. They've been talking about solar power since the beginning of the last century, and they haven't got it yet. Never will, I guess, because the power's too diluted. They can't build a big enough Sun glass. But if we can steal the secret of the Sun, and give them little private suns right here on Earth, that will settle the question. And give rockets some real power, too, incidentally.'

The old man chuckled. 'You know, John, when I started, it was the dream of my life that rockets should have atomic power so they could really reach the other planets. Atomic power! And now, here I am, close to three quarters of a century old – and I've never even left Earth. A grounder.

'And atomic power isn't so badly needed for rockets, anyway. They have good fuels now, safe ones and powerful ones like atomic hydrogen and oxygen. Atomic power is needed here on Earth, where factories are, and men labor in coal mines for fuel, and where they make the fuel for rockets. That's where mankind needs atomic power.

'And by all the powers of Heaven, if the Sun's the place where I can learn, the Sun's where I'm going.'

'But by that particular power of Heaven known as radiant energy, you can't,' objected Burns. 'The radiation makes it impossible.'

'Well, I'll kill that radiation, somehow. That's the real problem now, I guess. Wonder how – we've developed a lot of different radiation screens and blocks since we began this work here; we ought to find something.'

'Yes, doctor; we can stop any kind of radiation known, including Millikan, but we can't stop three or four million tons of it a second. It's not stopping it. Anything will do that. It's a problem we've never before attempted – the problem of handling it after it's stopped.'

'We'll stop it and handle it, somehow,' determined Mackay.

Burns gave up. Mackay meant it, so that was the new problem. It was obviously impossible, Burns knew, but so was atomic power, evidently. They'd run against all the blind alleys in the universe seeking that, so they might as well try a few more in a different direction.

Malcolm threw himself into that problem with all the keenness and determination he had shown through fifty-five years of active research on the main line. This was just another obstacle on the main track. It stood between him and the Great Secret.

He experimented a little with photoelectric cells, because he felt the way to do it was to turn the heat into electric energy. Electricity is the only form of energy that can be stepped up or down. Radiant energy can be broken down from X-ray to ultraviolet, to blue to red, to infra-heat. But it can't possibly be built up or transformed down at will. So Mackay tried to turn heat into electricity.

He wasn't long in seeing the hopelessness of photocells. They absorbed some of the radiant energy as electricity, but about ninety-five per cent turned into straight molecular motion, known as heat, just as it did anywhere else.

Then he tried super-mirrors and gave up within three months. That was the wrong way. So it must be some way of turning molecular motion of heat into electric power.

It was like threading the way through a maze. You found all the blind alleys first, then there was only the right paths left. So he started on molecular motion-electricity transformations. He tried thermo-couple metals. They worked only when you had a cool place. A cool place! That was what he was trying to get. So he quit that.

Then he got mixed up with hysteresis. He was experimenting with magnets and alternating current, and that gave him the right lead. He developed *thermlectrium* nearly a year and a half later, in 2049, of course.

The first fragment of the new alloy was put in the coil, and heat-treated till the proper conditioning had been obtained, and the secret of the heat-treatment is the whole secret, really. And finally it was taken out. It was dull, silvery gray, rather heavy, being nickel-iron-cobalt-carbon steel.

It looked like any of a thousand thousand other alloys, felt like any of them then. But they put it in the closed coil. In fifteen seconds dew formed on it; in twenty, frost, and the coil was getting hot, a current of fifty amperes flowing through it. Mackay beamed on it with joy. The obstacle had been removed! The way to the Sun was clear.

He announced his plans now to the news agencies, and to the Baldwin Rocket Foundry Co. They agreed to build him a ship according to his plans – and he made up his famous plans.

Thermlectrium is a magnetic alloy, the unique property being that its crystals are of almost exactly uniform size. When a magnet is turned end for end in a coil of wire, when the magnetic polarity is reversed, a current is induced in the circuit, at the expense of the energy which turned the magnet.

In any permanent magnet, the crystals are tiny individual magnets, all lined up with their north poles pointing the same way. In magnetized steel, if the bar is heated, the heat-motion of the molecules turns some of them around, with the result that the magnetism is lost. In thermlectrium, even at low temperatures, the crystals turn, but they all turn together. The result is the same as though the bar had been inverted. A current is induced in the surrounding coil. And, of course, the energy which inverts the magnet, and drives the current of electricity, is the molecular motion known as heat. Heat was conquered!

Dr Mackay drove his plans on to rapid completion. Burns insisted on going, and Mackay could not dissuade him.

The plans were strange. They were enough to dissuade any normal man. Only such a fanatic as Dr Mackay really was, and as Burns had become, could have imagined them. Either that, or a man with colossal self-conceit. The *Prometheus* was to leave from Luna. Then she was to circle down toward the Sun, down very, very nearly one hundred million miles till she was within three million miles of the million mile globe of incandescent fury, and stop her fall by going into a close, circular orbit.

That means less, today. No one had ever imagined attempting anything like that. Houston, who had circled the Sun, had actually merely swung in on a comet's orbit, and let his momentum carry him away again. That wasn't difficult.

But to break the vast parabolic orbit a body would naturally attain in falling from Earth toward the Sun would require every pound of fuel the *Prometheus* could carry and break free of Luna.

The *Prometheus* could set up her orbit around the Sun. That was going to be easy. But they couldn't possibly pull loose with any known power. Only atomic power could do it. When and if they found it!

Malcolm Mackay was eager to bet his life on that proposition. Atomic energy or – eternal captivity – death. And Burns, as much a fanatic as Mackay, was willing, too.

There were only two horns to this dilemma. There was no third to escape on, no going between them. So the Grand Old Man sank every penny of his fortune in it, and would have sunk any he could borrow had he been able to get it.

The *Prometheus* rose, slowly. And during the weeks and months it was being built, Mackay and Burns spent their time gathering supplies, instruments, chemicals. For one thing, every element must be represented, and in proportion to its availability. Radium, even, though radium could never be a source of atomic power, for power derived from radium would still be too expensive for commercial use. But radium might be the absolutely essential primer for the engine – so radium went. And fluorine, the deadly unmanageable halogen, everything.

Then, gradually, the things were moved in as the ship neared completion. The outer hull of the high-temperature tungsten steel, the space filled with hydrogen under pressure, since hydrogen was the best conductor of heat practicable, and in that interspace, the thousands of thermlectrium elements, and fans to force circulation.

The *Prometheus* was a beautiful ship when she was

finished. She glowed with the gleam of a telescope mirror, polished to the ultimate. Only on one side was she black, black as space, and, here, studded with huge projectors and heaters. The power inevitably generated in absorbing the heat in the therm elements would be cast out here in tungsten bars thick as a man's arm, and glowing white-hot in an atmosphere of hydrogen gas.

She left, finally. Struggling up from Earth, she reached Luna, her first stage, and filled her fuel tanks to the last possible ounce. Then, in August, 2050, she took off at length.

Reaching the Sun was no trick at all, once she had broken free of the Moon and of Earth. Day after day she fell with steadily mounting speed. The Sun loomed larger, hotter. The great gyroscopes went into action, and the *Prometheus* turned its silvered face to the Sun, reflecting the flooding heat. Nearer and nearer. Venus fell behind, then Mercury's orbit at last.

They knew heat then. And radiation. The Sun loomed gigantic, a titanic furnace whose flames reached out a quarter of a million miles. The therm elements began to function, and the heat dropped somewhat. Then the rockets started again, started their braking action, slowly, steadily, braking the ship to the orbit it must make, close about the Sun.

Hour after hour they droned and roared and rumbled, and the heat mounted, for all the straining power of the therm elements. Radio to Earth stopped the second day of the braking. The flooding radiations of the Sun killed it. They could still send, they knew, but they could not receive. Their signals were received by stations on the Moon, where the washing static of the Sun did not blanket all the signals that came. For they were beaming their waves, and the Sun, of course, was not.

84

'We must establish the orbit soon, John,' said Mackay, at last. He was lying down on his couch, sick and weak with the changing strains. 'I am an old man, I fear, and I may not be able to endure much more of this.'

'We will have to brake more sharply then, Dr Mackay,' replied Burns concernedly. 'And then we may not be able to establish the perfectly circular orbit we need.'

Mackay smiled faintly, grimly. If it is not soon, John, no orbit will mean anything to me.'

The rockets roared louder, and the ship slowed more rapidly. But it was three days yet before the orbit trimming could be started. They left the ship in an eccentric orbit at first, though, and counteracted for the librations of the ship, which tended to turn the blackened radiator side toward the Sun, by working the gyroscope planes.

Dr Mackay recuperated slowly. It was three weeks, actually, three, precious oxygen-consuming weeks, before they started the final orbit trimming. Then day and day they worked, observing, and occasionally giving a slight added rocket thrust for orbit trimming.

But, finally, at a distance of 3.73 millions of miles, the *Prometheus* circled the titanic star. The sunward side, for all its polish, glowed red-hot continuously. And the inside of the ship remained a heated, desiccated furnace, for all the work of the therm elements. Even they could not perfectly handle the heat.

'Ah, John,' said Mackay at last. 'In some ways Earth was better, for here we have strange conditions. I wish we could get a time signal from Earth. The space is distorted here by the Sun.'

Old Sol, mighty in mass and power, was warping space so that spectrum lines were not the same; their instruments were not the same; the titanic electric and magnetic fields threw their delicate apparatus awry. But they worked.

It was fortunate that the therm elements produced power, as well as getting rid of the heat. With the power, they kept the functions of the ship running, breaking down the water formed in their breathing to oxygen once more, and storing the hydrogen in one of the now empty fuel tanks.

And their observations went on, and their calculations. In six months it seemed they had never known another life than this of intolerable, blinding light if they dared to open an observation slit in the slightest; intolerable, deadly radiation if they dared to step beyond the protected walls of their laboratory and living quarters without a protective suit. For most of the ship was as transparent to the ultrashort waves of the Sun as empty space.

But it grew to be a habit with them, the sending of the daily negative reports, the impossibility of hearing any signal from Earth, even of observing it, for there was the eternal Gegenschein. It was blinding here, the reflected light from the thin-strewn dust of the Sun.

That dust was slowing them down, of course. They were, actually, spiralling in toward the Sun. In some seventy-five years they would have been within reach of the prominences. But before then – one of the pans of their balance would have tipped. Atomic power – or the inevitable end.

But Mackay was happy here. His eyes turned from deep blue-gray to a pale blue with red bloodshot balls; his skin turned first deep, deep brown from the filtering ultraviolet, then it became mottled and unhealthy. Burns' skin changed too, but his eyes endured better, for he was younger. Still, Mackay felt sure of his goal. He looked down into the flaming heart of a Sun spot, and he examined the underside of

86

a prominence, and he watched the ebb and flow of Sol's titanic tides of white-hot gas.

2050 passed into history, and 2051 and 2052 followed in swift succession. No hint of the great happenings of Earth and the planets reached there, only the awful burning of the Sun – and, in February of 2053, a hint of the great changes there.

'John,' said Mackay softly one day, 'John – I think I see some hint of the secret. I think we may make it, John!'

Burns looked at the sharp-lined spectrum that lay on the table before Mackay, and at the pages of calculations and measurements and at the data sheets. 'I don't see anything much different in that, doctor. Isn't it another will-o'-the-wisp?'

'I – I hope not, John. Don't you see this – this little line here? Do you recognize it?'

'No – no, I don't think I do,' he said slowly. 'It's a bit too high for the 4781 line. And I don't know what's in there—'

'There isn't any there, John,' said Mackay softly. 'There isn't any. It's a forbidden line, an impossible line. It's the impossible line of sodium, John. It's a transformation that just couldn't take place. And it did, so I'm going to find out how it did. If I can make the impossible release take place the same way—'

'But that tells so little, so very little. Even if you could duplicate that change, make that line, you'd still be as far from the secret as from Sirius. Or Earth for that matter.'

'I'll know more, though, John. You forget that only knowledge is the real secret. When I know all about the atom, I'll know how to do what I want to do. If I know all the changes that can take place, and why, then I can make that

87

other change. Ah, if only I could see just a few miles deeper into the heart of the Sun—'

'We've seen some of the greatest Sun spots in history, and at close hand. Do you think we could see any deeper? The light – that terrible light.'

'It blinds even the instruments, so there is little more we can do. But we can calculate and take more photographs for more of those lines. But now I must see what the instruments recorded when we got this line.'

They had recorded even more than the old man had hoped. It was enough. Mackay and Burns duplicated that impossible line, and then they produced some more impossible lines. It was the key. It wasn't impossibly difficult then. They could design the apparatus, and did, in September, three years and one month after lifting off for the final drop to the Sun.

They made it, piece by piece, and tested it January. It wasn't winter there; there was no winter. Only everlasting heat. And Mackay's eyes were failing rapidly. His work was over. Both because he could scarcely work any longer, and because, on January 14, 2054, the energy of the atom was harnessed by man! The Great Secret was discovered.

It took the intense light of the mighty arc to stimulate the old eyes when the thing was done. Only its tremendous blinding power was visible. His ears could hear the roar, well enough, and his fingers could feel the outlines of the hulking machine. But he could no longer make it out when it at last roared its lusty greeting to human ears.

His thin lips parted in a contented smile, though, as his tough old fingers caressed the cold metal and the smooth cold glass. 'It works, doesn't it, John? It works. John, we've done it.' A shadow passed over the old man's face for an instant. 'We haven't heard from Earth in over three years. Do you suppose someone else has discovered it, too? I suppose I ought not be selfish, but I do hope they haven't. I want to give this to the world.

'John, can you make the drive apparatus yourself?'

'Yes, doctor; I can. You had all the plans worked out, and they're simple to follow. It isn't really greatly different. Only that instead of using a high-temperature gas ejected at thousands of feet a second, we'll use a high-voltage ion ejected at thousands of miles a second. And because we can burn iron, as you predicted, we don't have to worry at all about power.'

'No, John. We don't have to worry at all about power.' The old man sighed, then chuckled contentedly. 'I always wanted to live to see the day when atomic power ran the world. But I guess I won't after all. I can't see, but it won't matter. I have so few years left, I won't worry about a little thing like that. My work's done, anyway. We don't have to worry about power, John; the world doesn't any more.

'Men will never again have to worry about power. Never again will they have to grub in the Earth for fuels. Or do things the hard way because it is less costly of power. Power – power for all the world's industry. All the wheels of Earth's factories driven by the exploding atoms. The arctic heated to a garden by it. Vast Canada opened by it to human habitation, clear to the North Pole.

'No more smoke-clouded cities.

'And the atom will lift the load of labor from man's back. No more sweating for six hours every day for daily bread. An hour a day – and unlimited, infinite power. And, maybe, even, some day it will lead to successful transmutation, though I can't see it. I mean, I can't see it even mentally,' he said with a little smile. 'The Sun showed me the secrets it held – and took away the impious vision that gazed upon them.

'It is worth it. The world will have power – and my work is done.

'You are starting the drive apparatus?'

'Yes, doctor. The main tube is to be—'

Burns launched into a technical discussion. The doctor's eyes could not follow the plans, but the old mind was as keen as ever. It pictured every detail with a more penetrative vision than ever his eyes could have. He chuckled contentedly as he thought of it.

'John, I have lost little, and gained more. I can see that tube better than you can. It's a metal tube, but I can see to its deepest heart, and I can even see the ions streaming out, slowly, precisely. My mind has a better eye than ever my body had, and now it is developing. I can see the tube when it is not yet, and I can see the heart of it, which you cannot.

'Make it up, John. We must hurry back.'

The lathe hummed, powered by atomic energy, and the electric furnace glowed with a heat so intense the old scientist could see it, driven by the power of the bursting atoms.

The mental eye he had boasted of was keen, keener than his old eyes had ever been. But still it was blind. Somehow, it did not see the white-hot tungsten bars on the 'night' side of the ship pouring thousands and thousands of kilowatts of power out into space. The power the therm elements were deriving from the cooling of the ship.

The drive tubes grew, and their great metal bed-bolts were turned. Then the great rocket tubes were sealed at the far end, cut, and insulated again. But now, electrically insulated, the great ion tubes took shape and were anchored, and the huge conductors ran back to the ion-gas chambers, and to the hunched bulk of the atomic engine. Day succeeded day, and Burns cut and fashioned the metal and welded it under the blazing power of the broken atoms in their atomic generator.

And at last the ship trembled with a new, soft surge. It must be slow, for the men were used now to weightlessness, three long years of it. But gradually, gradually, the *Prometheus*, bearing the fire it had stolen from the Sun, swung swifter in its orbit, and spiraled out once more, slowly, slowly. And the radio drove out its beam toward Earth.

They could not hear the messages that Earth and Luna pounded back at them, but gladly they guessed them. The ion tubes whispered and murmured softly, with a slithering rustle as of a snake in dry leaves, and the ship accelerated steadily, slowly. They ran those tubes day and night and slowly increased the power. There was no need for maximum efficiency now. No need to care as they wasted their power. There was plenty more.

Their only difficulty was that with the mighty ion tubes working they could not receive radio signals, even when they gradually circled out beyond Mercury, and finally Venus, slowly growing accustomed once more to weight. They did not want to turn off their tubes, because they must get accustomed to weight once more, and they were moving very rapidly now, more and more rapidly, so that they passed Venus far too rapidly for the ships that rose from the planet to congratulate Dr Mackay and tell him the great news.

They circled on, in the *Prometheus*, till they were used once more to Earth gravity, and then they were near Earth, and had to apply the braking ion rockets.

'No stopping at the Moon, John,' Malcolm Mackay

smiled. 'We and all humanity are through with that. We will go directly to Earth. We had best land in the Mojave Desert. Tell them, tell them to keep away, for the ions will be dangerous.'

John Burns drove out his message, and Earth loomed large, and North America came slowly into view. Then they were settling toward the desert.

The old scientist heard the faint, cold cry of ruptured air first, for his eyes were dark, and only his ears brought messages from outside. 'That's air, John!' he cried suddenly. 'We're in the air again! Earth's air! How far up are we?'

'Only another one hundred and fifty miles now, doctor. We're almost home.'

'Home – I should like to see for just this second, to see it again. John, John, I'll never see Earth again. I'll never – but that means little. I'll hear it. I'll hear it and smell it in my nostrils, clean and sweet and moist, and I'll taste it in the air. Earth's air, John, thick and spicy with green things. It's autumn. I want to smell burning leaves again, John. And feel snow, and hear its soft caress on a glass pane, and hear the soft sounds men make in snow. I'm glad it's autumn. Spring has its smells, but they aren't so spicy and clean. They're not so interesting, when you can't see the color of grass, so green – too bright, like a child's crayon drawing. Colors – I'll miss them. There weren't any out there. Colors – I'll never see the leaves again, John.

'But I'll smell them, and I'll hear the hum and whisper of a thousand thousand atomic engines making the world over for mankind.

'Where are we? The air is shrilling thickly now.'

'We're less than fifty miles up. They've cleared the Mojave for fifty miles around us, but, doctor, there are a hundred thousand private air-cars there – a new design. They must have developed broadcast power. They're all individually powered and apparently by electrical means.'

'Broadcast power? That is good. Then atomic energy will reach every home. The apparatus would be expensive, too expensive for homes.'

'The air is full of ships – there are half a dozen great stratosphere ships flying near us now; can you hear the *chug* of their propellers?'

'Is that the noise – ah! Men, men, again, John. I want to hear a thousand voices all at once.'

Burns laughed recklessly, carefree. 'You will, from the looks of things. You will! There are nearer a thousand thousand down there now!'

'The ship is slowing?' asked Mackay.

Burns was silent for a moment. Then, suddenly, the dry rustle of the tubes changed its note; it flared for an instant, there was a soft, grating thud, a harsh scraping of sand – and the ion tubes died in silence.

'The ship is stopped, doctor. We're home.'

Dimly, faintly, the sound of a thousand voices clamoring and shouting came through the heavy walls. Mackay had landed! The Grand Old Man was back! And half the world had turned out to welcome him, the man who had remade all Earth, and all Venus.

The lock opened, and to Mackay came the roar of voices, the thrum and hum and rumble of thousands and tens of thousands of propellers. There was the musical cacophony of a thousand air-car signals, and the mighty thunder of a titanic voice, rumbling, hoarse, and godlike in power, cutting through, drowning it all.

'They're welcoming you, Dr. Mackay – welcoming you.'

'So I hear,' said Mackay, half happily, half sadly, 'but I am so tired, perhaps I can rest a bit first. I am older than you are, John. You have done as much as I; you had better answer them.'

Suddenly, close-by human voices cut in, excited, happy, welcoming voices, and John Burns' swift answering speech:

'He is tired; it has been hard for him. And – you know he has lost his sight. The radiation of the Sun so close. He would rather be taken where he can rest.'

'Very well – but can't he say something? Just a few words?'

Burns looked back at the old man. Malcolm Mackay shook his head.

The man outside spoke again: 'Very well. We will take him directly to anywhere he wants.'

Mackay smiled slowly, thoughtfully. 'Anywhere, any-where that I can smell the trees. I think I'd like to go to some place in the mountains where the air is sweet and spicy with pine smells. I will be feeling better in a few days—'

They took him to a private camp in the mountains. A ten-room 'cabin,' and they kept the world away, and a doc-tor took care of him. He slept and rested, and Burns came to see him twice the next day, but was hurried away. The next day and the next he did not come.

Because even Burns had not gathered quickly the mean-ing of all this. Even he had thought at first it was in celebra-tion of the invention of the atomic generator.

At last he had to come. He came into Mackay's room slowly. His pace told the blind man something was wrong.

'John – John, what's troubling you so?'

'Nothing; I was not sure you were awake.'

Mackay thought for a few seconds and smiled. 'That

wasn't it, but we will let it pass now. Do they want me to speak?'

'Yes. At the special meeting of the American Association for the Advancement of Science. And – also on the subject of the thermlectrium elements. You have done far more than you thought, doctor. You have remade the worlds already. Those cars I thought were powered by broadcast energy? I was wrong. We were blind to the possibilities of that lesser thing, the thermlectrium element. Those cars were powered by it, getting their energy from the heat of the air. All the industries in the world are powered by it. It is free power.

'The elements are cheap, small, simple beyond anything conceivable, a bar of common metal – a coil of wire. They require no control, no attention. And the energy costs nothing at all. Every home, every store, every man, has his private thermlectrium element. Every car and every vehicle is powered by it.

'And the map of the world has been twisted and changed by it in three short years. The tropics are the garden-spot of the world. Square miles of land are cooled by giant thermlectrium installations, cities air-conditioned, till the power they develop becomes a nuisance, a thing they cannot get rid of. The tropics are habitable, and they have been given a brisk, cool, controlled climate by your thermlectrium elements.

'Antarctica is heated by it! There are two mining developments that suck heat from that frozen air to make power in quantities they cannot use.

'And rocket fuel costs nothing! Nothing at all. The tropical countries find the electrolytic breaking down of water the only cheap, practical way to get rid of their vast energy, without turning it right back into heat. They give the gases to whosoever will take them away.

'And Venus you have remade. Venus had two large colonies, already. They are cooled, made habitable, by the thermlectrium apparatus. A ten-dollar unit will cool and power an average house forever, without the slightest wear. By moving it outside in winter, it will warm and power it. But on Venus it is all cooling. They are developing the planet now. Dr. Mackay, you have remade the worlds!'

Dr Mackay's face was blank. Slowly a great question was forming. A great, painful question. 'But – but, John – what about – atomic energy?'

'One of the greatest space lines wants to contract for it, doctor. Their interplanetary ships need it.'

'One!' cried the Grand Old Man. 'One – what of the others?'

'There is only one interplanetary line. The lines to the Moon are not interplanetary—'

And Dr Mackay caught the kindness in his tone.

'I see – I see – they can use the free gases from the tropics. Free power – less than nothing.

'Then the world doesn't want my atomic energy, does it?' he said softly. His old body seemed to droop.

Frictional Losses

'But why, Hugh, do you insist on exploring always in these worst of the ruins for what you want?' asked Ban wearily. 'These sharp-edged glass fragments, and the thick ashes – surely there are other parts of this junk heap that would satisfy you. I can see little difference, save that some parts are churned more than others, and this is one of the worst places.'

Hugh Thompson shook his heavy, gray head slowly and straightened his aching back very slowly for he was getting old now, and the living conditions he endured were very hard for him. His back felt fragile, breakable. 'No, Tom. You are only thirty-two; you do not remember. New York was divided into many districts. Perhaps you can remember that they used to dig here for the food supplies? That was because this was a food-market district, too. But right in this section once was a great number of stores devoted to radio and electrical equipment. It is not as badly churned as you think. And here is our best hope, though faint enough it is.'

Ban Norman looked about doubtfully. Great mounds and heaps of semifused and disintegrated rock and metal sprawled as far as the eye could reach in one direction, to the river's edge in the other. Here and there a crumbling remnant of a tower remained, balanced by an occasional hundred-foot pock mark that, walled with glassy, fused granite, was floored now with a thin layer of muddy water and scum. The white masses of cracked stone were streaked with dark red, like the dried blood of the buildings they had been from the slowly melting iron skeletons.

'The Granthee treated this section to an exceptionally heavy lashing. Why expect anything so delicate as the radio tubes you seek, to survive?'

'Because we can do nothing else, Ban,' said the old man, patiently. 'I was no older than you are when this happened, and I first attempted to do what we have done for these thirty years now. Our little station has failed again, and all the people that have so faithfully sought to keep this thin thread of civilization are wondering again if the final break in the thread has come for us. Boston is gone now, has been for three months. Cincinnati is lost, we know, because Randolph Balling could get no man or woman to learn from him before he died.

'We are losing, Ban, and I hate it so. Man tried so hard for so long – and, now, in three decades – oh, it is so wrong to give up hope.'

Ban sighed, and moved toward the shade of some great tumbled blocks. 'Let us eat, while we rest and talk. What was this building?'

Hugh looked about him, at the great blocks, thrown down in a moment of petulance like a scattered child's toys. He tried to determine his location by the rotting remains of the docks, the tumbled heaps behind, the Jersey shore across the river. Slowly he shook his head. 'It is thirty years, Ban,' he said, seating himself gingerly, and pulling the hard, blackish bread from the bag of woven reeds he carried. 'I am forgetting how old New York looked. It has been so long I have seen it thus, it seems it was never otherwise. But there were few high buildings here, and this was evidently a very large one. It may have been the New York Telephone Company building.'

Ban looked about the ruins and shrugged. 'I see no cables, or wires.'

'No. But this was an executive building, and the central offices represented little of the equipment. It would be lost in this jumble. Besides, when the clans formed they stripped every fragment of copper they could find from every building to make plans. They could work copper more readily than any other metal, and all exposed cables were taken. There was lead, too, for the sling shots. We are fortunate, really, so much of the radio equipment was deeply buried for that would have been destroyed in those first years.'

'But the buried equipment was ruined so that was no gain.'

'It was not all ruined. And we can be thankful that much of the equipment had been refined to a ruggedness that resisted the strains. The metal tubes, for instance. They were but a few years old when the Granthee came. Had the old glass tubes been all we had, it would have been few, indeed, we could have salvaged.'

Ban looked about sourly. 'I can believe that. What was it that destroyed this section so thoroughly?'

'The atomic bombs. Some few of our own. That great crater I have shown you in the old park was one of our own, set off when the Granthee ship landed there. You cannot find even a fragment of that ship; even the metal of which it was made was ruined in that flare. The atomic bombs flared rather than exploded.'

'If we had the atomic power they had, why was it that they, with their little force of a hundred ships came, so near to conquering the whole world of man?'

'We did not have atomic power. We developed, toward the end, atomic explosives, which are very different. Grant Hubert has shown you explosives, and you know how different they are from fuels. We had explosives, but before we could learn to use atomic fuels, it was too late. The men and the laboratories and the machine shops were, it seems, gone.

'The Granthee ships appeared in April, over Russia, Chicago, Brazil and Central Africa. In July, the thing was a thing done. They attacked, with their fever ray – an intense radio beam – that heated men like an intense fever, till they died in seconds. They wiped out life in Africa in a few days, and they wiped out all life in Asia, nearly a billion humans, within two weeks. Japan was armed as a modern nation, and withstood the attack for a week, and destroyed seven of the Granthee ships. She might have done more, but for the Japan Deep.'

'The Japan Deep—'

'Yes. Japan was an island empire, of men somewhat similar to John Lun, yellowish, small men. But they had learned the ways of the whites, and fought more stubbornly, more heroically, really, than the others. They were a fatalistic race. They conceived the idea, and used it first, of the torpedo ships. I have shown you the wrecked airplane near Newark. They had many, smaller, but far swifter – little planes that could make six hundred miles an hour.

'They took those, and put heavy metal around the engine, and many, many pounds of explosive in them, and they filled the fuel tank with a substance known as picric acid in the gasoline. Their engines could not withstand that treatment for more than ten minutes, but for those minutes they were terribly powerful.

'So those planes took off from the ground, and flew like

great birds into the air, at a speed that would cover the distance from here to the clan in the Orange Mountains in less than two minutes – six hundred miles an hour.

'The Granthee ships were fast, but they were very, very large, nearly a thousand feet long. They turned their radio beams on the planes, and the engines sometimes stopped, and sometimes didn't, and the pilots always died, but not before they had lined the ship on its destination. So, several hundred ships that flew thus – great three-ton explosive shells moving as fast as the bullet of that short gun I showed you, the automatic – one might strike and penetrate and destroy the Granthee ship.

'Not all the Granthee would die then, but, of course, on the ground, without their ships, they were helpless against the many men and women, despite their poison fangs. They could run very swiftly on their six legs, but it is impossible to run far, or swiftly, when you are enveloped in men who do not in the least mind dying, if only you die, too.

'And, of course, there were guns. The Japanese had some ships, they were called battleships, made of steel, very thick and very tough, so thick and strong that the radio beam could not penetrate, so big that any beam the Granthee could throw would not seriously heat them.

'These ships carried guns, not like the automatic I showed you, but tubes two feet thick, and fifty feet long, and their shells weighed tons. Those great shells, when they succeeded in hitting a Granthee ship, caused serious damage, and sometimes brought one down. The Japanese brought down two of the seven they destroyed in this way, and, as they landed, peasants with scythes and sticks and stones attacked them.

'The Japanese were a peculiar race, but they fought as

all men fought in that day, with far inferior weapons – but enormous reserves. In the taking of one ship, with its load of a thousand Granthee, which fell near Tokyo, one of their great cities, approximately one million of the Japanese died. That is what was meant by the thousand-to-one ratio. Of course, not all that million ever got a chance to attack the ship, or tried to, but that number died in Tokyo because of the Granthee ship. Perhaps seven thousand actually took part in the attack.

'But had it gone thus, it would not have been too terrible for man's civilization, because there were only one hundred thousand of the Granthee. Had we lost only one thousand for each of the Granthee we destroyed, it would have been scarcely a serious loss. One hundred millions, of humanity – and in that day we had two thousand millions. But the ratio was fifteen thousand to one.

'And even that would be endurable, were it not that, sooner or later, the second Granthee expedition will come and destroy the rest of us.

'Man fought on capital then. For a thousand years the world had been building, and for a hundred thousand man had been spreading. In three months he spent all he owned, in defeating the invasion. Japan lost everything because the vast atomic bombs of the Granthee loosened the islands, and they slipped in the Japan Deep, a hole in the ocean floor where water went down, down, for five miles, a deep that could swallow the greatest mountain of Earth, and remain unfilled.

'And Japan was gone.

'But the Granthee had flown west, too. They attacked Europe, which was a very densely settled region of high culture and civilization. But the Eurasian Granthee fleet had concentrated on Japan, and the even more populous China.

'In China, one Granthee ship fell, and six hundred million men died. India brought down two ships, because of the British defenses there, and Australia, we know, must have brought down eight, though there never was any message heard. But Australia had few cities, and vast country, so it may be that thousands roam about, unable to communicate with us. The thread of radio is so thin, so fragile.

'Europe fought and destroyed the Granthee ships, all that had come over her, and her cities vanished in the purple-red atomic flares and her people died in the fever beams. But there were many, many forts, and armored vehicles and battleships. These fought, and the fever beams could not reach the men, and the atomic bombs could not be dropped, since even to the Granthee ships, a sixteen-inch armor-piercing projectile loaded with half a ton of high explosive was no futile pebble. The Granthee shot their bombs as shells, but they could not hit the small fleet tanks, and even their might could not beat to the forts buried hundreds of feet beneath rock and soil.

'Oh, they killed the men gradually, because they turned the whole region of the forts into a lava pool, bubbling thickly like a great pot of candy cooking, so the men died. But the ships died, too. The battleships resisted them, one, even two bombs sometimes, and they were mobile and hard to hit, and even the Granthee could not boil an ocean. They hid the warships in clouds of smoke so they could not be seen, while airplanes that flew like darting midges against the sun told them where the Granthee hovered.

'So, finally, was the last Granthee ship over Europe destroyed. And nearly five million people still lived to rejoice. They started quickly, though, to work, the munitions factories starting again, the hidden, buried plants.

'The Granthee fleet over Africa came, and joined with what was left of the fleet that had destroyed Australia.

'Europe fought again. They had vast reserves in that day, because a war was forever hanging over their heads, and their armies were trained and their guns were made, and their piles of ammunition.

'They did as the Japanese did. Their men died in destroying Granthee ships with their little planes – and some new ones, rockets they called them. They were hollow metal shells packed with explosives – save for the guiding man and the fuel that drove them on wings of flame instead of metal. The Granthee could not avoid them, for even swifter and more mobile than the interstellar cruisers were these tiny things. Frequently they moved so swiftly, the screaming metal shell did not explode till it was half through the Granthee ship.

'There were not so many men, then, nor women. The Granthee ships brought down were not always totally destroyed. Some Granthee lived to fight on Earth, and because even on the ground they were deadly, trained troops advanced cautiously and destroyed them carefully. No Granthee lived long, you understand.

'And, finally, as you know, the last Granthee ships landed, only three still in navigable condition. But they landed in England, which was an island off the coast of Europe. They had battered its every weapon of destruction. Now they set out to capture its humans, and did, for there were very few and no weapons whatever. The last three ships were destroyed by humans who let themselves be captured, together with packs of high explosives, of poisonous gas bombs.

'And in America here, the cities had all been battered as have these humbled blocks. There were no more cities, nor any government, but men needed no government to fight now. The first fleet that reached the United States we destroyed, as they had destroyed the fleet in Europe. More came from South America.

'This country is very large, so large you cannot understand. There is so much land the Granthee could not cover it all with their few ships, and everywhere there were humans who hated them. A man in New York discovered one way to release the energy of the atoms, and he made a great many bombs that would do what the Granthee bombs would do. He couldn't shoot them in guns, and they required a great deal of apparatus to set them off. But four Granthee ships were destroyed by them when enslaved humans, carrying food to the Granthee, carried those bombs instead.

'In three months the Granthee were all destroyed. The last few who were captured were tortured horribly. The few scientists among us who still lived, after the destruction of the laboratories where they had been working, tried to question the Granthee, but the people hated the Granthee too much. The scientists heard only the defiance that the Granthee screamed at men – that the second expedition would follow.

'Man had fought, and defeated the first expedition because though his weapons were far less powerful, he had so many of them, so much material, such immense odds in his favor so far as manpower went. And such colossal hatred that suicide was nothing to him. Willingly, a thousand humans would die if only they could take a single Granthee with them.

'It actually averaged about fifteen thousand humans for each Granthee, and still all the Granthee died, and there were humans left.'

'But there are only about two million humans in all the

world now,' said Ban. 'The second expedition will find that the first has done its work. Mankind is reduced to an easily conquered remnant. So what have we gained?'

Old Hugh shook his head. 'That is not the philosophy of mankind in the past. Not what have we gained – but what can we do to that second expedition to defeat them.'

'Yes,' said Ban bitterly, 'but you accent it wrongly. What can *we* do to the second expedition?'

'The scientists who survived have been working steadily. They have the secret of the Granthee radio fever beam, and they have atomic bombs, if they can only get a suitable source of power.'

'If!' said Ban. 'If – and we use an old Diesel automobile engine and a converted electric motor for our source of power. We burn weird fuels like the wood gas we used last spring, and we chortle our triumph of getting a staggering, weak signal into the air.

'There are no repair shops, no tools, no machines. There is nothing. We are still living on the capital mankind built up before the Granthee. We paw now in the ruins for strayed bits of that capital, helpless without the stored labor of men long dead. Only the things those dead hands reach out to give us this false flicker of civilization, a dying candle flame that splutters up once in extinction. We live because life is an automatic process. We have children because that is an automatic process we cannot halt. We grow food because we suffer hunger if we do not, and we fear the face of Death.

'It is false to delude ourselves we accomplish anything. What good is that triumph of the mind – that we can imitate the fever beam of the Granthee? Stolen idea from dead Granthee, made from stolen apparatus from dead cities. And even so the fever beam is useless when the enemy is behind a metal wall, and when does a Granthee come out to fight? What have we?

'Why grub in fallen ruins to communicate to people in no better state than yourself? Why try to build anything that the Granthee may tear it down? Men built a city here, a great city of steel and stone and beauty. They were far greater than we, they had a skill that is dead with them, a power that is vanished, too. And with all their weapons, with all their vast capital to expend – they are dead. We have not the skill, nor the capital nor the weapons. And the second expedition comes; they have told us that much.

'You old men who saw that civilization cannot forget it. You go on dreaming your dreams of rebuilding it. But we who have grown up since have no false hopes. We never saw it, and we know we never will.

'Man's capital is spent, his income is spent, he is pawning his last proud possessions. Man's civilization is done. He may still have pride enough and power enough in his shrunken body to destroy himself before the Granthee come to capture him. Man is the only large animal remaining on all Earth, and the Granthee must capture him. The you know what his fate will be. Man will be the horse to labor, and his child the chicken to eat. And it is sure for many alive now who have not the wit to see it, nor the will to escape it.'

Old Hugh sighed. 'I know, Ban, I know,' he said softly. 'I have felt it, and feared it, and understood that. And for two reasons I go on living and working: The first is that there are those who have not the wit nor the will; and for the sake of those who would become the horse and the chicken, we must try. There is a third reason, too, so I will say that my second is that the Granthee did not know when the second expedition would come. It was only a promise when they started – an empty promise.

'The greatest reason is that other men go on working still, with man's old courage and his old skill. You know that in Schenectady there are men who are not stealing apparatus from dead cities, but making new. And in Detroit they are making engines again – engines that burn wood and do not wear swiftly, nor easily, with bearings that are lubricated as we are lubricating ours, with oil pressed from castor oil beans we can grow here.'

'Do they make guns that can blow apart Granthee ships? Do they make swift rocket ships to drive a trail of destruction through—'

'Not yet, I know, Ban, but—'

'But the second expedition will put a stop to that. Old Hugh, I love you, love you as the only father I've known; but you struggle against impossibilities. The castor beans you mentioned – you know we will have oil but a little longer, since the frost destroyed last year's crop. Then our paltry little machines will slide and grate to a stop, as frictional losses destroy their efficiency and their metal. Friction has stopped man always.'

'Not friction, but inertia has stopped mankind, Ban.'

'Aye, the momentum dies, and the race glides to a halt as friction slows it. But come, old Hugh, I will help you, for I know the work is dear to you. What you are attempting now I do not understand, but I know you want more tubes, more apparatus, so we will grub among the ruins, you and I.'

Ban rose slowly, and picked his way over the tumbled stones and rotting wooden beams, charred and blackened by fires and atomic bombs had started and angered Nature drowned in ton on countless ton of outraged rain.

Wearily the old man picked his way along, head bent, sorrowful. He knew the truth of what Ban said. But Hugh was of a generation that had known and yielded to hope. His generation would always yield to it.

II

The sun was sinking into long summer twilight as they made their way down to the rotting dock. They were heavy laden and old Hugh was happy, picking his way along among the tumbled blocks. Cautiously they lowered themselves to the little rowboat, looking anxiously at the sullen flow of the river, a clean, clear river now, with sunken rusty hulls visible beneath its surface.

The tide was turning soon, and the water moved slowly, gurgling very softly round the piles of the pier. Gulls swung lazily on the little choppy waves, watching the men with keen, bright eyes. Men were a source of danger to gulls; to men gulls were a source of food – a rather strong-flavored soup, but nourishing.

'Lower them, gently, Ban,' said Hugh. 'I'm afraid we'll have to go farther afield next time. The instruments, thank Heaven, were in working order. Here's the receiver – and that other one. It's heavy, so be careful. Look, here's something we can use that I found just as we left.'

'What is it? It looks like a small motor or generator, but has no power shaft to take hold of.'

'It is both, a rotary converter. They used to use these on automobiles to run radio sets, it has a 6-volt motor and a 110-volt alternator wound on one armature, so that it produced 110 AC from 6 volts DC. We have lots of powerful storage batteries from old automobiles, and this is a 500-watt converter, so we have something very useful.'

'Hm-m-m – it may be. I've never seen one before. Well, are we ready?'

'I'm afraid that's all. I wish I'd been able to find that roll of copper tubing the old invoice listed. He must have sold it—'

Silently they rowed across the water as the long twilight settled. Stars came out, and the moon, as they plodded along, the little child's wagon behind them. They went over the rough cobblestones of the old Meadows road till they passed the torn section, then on their bicycles to the Orange Mountains.

The moon was high when they reached the lighted buildings of the clan. Ban's wife greeted them, slightly curious, as they returned. The neighbors came in, a few at a time, to look incuriously at the treasures Hugh had collected, and to ask news of the road, for few and seldom were the trips so far from the clan. They slouched out presently, only old George staying to help them, an automobile mechanic once, venting his love of machinery on their decrepit old engine.

'They were calling you today, Hugh,' he said. 'I couldn't do anything, and they couldn't seem to make it with the telephone thing.' He shook his head sadly. 'I never could understand those buzzes and clicks. I wish they'd talk language.'

'They can't always, George. Code will get through with less power, and we all have so little power. I'll send out a call and see if I can find who called me.'

The little Diesel pounded presently, with gnarled old George soothing its heavy knocks as best he could, and the transmitter, patched and jury-rigged, began to operate. But no answer came to their call from the silent ether – only the soft wash of static. Hugh shook his head and shut the Diesel off. 'No response, George. They'll call again. They always do. They always have time. I'm going to start working on that fever beam, I think.'

'Fever beam,' Ban said. 'You might give a mouse a dangerous fever and—'

'No, you don't understand. Fevers can cure, too. I'm going to build a curative fever apparatus, one with power enough to heal, though it cannot hurt. And that metal tube you asked about is no weakling, Ban. It will handle 500 watts, and we have six. If they are all in operable condition, as I believe they are, that is not insignificant power. It is more than we have had before, for a long time.' Hugh gently reproved him.

Ban snorted again. 'More than we have had for a long time – and enough to cure, but not harm anything, even a large mouse!'

'But I will learn. I will learn how to construct the beam. And you will learn. That is important, Ban; we must remember that. So help me now, while I test these tubes. Remember that they use 4,000 volts, and be careful, please.'

In two days they had finished the things, and set up makeshift apparatus. There had been a thyratron tube there, too, a thing that old Hugh brought along out of interest and a collector's acquisitiveness, for it was not a radio tube, capable of control, simply a type of switch capable of operating a near radio frequency in effect.

It was set up on a panel of well-dried, seasoned hardwood, for there was no more Bakelite or hard rubber to be used, and slate was hard to get. And the wires were never insulated, merely spaced, because insulation had rotted and fallen off in the years since wire was made.

But they tried it, and it worked to some extent. Not as well as old Hugh had hoped, but nothing ever did, for his apparatus could never be quite the right apparatus, but the nearest equivalent to hand. By radio he held long conferences with those men in Schenectady who had not forgotten their craft, and developed ways and means to measure what he had no instrument for measuring – wavelengths and frequencies, waveforms even, after great difficulty, from an old television tube that had somehow maintained its vacuum. Television they could have no more, for television required waves so short they could be sent only with horizon distances. But the old cathode-ray television tube became an oscillograph.

Old Hugh looked at the result in dismay. 'Ban, I'm afraid our apparatus is very faulty. That's not a sine wave, but a waveform for which man has never invented a name. Well, it can't be helped. We must do what we can with what we have. The men in Schenectady have sent one of their young clansmen on foot and in canoe clear out to Detroit to help the men there.

'Presently, radio equipment will be made there, too, where they have production machinery still – and again, and vast cargoes of raw materials. Maybe then we will get new, and good equipment, tubes that always have their vacuum, and haven't gone "soft." They will make caterpillar tractors that burn wood gases, and use castor oil beans for lubricant. Then they can break through, and start commerce again. They are going to make big boats again, and try to ship things on the Great Lakes, and finally, even a huge Diesel of hundreds of horsepower to the men in Schenectady.'

'Hugh!' said Ban. 'Hundreds of horsepower! The locomotive those men at Schenectady once made stalled outside of Montclair, and it used fifty thousand horsepower, a mere fraction of the load of one substation!'

'It is huge,' old Hugh maintained, hurt somewhat by the tone of Ban's voice. 'We are rebuilding with a very little start. We have a great task, and that will be a huge accomplishment, Ban. Men will try very hard for that, and work with a great love and pride and honest effort that man never exceeded. It will represent the hopes and thoughts and labors of many men, an accomplishment they can be as proud of as any ever done.

'The giant machines are gone, and man labors again with the sweat of his brow and the craft of his hand. That engine will release many hands and many brows to greater, better efforts. Did I not know it useless, I would urge you again to go to Schenectady, that you may get real training and do your part in this greater labor ahead.'

'The labor ahead is useless. The second expedition is ahead.'

'I know, Ban; I want to show you something of interest. You remember that neon bulb I brought? Take this terminal of the new power set in one hand, and the bulb in the other. So I will turn it – no, do not loose your grip, hold tightly and remain on that insulating plate. Do not touch the ground, though that would probably harm you little, but stay there and hold the tube. So – and see.'

'Eh – it lights!' Ban stared at the brilliantly glowing tube. 'With but one connection – through my body. How can it be so? My body has very great resistance, you have schooled me, and for power to flow, always there must be two connections.'

Old Hugh chuckled. 'I shall show you something perhaps yet more remarkable. See, here is that coil I wound yesterday.

I told you it was a furnace, and you looked at me askance. So. Now, will you hold this metal cylinder, and I lead the wire here, to the coil, and again to the set here. You are in the circuit, see?'

'Aye, I'm in the circuit right enough, and I like it very little. Old Hugh, are you sure of yourself?' Ban asked dubiously.

'We shall see. Now, the furnace is set on this table, and in my hand I hold a bit of asbestos, hollowed to hold a few scraps of aluminium metal. Now – I turn on the power set, and thrust my hand in the furnace—'

'By the gods of time! It's melting! Your hand—'

'As cool as you please, my son.' Quickly the old man shut off the set, and tossed aside the molten metal. 'The radio-frequency currents play strange tricks, for they run not through your body, but across it, like water. These extreme frequencies cannot go through any conductor, but always across its surface. It is called the skin effect. When it passes as a flow of current in a wire, or any conductor, it is only on the surface; yet when acting through an insulator, it acts all through it. In the furnace, it attacks the metal, but not my hand, for my hand is a very poor conductor, and a hard path, while the metal is a very good conductor, and an easy path.

'It is very interesting, but not useful I am afraid,' he said. 'Come, we must see what we can do to correct the fever beam hook-up, to get better efficiency, and the correct wave form. I wonder if the waveform can have any peculiar effects – something unusual. I wonder perhaps—'

'What? What might it do?'

'I was thinking – thinking of the time I worked with a quartz-crystal oscillator, and built up the frequency till it exactly corresponded with the crystal's natural note and – the crystal was white dust. Maybe I could develop a waveform that would pulverize even hard steel that way—'

'Maybe. Then you could break all Joan's sewing needles, and maybe even get enough power to crack one of her knitting needles. There are many things you might do – if you had power.

'Old Hugh, I do not like to see you spend your time uselessly.'

'I have nothing else to spend, Ban. Let me work. Who knows – but let me try, it costs little, and might be worth much.'

'It costs a mouth to feed, and work to gather oil for the engine, and wear on the engine and tubes. It does cost us time.' Ban looked at the old man sorrowfully. 'The others complain. I do not; I know what you are attempting. But it is they who must work to feed you, and, as yet, the communication they have maintained all these years has brought them little good. Twice only it has warned them of a killing frost, once of the great storm. Beyond that – since the bandits have all been destroyed, it has done them little good. They grow restless, Hugh.'

Slowly old Hugh looked away, out through the window toward the hard-working men in the fields, women weaving again on hand looms. It had been a fad once, in the world he had known, before the Granthee. It was no fad now; it was protection against the winter, and, because the wool was never cleansed completely free of its grease, against the rains.

'I know, Ban. I told Dr Ponting I would call him at noon today. I must call.'

'And I must go,' said Ban. 'I will be back this evening.'

III

Old Hugh sat silent, fingering slowly the crude key of his transmitter, a bit of brass spring he had cut himself, mounted with a scrap of a platinum wedding ring above and below for contact points. The platinum wedding ring had been found on a slender, bleached bone, protruding from beneath a great tumbled block of stone in the city. His lined old face grew more and more sorrowful. Finally he buried his face in his gnarled old hands, and his body rocked slowly.

'Three groups,' he muttered, 'three groups in all the world. So far as we know. Never have we roused Europe, never Australia. Three little groups against the vast inertia of two millions. The first expedition was destroyed, and utterly defeated – yet it has won. Ah-h-h if only—'

Hours later he fussed with his apparatus, setting up the parabolic netting of wires he had contrived after Dr Pointing's radioed directions that noon. He was working over it carefully to align exactly the bit of copper tubing a few inches long that was its aerial, designed to radiate these ultra-short waves. Multiplex ultra frequency they called it in Schenectady. It was ingenious, perhaps too much so for him, his wave form was so poor.

Carefully, because he had much time, and no real aim, he checked his work by the plans he had copied down from the messages over the radio. The triple generating oscillator set, the power set, the mixing oscillator, the phase indicators were all in order. But somehow they did not combine properly.

Then, quite by accident, he noticed that he had connected one of the tubes slightly more than 185 degrees out of phase, instead of slightly more than 5! And a screwed connection near it had come loose. No wonder his waveform was peculiar, his efficiency low: one tube fighting the other two!

Muttering to himself in vexation he brought a screwdriver and tightened the connection down firmly, solidly. Then, just to test it really, he turned on the set. The oscillograph began to move as heaters warmed up, then abruptly struck a weirdly shaped wave, and broke again, abruptly, into the peculiar wave he had been getting just as there sounded in the quiet little room a very sharp *ping*.

Hugh looked curiously, and shut off his set hastily. The loose connection was not merely loose now. The screw had vanished!

Vaguely worried and surprised, old Hugh replaced it, and turned on the set. This time he watched that screw. The tubes were warmer now, heated more quickly. *Ping!* Very sharp. And the screw was gone.

Old Hugh brought the soldering iron and soldered that connection in place, and wondered. Again the set started. There were five distinct *pings* this time – and a little tinny clatter of falling metal parts. The beautifully constructed little paraboloid director lay in disassembled parts on the table, quite scattered and crumpled – not harmed, merely taken apart in a hundredth of a second, with a little stinging *ping* of metal.

A man trained in research through a lifetime would have stopped there, and worked very hard with his mind, and sought some explanation, some theory, then devised a theory-testing experiment to prove or disprove that theory. Old Hugh had not done research work, real research, for thirty years. He had simply tried to make delicate mechanisms work with defective apparatus. To him, this was simply more defective apparatus. With the patience a generation of troubles had taught him, he kneeled down on the floor and hunted about the little shack till he had found five bolts, four nuts and two tiny screws.

These were precious things, these little screws, because they couldn't be made any more, and they were so hard to get – such little things, they sifted down among the debris to unattainable depths. One nut was missing and he had to replace it from his hoarded stock. Then, patiently, his stiffened fingers assembled again the little thing that had fallen apart, and bolted it firmly.

Then he started his apparatus again. But he made sure this time that the thing would not be so defective. He wired the tiny nuts in place. And now in all his circuit there were only soldered joints or bolts with nuts wired solidly in place. And he turned his projector where it would send its beam harmlessly into the mountainside half a mile away, and so started the set.

He watched his set, and it worked, so he did not look through the window where, half a mile away, a mighty mass of rock and earth and giant trees began to move in a ghastly silence down the hill. For seconds the thing moved in majestic silence, a whole section of the hill gliding downward, swifter and more swiftly. Then it broke in flying, smoking rock, crashing and roaring in monstrous shock. The shouts of men and screams of women made him rise suddenly and step hastily across the room, not even pausing to shut off his machine.

He fell with a sickening jar, heard the dull snap, felt the meteoring pain that shot up his leg to become a vast, unbearable ache. He tried to rise, and fell back whimpering softly, calling bewilderedly, mercifully numbed, as yet.

It was hours before Ban found him there, in the dark

little room, with only the faint glow of the heater tubes shining in the dark. The steady pounding of the Diesel had attracted him from the mystery there on the hillside that the men were looking at in awe and vague fear. They wanted old Hugh, suddenly wondering where he was, who might explain this to them.

Gently they lifted him up, unconscious now, and the old doctor showed them how to set the bone again, giving in words the skill his hands possessed to hands that had the strength his no longer held. Then they bound the leg, and straightened it, and beside him two women watched. They fed him when he woke, feverish, mumbling.

Ban shut off the experimental set, and started the transmitter. Through space his message leaped to other sets and found them deaf. This was not communication time.

Morning came, and again Ban tried, but now the men came in. The mystery had vanished in the night. The rock slide was there, and the more distant, strangely truncated slope was visible beyond it, raw and harsh. But the strange thing had vanished.

Ban called again. Schenectady answered finally, and to them Ban poured out the message: Hugh Thompson feverish and sick with a broken leg; the mountains moving and stirring, strange rocks down which Jeff Hurley shot, slipping without resistance till brought up against a broken hull of a great boulder outside the area of damage, damaged himself beyond repair – dead; the broken mountains—

And no mention of the set. For the men of that later day, even when trained somewhat, did not so rapidly connect cause and effect. And in every mind, anyway, lurked the thought: the second expedition.

Old Hugh woke late that afternoon, and they told him of

the mystery, at his insistence carried him to the little room and his key. And from that position he saw the meaning of the thing.

'Ban,' he said suddenly, quite softly, 'Ban, look along the axis of the paraboloid there, and tell me—'

'Eh,' said Ban, 'the slippage is along that line. What do you suppose made that paraboloid line up with that damage? Some magnetism—'

Old Hugh groaned softly. 'Oh, Ban, can you believe nothing you see, either? Move that paraboloid one degree further toward the mountain, making sure no man is in its path—

'But no, there will be half a hundred out there now. Never mind. I must think why. But first – start the transmitter.'

At the key he called, called vainly for a long time. Schenectady answered after a while, and rapidly he told them of his mistake in the connection, and the damage involved. They would try it, on a barren mountainside.

His description was too accurate. Old Hugh said, 'Right through the wall.'

They did not hear from Schenectady that day, or the next, as old Hugh grew more feverish, became delirious. Ban caught the weak, broken signals the third day. '—building as – gested. Something – ent wrong, for the entire building – lapsed. Transmitter ruined, as – ell – set we – ade up. No power. Will – d more later. Greatest – covery – as ever made in hist—' And no more could he catch; so he put down what he got, and turned back to old Hugh, uncomprehending.

IV

Thirty years of harsh, rugged life lay behind old Hugh. Somehow the fever abated, the pain lessened as his sturdy old body rallied in defense. Slowly, he began to recover, and still no message came through from Schenectady, though two weeks passed. The women who cared for him had cleaned the room, and Ban told old Hugh, negligently, that the message he'd been unable to clear up had been thrown out.

Old Hugh was busy thinking. But the problem eluded him. Somehow, he was sure, he had destroyed some of the rock crystals to powder as he had hoped, yet he could not understand; it was beyond his belief that so tiny a power, a bare three horsepower, could do so much damage. Surely, it seemed, it would have taken vastly more. But, perhaps it was some really rare constituent of the rock, rare but vastly important that held the secret, some unconsidered crystal that was the key log in the jam that made rock solid, vibrating in chance tune to his set, and vibrated to powder.

He cursed that lost nut he knew must be guilty for his fall. A little rolling nut – but the feeling as he fell had been so strange—

He didn't see his ragged, raveled clothes. When the women brought them back to him they had been carefully repaired, as all things must be where all things are worked for and made by the sweat of man's brow and the craft of his hand. Perhaps they would have given him some little hint.

But he itched to be at it again, determined now that, pointed to the skies, the thing must be safe. So he had the men bring in samples of every rock they could find at the great slide, and, when he could hobble again on his crutch with Ban's aid, he set the paraboloid on its back, and the rock specimens above it on wooden shelves, turning the power to a very low degree. Then he turned on the set that had not operated since he had fallen there by the window, and broken his leg as the mountain slid down.

Slowly the tubes warmed up. He watched with interest and care the little stones on the little platform just under the low roof of the little wooden shack.

Then the tubes were warm, and there were a great many slight *pings* of sound, and a very quiet, swift slip of the roof and the sudden heavy thrashing as the roof fell in. It was fortunate that the device was so effective, for the roof came in as separate shingles and boards.

Old Hugh groaned as they dug him out, and reached a hand to feel the device that had done this. His leg hurt, his head ached abominably, his laboratory was a ruin, evidently, but he was not seriously hurt, nor was Ban. Ban's wife was crying and dabbing at his bleeding face, questioning frantically and tongue-lashing old Hugh simultaneously. She was pale, and very scared, for the shack looked as though a monstrous giant had stepped heedlessly on it.

Ban stared dazedly and bewilderedly at the wrecked laboratory. 'I know,' he said suddenly, looking owlishly at old Hugh. 'What they said was "building collapsed." That was it.'

Old Hugh laughed shakily. 'A fine time to remember it, my boy. We can confirm their report.'

'And they said it was the greatest discovery in history. I'll bet that was it. Yes. I know it was. You've got the disintegration ray, Hugh!'

Old Hugh shook his head. 'It doesn't fit, Ban. It does the job, but I don't know why, nor how. That's never really safe. We must find out why.'

'Why? We can work it.'

'Eh? How well? How much? I'm going back in there.'

Silently, other men began to clear the wreckage away, and with their efficient taciturn movements, more and more apparatus began to appear. Old Hugh interfered with them as he brought forth coils and condensers and little metal tubes, his soldering iron and the precious little alcohol soldering torch, a piece of dry, seasoned wood, a few condensers, the rotary converter. Miraculously, from the ruins, Ban brought the oscillograph.

With gnarled, skilled fingers old Hugh built up the thing on his bit of board, a foot square with one-inch tubes and a gently hammered piece of annealed copper in the form of a bowl. They brought him, silently, the things he asked for, and silently stood watching.

It formed under his fingers. At his command, Ban brought the storage battery they had built up from the sound parts of a dozen decrepit wrecks. Hugh attached his terminals, and the little converter whined. The tiny tubes grew warm and a wave form built up in the oscillograph.

'A good research student would know just what to do. I think I know just what happened now, Ban, and the way to test it is to see if my theory will predict results. I have aimed this at the horizon. Ban, will you catch that little kid over there, and place him on that bare patch?'

Ban tried, and with the aid of three other men the struggling kid was brought and placed on the bald knoll. 'He won't stay, Hugh.'

'Leave him and run at right angles to the beam, Ban. You others step away now.' In a moment Ban ran – and old Hugh pressed his key. The running goat bleated suddenly, tumbled and slid along the ground, his feet threshing and struggling, bleating louder now, mortally terrified. For half a minute he struggled, flashing legs flying without result – then he was up and bouncing away like a thrown rubber ball. In moments the kid was nibbling grass, tossing his head back toward them, bleating defiantly.

'Yes,' said Hugh, eyes flashing, 'I was right.'

Open-mouthed, Ban stared at the little animal. The lean, silent men moved restlessly. 'What did it, Hugh?' asked one at length. 'That goat acted like he got on a cake of ice, and even then I never saw one of them sure-footed little beasts slip like that.'

Old Hugh was disconnecting the battery. The rotary converter slowed from a whine to a drone, and stopped. He looked lovingly at the foot-square board and the copper bowl and the little black tubes, like dull metal acorns, less than an inch high. 'Yes, that's what broke my leg that day. I know now. Old Jim Duncan, you've been wanting to tear down the old wooden house there and haven't had the time to do it right and save the nails. Well – Ban, you pack the battery, will you?'

Hugh set off down the grassy lane that was all the main street the clan had. At the end of the row was the old, rotting house, deserted, broken, preserved only so long by the original sound construction, and the fact that men who grubbed for every grain of food they ate had no time yet to tear it down carefully and pull the nails out straight and usable, keeping the boards, most of them, unbroken and sound.

They followed him silently. Talking was not a highly developed art among these people, not as it had been when old Hugh was young Hugh. Ban set down the battery at Hugh's gesture, and the old man laboriously set himself on the ground, his game leg sticking out before him. He connected the set, and the converter whined again. Old Hugh lined the copper bowl on the tumbledown house and pressed the key. A thousand, thousand sharp *pings*, a sudden settling, a clamorous rattling of boards – the building was down, and dust swirled slowly.

'Great heaven!' gasped Ban. Suddenly he was running forward, toward the house and – through the beam. In an instant he was down, skittering along the ground, threshing arms and legs. Quite unhurt, evidently, but surprised, and suddenly embarrassed.

Old Hugh cut off the key. Slowly, flushing, Ban rose to his feet, absolutely nude save for his leather belt, his leather shoes, a mass of thread and lint that reduced itself, as he moved, to individual hairs, all that remained of his clothes. A slow roll of laughter welled from the people. Then his wife was running forward, her face crimson, her eyes blazing wickedly at old Hugh as she glanced toward him in her swift passage.

'Wh-what happened?' asked the unhappy Ban Norman.

'I sort of think you better get dressed again, Ban, before you start gettin' questy,' said a laconic, faintly humorous voice. 'Looks like you wore out them clothes in a hell of a hurry.'

Ten minutes later Ban was back, his angry wife bristling at his side. A soft murmur of chuckles ran through the folk as they straightened from their work of gathering nails and screws and useful bits of metal from the old house. Long, straight boards, mostly unharmed, were being stacked to one side.

Old Hugh looked at Ban with twinkling gray eyes. 'Maybe my puttering will be some use, yet. See?'

On the ground before the humming little set a pile of lint was accumulating. The women were at work. Every old, worn-out bit of clothing in the clan had been brought and reduced to its original fibers in moments. 'They can reweave them now, into new and useful material. And Ban, they are beginning to feel something else. Do you see all this little, little thing means?'

'I see something it means, you old fool!' snapped diminutive, peppery Joan Norman. 'It means I have to weave Ban Norman a new suit! First you tear down the house about Ban's ears, then you tear the clothes off his very back. I had to make that, and those you're wearing too, you muddle-witted ingrate. You have less sense than two-year-old Junior and don't use what you have! You and your messy batteries and coils and wires. Every day Ban comes home with holes in his things, and now – now you're not content with just making holes in them, you tear them all to pieces, right back to lint, and make a spectacle out of my Ban. And will you—'

Gently, Ban picked up his wife and carried her back to the house. Ten minutes more and he was back grinning. 'She's peeved. But Hugh, what in the name of the heavens have you got? I don't—'

'It's the skin effect, Ban. I've figured it out now. That's why so little power does so much, so very much. Look, it induces those extreme frequencies in any conductor, and almost anything is more or less of a conductor because of moisture in it, and those frequencies go, of course, to the surface. How they do it, I cannot guess. Yet, somehow, they rearrange the molecules so that they become perfectly fluid, there just on the very surface, and absolutely destroy all friction.'

'Friction! But—' Ban gasped, and fell silent for a second. 'But I do not understand – friction—'

'Man has always thought of friction as his worst enemy, yet he cannot do without it. Look, your clothes fell apart in a moment, because the woven strands were held together by their friction. Even the knots were held by friction. The shed fell on us, as the house fell, because the friction that held the nails in was gone, and the nails, of course, sprang out. I was vastly tempted to turn it on the Diesel, and get along without oil, till I remembered – every bolt and nut would fly off as though a charge of explosive lay beneath it, for each bolt and each nut is held in place only by friction. In a hundredth of a second, the Diesel would have become a mass of disassembled, oil-splattered parts.

'They know it over there, I think. We have lost some of our fear now, Ban, because—'

'Then – then that little set there could tear down a small mountain! It needs no power, the weight and force of the mountain would do it all!'

'This needs no power,' said old Hugh, brushing about his head at the dull hum and buzz he took to be a fly.

Only the low cries of the men over by the fallen house made him look up. Some five miles away, two or three miles up, hung two great, blackened, pointed cylinders. They buzzed like vast, angry insects, and pale, lambent flame rippled and played about their atomic exhausts.

They seemed to move slowly, so far and so high there, as they drifted across country. Then one twisted and dipped in its course. A thrilling wave of warmth seemed to reach down to them; the men by the house dropped their tools and the lumber they carried. They ran to their homes. Already women and children were coming out, joining their men and vanishing in the green depths of the wood.

Old Hugh's eyes were keen and bright as he looked up into Ban's dull, racked face. 'Oh, Lord,' said Ban, and turned suddenly toward the clan center, toward his home. His wife was coming out, crying for him, little Junior in her arms. Ban ran swiftly to them. The feeling of warmth and heat made him sluggish, he realized suddenly as he ran to them.

Old Hugh looked after him, and turned back, a lone little figure squatted awkwardly with his broken leg stretched out before him. From the wood came softly muffled cries. Only two words seemed to filter through – 'second expedition.'

Old Hugh stirred beside his softly humming little board; the old, patched battery; six little metal acorns, warm to the touch; a little copper bowl. Old Hugh's eyes were bleak and dark as he looked along the edge of the board and wondered what power he actually had in his tiny, futilely whining bit of wood and metal and insulation.

An unbearable violet flame leaped suddenly in the skies, shrieking a thousand feet in the air. A rain of black metal separated from a solid clump to spread in a long, stretching line that reached down and down in masses to the waiting earth. It settled at the base of a giant rock, finally, as a second long rain of metal reached down and down.

Somehow, miraculously, living, moving parts separated themselves and stood a moment, bewildered by sudden helplessness, perhaps, pawing at the broken wreckage, glinting peculiarly like an iridescent metal in the afternoon sun. The old man hobbled to a higher knoll, dragging the heavy battery and the little bit of wood and metal and insulation.

The great cliff stirred, moved. The afternoon quiet echoed to the vast, angry mutter of the mountain. Annoyed, it seemed to settle more comfortably over the spot where, iridescently, purple things had moved.

V

Ban looked in at the doorway of the wrecked shed cautiously. The Diesel was humming rhythmically, and the whine of the generator sounded sleepily on the quiet, late-afternoon air of the deserted little settlement. Old Hugh was propped up on three broken boards; his game leg tenderly rested on a fourth. On the bench beside him was the rough, dry board, and on the floor the old, decrepit storage battery. There were soft, quick hisses and buzzes coming from the loudspeaker on the table – a rather dented and battered loudspeaker, but functioning.

Ban listened to the familiar code. '—already,' it spelled out to him. 'There were eight here, thirty more came this morning. Detroit has sent three of the rocket machines, and five of the frictionless, welded tank machines have crossed the country. They left an anti-friction projector set in each clan village they passed.

'We believe those two ships you destroyed were the last of the American fleet. Our new set, though, caught a European station never before heard. We cannot get through to them, apparently, till the new transmitter is finished tomorrow, because they have no receivers as sensitive as ours. But one of the Detroit rockets is making the one-way crossing tonight, though unable to return till fuel is developed there.

'Undoubtedly, however, our strong point of resistance here will protect Europe by drawing all the Granthee fire. The tank machines ring up at a distance of thirty miles, and the rockets are waiting.

'Detroit is preparing thirty-five more now, for production has been vastly speeded since the frictionless machine tools went into operation. Have your clansmen returned?'

The speaker fell silent. Old Hugh reached out a firm hand to the key, and Ban listened to his swift keying. 'One, so far, at any rate. They will drift in now, for their fear is gone. He has brought in a sample of the Granthee hand weapon, powered by atomic energy, I see. He is beside me now – Ban Norman – so, if your rocket will come for me, I can join you in three hours. Ban Norman knows the language of the key; he can teach it to others.'

'You said no others would learn, and Norman was weakening,' spluttered the little dented speaker.

'Others will learn now. Another has come, and is watching through the broken window. He is trying to understand now. In six months we will have fifty trained operators, and perhaps ten men who can hook up apparatus.'

'That is good, Hugh Thompson. Detroit just sent word that the rocket has taken off to pick you up. We will deliver the tank machine and the medicines you asked for in three days or so, the gang plow in two weeks. Can Ban Norman take the key now?'

'Yes,' said Ban Norman softly. 'Going to – Schenectady – Detroit – in three hours. Old Hugh—'

'What – what does it say?' asked the keen-eyed face at the window.

'It says, young Jim Duncan,' old Hugh replied slowly, as Ban Norman slipped eagerly over to the key, 'that the Granthee have suffered severe frictional losses, and – that man's hesitation is over, and not his civilization.'

Dead Knowledge

The sun was a red ball sinking at the end of the broad, paved avenue that ran straight to the east. Its long rays slanted down across the city, across the towers, gilding their clean-lined hulks with a parting gold. An absolute silence wrapped the whole majestic city, a silence that had settled on, and into the three men standing immobile on the short, green grass of the Circle that was the city's center. In a dozen directions great arteries radiated through vast chasms between artificial cliffs that lifted a hundred stories, a thousand feet into the dark blue of the sky.

A restless breeze, stirred by the approaching chill of twilight, soughed softly down the street, around the immense bulks of towering buildings leaping upward, sweep on sweep of fine-drawn graceful line. Bar Young stirred restlessly, obliquely eyed his companions with an uneasy tensity. 'That – that's why nobody noticed us.'

'There were lights in this city last night,' Hall said in a voice lowered unconsciously by the pressing weight of silence. 'It can't – can't be deserted.'

'I thought for a while that the people might be a race of day-sleepers – an owl people – but even at 4 a.m. no Earth-city could be this quiet, so motionless. And however alien these people of a strange solar system may be, they must be in many ways similar to man. Those buildings – this park – all their works might be those of some city of Earth.

It's a ghost-city, deserted place like the abandoned mining camps.' Ross looked about with a vast unease.

'We could try one of the other cities—' suggested Young. 'We have to find them – the people – somehow. Twenty-seven light years – three years of traveling – to reach this system, to find five dead worlds, and only this one habitable. And inhabited; such cities as this cannot be simply – abandoned. There was no place for the people to go, no other planet they might have migrated to. And no signs of space-travel or space-ports that might accommodate spaceships, even such small ones as ours.' Over his shoulder he glanced back toward the 300-foot bubble of steel and quartz that had brought them across vast gulfs of emptiness.

The swift-sinking sun shrank below the eastern horizon, its beams lifting from the level of the park, climbing slowly up the sides of the towers, painting green and blue and pale-yellow stone to red. Polished metal reflected its brilliance in flashing gleams from the curving, rising buildings that towered about them, a ring of 1000-foot giants dwarfing the low trees of the park, and the 100-foot sapphire needle of crystalline light at the center of the circle. Slowly, the lifting light left the feet of the buildings, the deep blue of the sky overhead darkened with a fast-running twilight.

Still darkness crept in to replace the silent daylight, welling up from the pavements into the shadows. The thin, clear air of the planet, utterly quiet and dustless, held no light within it; the shadows became black and sharp. The deserted city of daylight began to people itself with unseen things that moved soundless in the silence, pressing the lengthening shadows toward the three men with a sound-less, eager menace.

Ross shook his head slowly. 'We've got to find out

what happened here – why this city was deserted. There is something – wrong. A ghost town is something understandable – a town, built by a lode of mineral, that ceases to be when the mineral is gone. But a city – a magnificent city of thousand-foot towers and ten million homes stretched over fifty miles of meadowland cannot be deserted. It's impossible. Even – and I thought of this for a moment – even a plague could not drive out every man, every woman and child. There would be watchmen, caretakers, there would be sanitation corps men to work and rehabilitate the city. It is too much, too much of labor and thought and effort to be neglected utterly, however fearful the plague might be.

'There is something wrong.' He watched the uneasy shadows creep across the pavements toward them, engulfing them as the light of the city faded, the last faint sunrays touched the tips of the highest towers for a lingering instant – and vanished. The night-wind grew, murmurous and mumbling behind the buildings, freighted with the communications of the unknown rising on the flowing tide of dark.

He turned abruptly; a soft, blue light was growing on the building walls – something behind them— At his start the others turned, nervous hands grappling suddenly to heat-guns. The sapphire needle behind them was a crystal of living fire that wavered, grew in a rising rush, and retreated for a moment to gather strength for another upward rush in the dusk. Waves of shadows forced back by it seemed to gather denser in the buildings' outskirts, spreading invaders hurled back by the light.

With a rush the light mounted suddenly to a needle beam that stabbed into the dark sky, to winking, unfamiliar stars, in strange constellations. Simultaneously with the jetting light beam, a low, sweet hum built up, up to a ringing music that floated out across the silent, darkening bulks about the park. It rose and fell and rose again in sweet cadences, to fade away in plaintive notes. As it faded, light, a million lights on a thousand streets grew, a vast lighting system coming to life to drive back again the shadows crouching angrily at the feet of the towers.

Swift darkness fell with the sun's disappearance, a darkness that made the unlighted buildings vanish in black needles against the black, star-flecked sky. Only their lowermost levels were clear in the soft rays of the street lights, fading into rising dimness of black, lightless eyes – polished glass that gleamed dimly without being illuminated, unexpected winkings of light from ranges far above the effective limits of the lamps.

Bar Young's breath sucked softly. 'Automatic – automatic lights controlled by the coming of night. No light – no window shows a trace of illumination within. Only the city's mechanical watchman functioning to turn on the lights of a deserted waste. That was the light we saw last night from space, as we came in. Those were the lights we saw in the western cities already in night when we were landing.

'They are gone – gone, it must be, forever, and gone not hurriedly, but calmly, putting away all cars, all traces of their occupancy in neat order. But why, *why* have they left this place?'

Hall moved forward into the light of the crystal and out of the lean shadow of their cruiser. 'I don't like this city – particularly at night. There is something wrong with it, the same thing that made the people leave. It was the city, I feel somehow, not the people that made this desertion necessary.'

Ross moved his head in a vague gesture, half agreement, half negation. 'The city – well – I have the feeling you do, the oppression of the silence and the dusk. Those buildings standing there, crouching in the darkness, half-seen things that have a suggestion, in this city of deserted mystery, of some menacing thing. But isn't it more our own vague feelings – strangers from an alien world and solar system, who have stumbled on this cosmic mystery as the quick dusk of this planet set in – that are to blame?'

Young looked at him under frowning brows, a wry grimace twisting his mouth. 'The original builders deserted it. Something, human or inhuman, forced them to a course unbelievably extreme. Yet – there is no sign of wreckage, of invasion, of trouble. The city is clean, so clean that even the normal litter of a great city does not appear. We have to investigate, but – I don't like this city of night. We can go to one of the daylight cities.'

'This is one deserted city,' said Ross abruptly stubborn. 'I feel I'm fooling myself with man's instinctive, age-old fear of darkness, and unknown things. The others probably aren't deserted, and this is our opportunity to study the race unhampered. Their language, perhaps, from books and pictures. I say we should investigate, visit some of the homes we saw on the outskirts. Our ship is slim enough to move down that main artery without striking anything, and in a few moment we can get some indication of what the people who deserted this place were. Therein may lie the whole answer, a vagrant, migratory people descended, perhaps, from birds, who move en masse from city to city as the seasons—'

Young looked at him keenly, and his voice trailed off apologetically. 'You know as well as I that no civilization of thousand-foot towers would rise from a race of migratory habits. No, the people who labored for this city intended to remain, generation after generation, and they built with lofty permanence in mind. Hall, what about that language? I think – but you're probably the expert.'

'You saw what I did – you're probably right. As a guess – the signs, that posted notice on the tree, looked to me like an ideographic writing.'

'Ideograph—' Ross repeated vaguely.

'Picture writing, like Chinese or ancient Egyptian. It is a sort of completely conventionalized rebus writing. In a civilization such as this, it must be highly idiomatic, impossible to decipher without a hundred years of study.'

Ross shook his head stubbornly. 'Then we'll have to investigate. We can go down that main avenue, out toward the suburban districts, and stop at some apartment house.' He pointed down the great avenue that stretched out straight toward the east. A faint lingering of lighter sky gave substance to the vast, hunched shadows that waited down the long passage. The night pressed down on the thin line of lights, crushing their illumination to the ground, obscuring the unseen things that went on in the higher, darker silence. The silence of the city brooded again, unbroken. The dusk-wind died away as night gained full sway. A moonless sky – sprinkled with the myriad bright, blind eyes of the stars – looked down sightlessly.

The silence held them in its grasp, froze them for long seconds before Ross moved, half-angrily. 'Let's go down there.' He spoke in a voice that echoed in startled protest against the blind, high walls. 'This silence gets you.' His voice was suddenly softened. He turned and walked to the open lock of the ship, his rubber-soled feet seeming noisy in the ringing corridor.

A silent ghost, the ship lifted on her antigravity field and drifted down the broad avenue, the space-fields meshing in the soundless structure of space to pull it forward, as noiseless as the city itself. Only the soft purr of the atomics, the familiar whine of the circulators, changed the soundless menace of the city to a world of reality, of living things moving in the light.

The hot, white beams of the forward landing light swept brilliance down the avenue ahead as the silent, waiting towers moved by in stately procession – broad, brown-paved streets, gray concrete sidewalks, a thousand shops, their broad windows sparkling in the light of the ship. Goods of strange pattern and unguessed purposes lay still behind the windows of the locked, dark stores. 'They did not take their possessions,' Young said softly.

Ross' fingers flickered over the controls, his iron-gray eyes level and intent on the avenue before him, his powerful, stocky body hunched over the controls in self-determined blindness to the dark mystery beyond the windows. Hall's lean face looked strained and tense; to him the presence of the goods seemed no surprise, nor would its absence have changed his opinion one iota. His dark, keen eyes followed the moving windows silently, watching them slip behind.

The towers shortened, pulled down from the skies to became squatter, smaller buildings as they left the city's heart. Swift miles fled behind the cruiser's sleek, bright-metal form. Ten times the speed of light lay within the powers of her fields; she idled now, and the wind of her passage chuckled meaningful laughter in her wake. The shops gave way to blank-walled business houses, then again as five-story apartment houses, set back from the avenue, spaced by green, tree-dotted lawns, appeared.

The cruiser slowed, halted in the street. The burbling of the wind died away and the silence of the city wrapped it again. No cheep of insect or ruffled piping of birds disturbed the utter quiet as the purr of the atomics died away. Ross rose, his feet scraping noisily. 'Bring your camera, Hall, and let's see what we can get. There must be some indication in there – some reason for this desertion.' His voice echoed pleasantly in the ship, breaking the pressing silence in rolling sounds that continued, gave life to his voice. The vastness of the city's ways drank in the sound, made voices flat and as unnatural as the city.

There was no door, but a grilled gateway that led into a courtyard open to the still night sky. A dozen doors opened from that; a fountain pool lay with unruffled waters, reflecting the starlight save where the smooth surface was broken by the spider-web fronds of some water plant show-ing minute red flowers in the light of their atom flares. The three floors of the building were terraced back from the courtyard, so that each story had a small, railed terrace run-ning entirely round the court. Onto these the doors of the apartments opened. Pale-blue wash of some sort laid over a plasterlike material reflected the light of their flares, limning each detail of the patio clearly – the winding stairs that led up from terrace to terrace, the bright blue and white tiles of the fountain pool—

'They knew how to live,' said Young softly. 'Three years in that metal bubble and this place, even in the silence, looks attractive. Why – why – *why* should any being, who loved life and beauty as the creators of this must have, leave this building, neat and ordered, a perfect home?'

'Try that first door, Hall,' said Ross steadily. 'I'll try the one on this side. Young, you want to take the second one?'

Ross reached his goal first, studied the knob of the portal of golden metal for a moment, pulled at it gently. The door opened toward him, and his call brought the others.

Curiously familiar the furnishings seemed, chairs of gracefully curved, glowing metal – an aluminum bronze with a matte, golden glow – upholstered in bright blue and white, a studio couch in similar materials, a desk in a dully glowing, dark-red wood. The silence of the city seemed to leak into the place with the opening of the door, making these ultimately human things more deserted, more poignantly alone, than had been the vast masses of the City, towering into the black hush of the night skies.

The room was lived in, the desk untidied by a torn bit of paper, scattered sheets of faintly yellowish parchment like material, a few scattered instruments evidently – humanly-pens. Hall moved toward the desk soundlessly, on rubber-soled feet over a carpet of bright, dark blue. A dozen lines of characters ran smoothly across the exposed sheet, from right to left, many-dotted, rounded characters, curiously like Arabic script; unfamiliarly dissimilar to Hall who read half Earth's polyglot tongues with ease.

Ross turned his head slowly, seeing the lattice-fronted cabinet faced with meters and three small knobs, the well stocked bookcase, scattered pictures on walls, small tables. Discarded a moment before, it seemed, a newspaper in a strangely curved, many-dotted characters slashed a message across all its front page. The entire page seemed devoted to that one item – the secret?

Hall looked up at Ross' low word and followed his pointing finger. Slowly he shrugged and shook his head. 'It's ideographic. I'm sure. The secret lies there, all right, open to be read. In full detail, no doubt, the story of the silence – the dark city under dark skies.

'We'll never know. These people, when they left, did not prepare for visitors. Why should they? They alone on the only habitable planet of their system, alone in a gulf of space we never would have guessed could be crossed by living intelligence, but for Hargreave's Accident and its consequence, the speed-drive.

'They left no primers for those to come, in their ordered – ordered? Why this paper dropped so carelessly, as though suddenly?'

'There is a door there,' pointed out Young, quietly.

Ross strode forward, his square, blocky body determined in its movements. Slowly he opened the door, letting the strong white light of his atomic flare reach in. Abruptly he stiffened, his breath sucked in sharply, then slowly he relaxed. His head lifted slightly, and he seemed to look without seeing at the ceiling of the room beyond, his body curiously half-tense, half-loosened. 'They were very human,' he said softly. 'But for that bright blue hair, she would seem a girl of Earth.

'Hall – Young, they did not leave. Here, here everywhere in their homes throughout the city they wait in silence. They are here, forever – everywhere, all about us, the ten millions of them who loved life and beauty.'

Silently, slowly, as though reluctant minds dragged on by bodies captured by an alien will, the two moved toward him. Over his shoulder they saw the little room, the low, broad bed, two figures seeming asleep only now that dusk had fallen, wrapping the city in its silent cloak. A girl – twenty, she might have been if of Earth – slim and young, her smooth, warm face still now, with a look of tired unhappiness half smoothed away. From beneath the white, closed lids, tears had trickled and dried long, long since. The arms of the man who had held her close were stiffened forever, yet so quiet, so easy had been their passing that no sign of death save their soft, gray blankets indicated more than a nighttime's sleep. Soft, gray fabric of dust lay deep over them, as it lay over all the furniture in this place.

Something gleamed with a brilliant ruby light on the bed beside the girl, dropped from her relaxed hand. Softly, on tiptoe as though to save disturbing this sleeping pair, Ross plucked it from its place, and brushed the dust from its surface – deep-cut sparkling red glass, formed in a graceful bottle, labeled in bright green characters on whitish background on an inlet smooth surface of the bottle. Enigmatic, rounded characters, made plain by the blurred thing below – a rounded, evident skull, framed by a pair of fleshless hands.

Softly the three left the room, went out to the courtyard of pale, pleasant blue under the sparkling night sky. Far off, the mighty tower of a building rose a dark finger against the pattern of the stars. Silently, Young lifted a pointing finger toward a strange constellation, a leering devil's head, with crooked, twisted mouth, and one winked eye. A bright star, and a lesser one for eyes; blind eyes, of which Sol, the ruler of a certain planetary system twenty-seven light-years distant, was the lesser.

'Three years,' said Ross dully. 'Let's try these other doors.'

Hall moved slowly toward another golden panel and opened it. The glare of the atomic flares lanced in. As the others came up behind his motionless figure, their eyes, too, saw into this room – this once lived-in room.

A child – a boy ten years old? – slept in a chair, sprawled carelessly. Slowly Ross led the way in. Not till they rounded him did they see the dark hole in his temple. The door of the room beyond stood open. And as their lights moved, beams reached into the space beyond. Another child, a girl perhaps two, lay in the lap of a hunched woman's figure. Each was marked with the dark hole of a bullet wound; Hall saw the other marks first, small pricks in blanched, whitened areas – one in the child's thigh, one in the mother's throat. Only when they entered the room did they see the twisted, contorted body of the man, his lips drawn back in a toothy, hideous grin, his arm swollen, enpurpled still, clasped in the death-loosened grip of the other hand.

'Preservative,' said Young softly. 'Effective, a poison that killed in agony. He shot the others and protected them; himself he could only protect. That other couple – that poison must have had the same effect.

'Need we see more apartments – more of the tens of millions who built and labored and loved this city – and left, to go beyond the stars in the only way they knew?'

'No,' said Ross softly. Then his voice became sharply agonized. 'But why – *why*? No sign of danger, no sign of damage. What struck at them, forced them to this? A foreign state of this world? But what could war, or attack of any sort, offer that made this preferable? And this is the greatest city, by far, on this planet. It would have a greater backing of manpower and machines than any other, if there are those silly artificial boundaries no visitor from space could see.

'No unproven threat could do this; no *threat* of death can make ten million people seek death.

'I know – we do not *know* that they have all killed themselves, but—' He stopped, and the silence of the city poured in, drinking the little sounds they made and washing them away.

'There could be no invasion from the other worlds of this system. We know them – and they're dead rocks. Two blistered in unbearable heat, one an airless boulder too small for atmosphere, and two frozen utterly. No alien race could menace them from their own system.

'Is there some other ranging race in space, some stock of slavers perhaps, working on a cosmic scale? No race that fought its way from mud to magnificence as these people did would kill themselves without fight. And fight of the magnitude that must result – they have atomic power, I'm pretty sure, for the city power is still functioning and gray dust gathering half-inch coats over the people – that fight would leave scars we couldn't miss.

'Why? What deadly thing could drive them to this, a century or ten centuries ago?'

'That long?' asked Hall softly.

Ross gestured, and again the silence welled in. 'No sounds, no action. This is a cloudless, almost rainless world, the temperature so constant, the air so clear, only a few light showers can have fallen. There are no seasons, and no winds or living animals to damage buildings. The grass grows on, the trees we saw seem long-lived. I don't know.

'But we must – we must—' He looked about him jerkily, his face whitened by three years of sunless spaces, whiter still in the flame of the atom-flares. 'The menace cannot be from this system. It must have come from outer space, a power that wanders from star to star – a power that could wander to Earth.

'That may *have* wandered to Earth—' He stopped aghast, looking at the other two. 'Three years – and it will be six years before we get a word of news from Earth.'

Earth – a planet of silent cities, its wandering ships stilled

143

once, forever, the soughing wind alone whispering through crumbling cities—

'No.' Young spoke sharply. His voice bombarded back from the shocked, protesting silence. 'Let's go out – go to the ship,' he muttered, turning sharply. The room fell dark behind them, a quiet, dark hush that was accustomed here stealing back as the flares passed out.

'We can try other cities. Somehow, crazily, I had not thought of nationalism. I had more the idea of a world state, such as Earth has now. But ours is only half a century old – long to us, but not to history. Other cities here may have different languages, as different nations on Earth did have. Those other languages might be such that we could translate them in time, and a lot shorter time. Primers not, perhaps, for people of other worlds, but for people new to this world, learning the story of its development from as little background as we have. Children come with no more language than we.'

'No,' Hall shook his head. 'That isn't true altogether. For a phonetic language a child's primer might serve, but not for an ideograph. An ideograph is a rebus, a symbolized, conventionalized puzzle, from which all trace of origin has fallen away, tacked onto a highly modern idiom. That is not for unlearned children, but for those who know already the spoken language from which the thing takes start.

'We can try those other cities, there might be a living people – incredible – but if there is another language, a phonetic one, we have some hope of gaining essentials in a city where books for children might exist.' The silent ship gained life and sound as the lock took them in. A circulator whined into soft sound near them and the silence of the city rested, knitting up its briefly tattered fabric as the shining metal bubble leapt away in startled, frantic flight. For an instant, the delicate fern-like fronds of the trees waved in the vacuum of its passage. Then the stillness and dark crept in and regained a long-held sway. Vague things stirred busily in the shadows that reached out again with the vanishment of the white, clear atom-flames.

The silent world fled beneath the slanted rise of the ship, darkness giving way to a swift-returning twilight as the rise and movement brought the sun again above the horizon. Wordlessly, the three watched mist-shrouded hills rise from the plains, climb, and fall behind in diminishing foothills. A vast river-valley opened out, shadowed at one edge 100 miles beneath, sunlit at the far side.

The ship angled down again toward the soundless planet. The patchwork of farmed land mottled the green-brown of the ancient river-system's valley. Where two tributaries joined the stream a many-colored blot of steel and stone shadowed the land. The ship slanted down and the city below gained reality and a third dimension as their altitude diminished from miles to feet.

Slow as a settling dust-grain, the interstellar cruiser drifted down on her antigravity fields, down toward a park-land in the city's heart. Dense, dark-green trees around a small lake, fed by a tiny meandering stream. Flowers had run riot, spreading in the unattended years back from the stream, around the borders of the lake.

No sun-tipped 1000-foot towers ringed this park; the buildings were broad and low, colonnaded structures of white and green and pale-blue stone. Glinting walls of glass brick poured the rays of the setting sun into the buildings to escape again through other glass walls as a mockery of internal illumination shining out into the evening sky.

Slowly the ship settled while Ross' gray eyes tightened. This park was not deserted. On smooth lawns, under clear waters of the pond, at ease in a hundred places, sleeping figures lay. Tiny, graceful cockle-shell boats lay upturned beneath the waters, beside their spilled occupants. On the lawns couples, trios, lay in an eternal sleep. The warm strong rays of the sun, heat, the soft rains had bleached away the bright colors of the clothes they wore. Slow oxidation and time had embrittled them and the stirring breezes had torn the fabric to broken tatters.

Young moved toward the lock, out onto the soft turf, yielding under his feet. A group of four lay beneath a grotesquely gnarled, gracefully twisted tree. Two elderly people, man and wife, and a younger couple, the girl's bright blue silkens faded now to a color as soft as the wall of the building that rose two hundred feet away, beyond the brown-paved highway. Long rays of the setting sun reached down to illuminate her body, bent forward over the head of the man in her lap. Nestling beside it lay a ruby crystal green labeled flask.

Hall walked past them and automatically Young and Ross fell into step behind him. 'That building,' said Hall slowly, 'must have been an office building, or a public building. There must be written material there, and we can find in five minutes whether there is any need to stay in this city. These people took their poison – the same one apparently – in the parks, in many places. Look – parked cars. Their psychology was, in that degree, different. Their language may have been.'

'If it is – the menace was not national, but planetary,' Ross added.

Broad doors stood open, a layer of sifting dust laid down

in the farther passages where the other breezes had not stirred it. On one white-stoned wall, between a series of small bronze doors, an inset panel of dark stuff behind glass covering, showed the curved, many-dotted characters of the strange, yet familiar language. Hall sighed. 'The language is the same. We could try once more, say half around this world.'

Silently, the three walked back, the smooth carpet of dust tearing beneath their feet. The quick dusk was setting in once more, the sun's last rays lighting the sky, but lifted already above the city's streets. Moments later the spherical ship lifted once more into the light, and rose beyond the atmosphere's dim carpet to race around the world.

Shallow inland seas, their smooth waters darkened under night skies, fell behind; the glowing patches of great cities operating long after their creators had given way to death and some unknown that hovered still about this dark world. Great cities, like mouldering patches of phosphorescent decay on the dark trunk of a fallen tree, and lesser towns that sparkled only faintly.

'This is a temperate zone,' Ross suddenly. 'I'll head for the tropics. If there were two races on this planet, the difference in climate would be the most probably dividing factor, and this our best opportunity to find a second language and a clue.'

The sun rose again with the fleeting ship's motion, rose and held as they cruised a thousand miles around the bulge of the planet, to slant down once more as the dark green of temperate foliage gave way to the brilliant colors of a tropical jungle. The ship slowed over a broken patch in the spreading jungle growth, a city whose buildings lay in broken ruins beneath the thrust of climbing plant-life.

Shattered stone and glass half-hid, half-revealed the crushed bodies of the people who had built and died here. Broken rubbery pavements twisted and writhed over thrusting roots of giant trees towering half a thousand feet above the low white buildings. There was sound here, the faint rustle of a billion leaves in the slow-stirring morning air, and sharp tinkle and crack of masonry disturbed by a life that thrust out blindly, voraciously for more, and yet more room.

Hall pointed silently to a broken, tumbled wall of glass bricks, fallen to jagged splinters in the sunlight, half obscuring the metal shelving it had protected. A crumbled, sodden mass of books bleached under the hot sun – the color and printed symbols lost under soft tropic rains and harsh, white sunlight. 'The same language,' said Hall briefly. 'It was the universal language of this planet. We will find no comparative tongues to give clues and hints. There can be no Rosetta Stone in three languages. Everywhere there must lie a thousand, written complete accounts – a million notes of explanations, a thousand printed accounts complete and exact, written by dead scientists.

'The answer of a million eyewitnesses from the views of every type and class of man or woman. Why it was that parents murdered children, and then themselves.' 'Why it was,' added Ross thoughtfully, 'They all, each one took such precautions their bodies should not decay. There is that which puzzles me. They went out of their way – the one we saw who shot those he'd tend to protect and injected some preservative, but poisoned himself – unpleasantly.'

Hall shook his head uncertainly. 'I don't know; a lot of races made a fetish of preserving the body, for rehabilitation in another time, a reincarnation in that flesh.' Hall looked about him. A thousand bodies, some crushed, but none, never, a skeleton. 'The red-flask poison must have been rare and hard to obtain, the injected stuff a common substance any one could get.'

Ross shook his head with an air of ending the subject. 'There is more to it than that. These people died, a world of them, by their own hands. Why, in a world without war, without threat of damage? And why in a world of scientific achievement should this fetish of body preservation have survived, and it alone, in the face of acts that denied every other custom, even the law of self-preservation?'

Hall shrugged wearily. 'Let's go out to space. We are tired now, and in the atmosphere of this world our thoughts are mixed. Perhaps after rest, we'll understand it better – perhaps not. But we'll have to make a thousand photographs and ten thousand reports. There must be samples of soil and air, water and minerals.

'We aren't through. We'll have to study this morgue world for three months at least. Come on.'

The ship floated up as silent as the world it left, the anti-gravity field increasing, and the slow throw of the planet's spin sending it again into space. The drive-fields gripped, and the cool and dark of space received it. The spinning world shrank away in distance, the vastness of its puzzle contracting in their minds as the planetary ship with its cargo of death, stilled happiness, and unguessed mystery shrank in size.

Young and Hall sat beside Ross, watching with unseeing concentration the skilled manipulations of his fingers, lulled by the soft purr of the atomics aft. Slowly Hall rose to his feet and turned down the corridor toward his room.

Young shook himself, the dark horror in his eyes fading

suddenly, his tense mouth relaxing in a startled, half-sheepish grin. 'Ye gods, that world gets you! I'll start the galley; *they* may be dead, but *we're* still living.'

Ross nodded wearily, then nodded again abruptly as his eyes, too, cleared. 'Gets you, is right!' he exploded. 'Yes – go ahead. I suppose I do have an appetite, but—' He shook his head with the jerkiness of a boxer trying to clear away the fog of a blow. He looked up with dazed eyes, a new intentness and questioning in them.

'Back there, it's a dream. It's been three years since we saw a living soul, Bar, and something of the wear we've had on each other in this damned tin bubble eats down your resistance and appreciation of reality. Already that whole thing back there is beginning to seem a dream, another of those damnable nightmares you get from sleeping while the speed-drive is on. A world – cities, their millions dead by suicide, without a sign, an indication of the slightest trouble that might have affected them to make them do it. And – Lord, the silence! That silence is as unnatural as those almost-living corpses. Weren't there ever any birds to sing, no insects at all?

'That great dead city was too unreal to make the thing comprehensible; it seemed more like a posed question visualized with a ghastly accuracy.'

'That was no vision, or if it was, we have to live and labor in it for three months or more. And think it over for three years going back.' Young stared down from the port toward the slowly turning, mottled world, not 50,000 miles away. The faint blue haze of its atmosphere drew a blurring veil over its features, disclosing the gross outlines of land-locked seas and mountain ranges. The great river valleys showed as wide depressions, while the mantling, faint haze of blue reflected from the atmosphere veiled the thin silver threads of rivers that had caused them.

Young turned sharply and strode back to the galley. Presently he heard the strains of one of their stock of records grow in the ship as one of the others – probably Ross, he thought – started the amplifier. The lifting, quick-paced song caught him for a moment, and speeded his movements. The mystery floating there in space contracted into unreality; the strong, deep channels of familiarity and accustomed work diverted his conscious mind. Somewhere deep beneath the surface a vast weight of impending trouble stirred, and rose to bother him into uneasiness and haste as the record stopped and another started – a faint-toned plaintive song of the Martian colonists composed of the thin whine of Martian dust-winds and the sough of compressors. Surely, the composer had woven into it the same sphinx-mystery of the Martian sands, the scattered, cut blocks that never could have been assembled to form anything, but were shaped and cut on a world that never, in all its history, could have supported intelligent life—

His mind stirred uneasily. 'Hey, pilot! Hall! Come and feed.'

The song died jerkily as the needle-light died and the record-reel rewound automatically. Ross' heavy feet came down the corridor, and his stocky body swung round the corner. With half-unconscious eagerness, Young found himself watching him vaguely; he sighed gustily, familiarly, as he seated himself and Young turned away, vaguely satisfied. Three years of familiarity in the cramped 'tin bubble' – that unimportant thing, the invariable sigh as he seated himself. Always, Young caught himself watching for it; always it came. His eyes swung to watch for Hall. He would pause in the doorway, lift his head just-so and sniff. As unconscious as Ross' sigh. Then he would enter.

'Hey, Hall – come on,' Ross called. Leisurely Young slid the metal plates across the table, pans of food. In a momentary pause, the ship was suddenly silent, the air mechanism off, the atomics cut down to soundless idle.

'Hall—' Young stepped into the corridor doorway. The vague unease welled up in him as the silence of the ship stirred strong memories that had seemed to fade into the limbo of nightmares and things of unreality. 'Hall—' He walked with spaced, hesitant steps toward the closed door of Hall's cabin, threw it open and grunted in disgust. 'He's asleep,' he threw over his shoulder to Ross, peering round the corridor. 'I don't see – how he could have—'

'Ross,' Young's voice was very low and still in the corridor, 'he's got—'

Ross' bulk edged by him somehow, darting into the little room. For an instant his great, thick-fingered hand clutched the green-labeled ruby bit of glass, then dropped it to crashing fragments on the metal floor-plates. Roughly he turned Hall's quiet figure to the light. It moved with a curious solidity, as though in one stiff, solid piece – legs, arms and head in the same rigid position. Ross jerked back, rubbing his finger stiffly on the tough fabric of his trousers, darkened eyes tense on the face before him.

They of the planet had died, always, with closed eyes. Yet Hall lay with eyes wide-opened. Jerkily, Young snatched a carelessly dropped shirt, and threw it over the white, staring face, over the black misery of horror in the eyes.

'It got him,' Ross gurgled unpleasantly. 'Hall – it got Hall. Hall's a man—'

'Notes,' – Young clawed frantically at the little desk let into the metal wall. 'This thing's locked – get his keys. Notes—'

'No.' Ross shook his head groggily. 'No notes – if he wrote a note it'd be out – open for us.'

'If it got him he must have known why – why they died, why he was dying,' Young pleaded. 'He must have. Lord, Ross, he didn't lie down and drink that to see what it was.'

'Maybe he did!' Ross straightened slightly, then slumped again. 'No. He's the chemist. He knew. He knew what it was and why – why they died, why – we – will – die.'

'He couldn't have! No, we won't die. We have to find out.'

'So did he. He didn't even tell us. Didn't tell us to warn us. Why? That's another why.' Ross looked at the still frozen figure. A queer hatred was growing in his eyes, bitterness and horror, hatred and a bit of madness. Suddenly all the weight of oppression that had ridden them in the city rose again and crushed him. The comforting, shock-proof feeling of unreality was rent and cast aside. Hall did that; Hall laid his mind open to that deadly pressure of realization and reality. His lip lifted slowly, lifted and snapped down.

'Will you stop that,' snapped Young. 'Stop grinning, you crack-headed ape.'

Ross glowered at him. 'It's damned unfair of Hall. If he knew – he must have known. Why didn't he tell us? Why did he make another "why" to bother us? Why – why—'

Young shook himself, and looked down at the figure under the shirt. It looked contorted, agonized now, because it was rigid and stiff. It should be lying on its other side, so he grasped it abruptly and heaved it back.

Ross stalked out of the doorway. Suddenly the amplifier began to roar out a recorded storm of music, blaring forth an echoing shock of sound that shattered silence.

Young joined him in the control room. 'What do we do?'

For answer, Ross' fingers flew over the controls. Behind them the slumberous atomics woke to a straining throb that drowned the roar of the speaker for a moment, then died away as vast potentials built up. A dark mantle, a trickery of unseen lenses had acted. The sphere of space about them rushed in suddenly and contracted close to them. From the port, in one single direction, Young saw the planet that had been below them, the sun that had been ahead, and all the field of stars that had been on every side. Yet they did not overlap. From every other port, he knew, he would see the same. Abruptly, the planet puffed, and vanished. The nearby sun puffed and snapped down to dwindle at crazy speed.

Tense eyes in white face, Ross labored over his controls. The calculators hummed and clicked softly under the protecting screen that kept out the clawing silence that struggled to reach them, gnawing at the walls of the ship, pressing savagely—

'We're headed back,' said Ross. Slowly he straightened, then slumped forward to look at his work. Minutes passed; the record ran out, stuttered, and a new one fed itself in. White-faced, Ross looked up again, a saner terror in his eyes. Slowly that submerged as reason and courage came back. 'I guess that's best, at that,' he said quietly.

Young nodded vaguely. 'We need help. I wouldn't stay there. That planet is *wrong* – and Hall knew why.'

A light of bitterness blazed in Ross' eyes, his face set angrily. 'No matter what the thing might be, he should have told.'

'I wonder if it could have been a thing – that isn't tellable. An explanation that does not exist, without the lack of explanation.'

Ross glared up at him. 'Talk sense; stop words and make sentences.'

'I mean – an hysteria. It nearly caught us. Hall was a more sensitive man than you and I; we know that. We lived with him – damn near inside his skin – in this bubble for three years. It might have been an hysteria that, mounting and growing, swept round that world and destroyed them all. Made it a morgue world without reason or sense.'

Ross muttered vaguely. 'It isn't sensible. Some few in any race are too utterly selfish to permit the thought of possessing all the world to be overcome by an hysteria of death. No. The misers and the antisocial would be dancing in joy. No, it doesn't explain. Hall knew. Hall knew the secret, the answer to all those "why's," damn him. He died as all those millions did – sealing the secret forever.' Ross swung abruptly, a sudden fierce flame in his face. 'And listen, if you get it – get a hint of it – and don't tell me before attempting suicide— If I find you still alive, I'll roast you slowly. I'll tear each separate nerve out of your carcass one by one. I'll—

'Hell. You tell me. That's all.'

Stubbornly, Ross turned back to his controls and pecked at them as a small blue light gleamed. The light winked out. A green one lit, faded, and finally a white one lit and burned steady on the board. 'We still have to eat.'

Only the tinyness of the star they had left indicated the motion of ten times light's speed, hours later. The stars from every port appeared the same; there was no shifting of position, no changing in constellations of the vastly distant suns. The ship plunged on, a silent, darkened metal bubble in a silent immensity of space. The atomics were silent now, the speed-fields built to saturation. Ross stood at the port-light motionless, his eyes unseeingly staring into the strange, twisted maze of stars compressed in unnatural clarity to any line of sight.

'It must have been hysteria. It must have been. Hall would have spoken. He'd have told us, sure, if he knew and realized what struck him.' Ross blurted out the words, swinging to Young.

Young looked up from his lab bench, fragments of ruby glass and a dozen drops of liquid beside his microscope. 'Nothing I recognize.' He shrugged morosely. 'I'm no chemist, just an inept physicist out of his field. I wouldn't know anything more complex than a few muscarine derivatives – and this is complex and new to man, I suspect. Surely we know of no such precipitation. One fragment of a drop of it solidified an egg white like lightning.

'And – it may have been hysteria. Hall was 50,000 miles in space when it got him. How many millions—' He stopped and looked at Ross with a twisted grin. 'One of us will fail to reach Earth, in all probability. Stop to think of that?'

Ross looked at him in sudden suspicion. 'Listen, if you get some idea of what this is all about—'

'No, damn it. But why were there three of us sent in the first place?'

'The energy concentrations needed by a larger ship couldn't be built up by known means. The atomics couldn't handle the potentials. They couldn't carry food, air, supplies for more than three men.'

'Why not two men?' suggested Young smoothly.

'Why, two men—' said Ross blankly and stopped. 'Because,' he went on in suddenly tense, hard voice, 'two men for three years, in a tin can, makes one man. Nerve friction, as they call it.'

'Two men in a sealed tube for three years. Two men, one

corpse, and one – vast – mystery. The mystery of a dead planet and a dead man. The cargo of this ship won't stay that way.' Young rose and went abruptly to his room. The air recirculator cut off with a soft pop as though to emphasize his words.

For a long time Ross sat silent, listening to the creak of Young's feet on the floorplates. He began to move restlessly, his fingers twitching slightly; then his arm. A vague uneasiness seemed to stir him. Then the unseeing lethargy seemed to drain from his eyes, a sharpening, widening horror flooding in—

He rose to his feet, and on soundless toes moved past the laboratory bench, toward the corridor leading to the rooms.

Hours later, Young looked down into his face with a look of frozen bitterness. Ross stared back at him, his face relaxed in a gentle smile of complete satisfaction. 'You damned, sneaking rat. You rotten louse. One man to operate this ship for three years – and you *knew* you unutterable skunk, you knew. You, *you* shouting about knowing and telling, and then ducking like that—'

The cold smile on Ross' lips remained unchanged; growing wildness in Young's eyes matched the tic that formed in his cheek, jerking the muscles in little, rhythmic twitches.

He straightened slowly from the cooling corpse, and slung down the echoing corridor of the ship, a dull hatred and hopelessness in his mind. Nightmares – nightmares of a horror planet riding in a death ship with the speed-fields up. He wouldn't dare to lower them for three full years, until they cut off of themselves. Ross and Hall were the pilots, the ones who knew the manipulations of the speed-field finders. They had escaped, had escaped with the infinite velocity of death.

And Ross had known. Somehow, he'd guessed the secret of the planet and its dead millions, guessed it as Hall had. But what clue, what unremembered thing, had given them the path that led to understanding? And what was that understanding that drove these men, sound and safe, already trillions of miles from that world, to follow the builders of the ghost cities?

Young started at the tinkling of a falling water drop, and jabbed at the tap angrily. A sudden tinkling stream of water bubbled down and stopped. They had known – and said nothing.

And more than that – knowing, realizing that some menace hung there still, a menace they escaped by death, and death alone – Ross had taken the last few drops of that sudden poison of the death world, leaving none if he—

A cold fury settled on Young, a seething anger that cleared his mind and filled him with a determination to bring this ship, bring it back to Earth, and know the full story of the planet before he did. If, somewhere, both Hall and Ross had picked up the clue that gave them understanding, then he, too – by the gods – he, too, would find that clue!

Some understanding of possibilities came to him slowly. He moved with a swift surety to his room and gathered a few things he needed. Then, to the pilot's bench and the ship's log. Swiftly he wrote into it the account of what had passed since Ross' last entry after Hall had died. Then laboriously, he calculated many things – the exact specific heat of the ship as a whole, the energy content of the ship at 700 degrees absolute, and studied all the ship to determine what might and might not happen.

He was a physicist and atomic engineer. Piloting this ship from the closed space of the speed-drive was beyond him; a practical knowledge he didn't have. But not the designing and building of the controls he wanted or the construction of the cylinder he would need – if things happened.

He made his connections, pressed a small switch. A tiny synchronous motor turned slowly to the low, smooth hum of a tuning fork; a slow creep of the rotary switch assured him. In twelve hours that must be reversed to halt its action.

Then he went again to the pilot room and stared unseeing at the queerly clustered stars. Slowly, every item that they had seen, had touched, went through his mind. The cold hatred for the two blankly unspeaking, yet informative corpses he suppressed; they told him only this – that it could be known. It could be, knowing the why of those dead millions the reason for that suicide, the nature of the cosmic menace that had overcome them so utterly that they, the supreme fighting type of their world, had gone down unresisting. And that, somehow, that knowledge impelled a bond of final secrecy.

It came to him with sudden surprise the numbness of his hand. The faint ticking of his finger nails in the startled silence of the ship brought a slow fading of that intense concentration. Idly at first he rubbed the numbed hand to restore circulation – and paused.

A tremor shook him, and a shocked horror flooded his mind. A million voices shouted and commanded deep within him, a growing clamor that was, somehow, united and fiercely determined. A conscious force growing discoverable abruptly, noticed for the first time—

It seemed, then, to take long minutes of slow growth, yet in the confusion he knew simultaneously that it was like the time-rate of a dream, started by the slam of a door, ending with the slam of the door as the closing sequence of the dream. A flash of mental action of incredible rapidity vouchsafed him in the infinitesimal instant of time between his awareness of attack, and his defeat.

In that atom of time, he saw through other minds, a million billion other minds, and yet thought with his own. He lived in another universe, a universe of infinitesimals, thinking, conscious, intelligent molecules. Single molecules of a vast complexity driving forward to a racial goal through the medium of countless billions of keen-thinking units – units that were single, conscious molecules. What body cells were to Young, single atoms were to them. Their thought was a swift shifting of atomic strains within their molecule-bodies; their senses not sight, nor sound, nor any thing humans might know, but finer, subtler things of electric, magnetic, gravitic strains. A fineness that made chemical action a stupendous, gross thing.

Light came to them as great blundering, fuzzy balls of energy which they absorbed as food. Their thought processes, flashing with the speed of electric stress, outstripped man's clumsy mechanism a million times. Yet one great thing they lacked; they could have no control of gross matter, their very minuteness made that thing to them unthinkable. A hundred million atoms composed each molecule-body. A vastly swollen intelligent molecule – yet withal so minute that a hundred million of them were indetectable to man.

Intelligence, swift, keen intelligence – unable to control their own environment by the handicap of size. Yet, eating the hurtling quanta of light and radiant heat as food, they could ride the streaming light-currents of space from world to world. For temperature was unknown to them, light, food enough. Only the extreme battering of high-temperature molecules could destroy them. Beyond that one thing, their conscious control of their own molecular forces made them immune, eternal.

But the delicate, immensely organized chemistry of intelligent beings like man were susceptible to the race control of billions of them. Immense organizations of them, working in planned unison, could affect the delicate chemistry of nerves and brain to give orders, relayed by the grosser, greater organism into action that could control that physical environment beyond their own control.

And, like many high protein molecules, they had this other attribute; they were, chemically, enzymatic. They could force lesser unconscious proteins that to them appeared as lesser animals, to shape and form themselves into replicas of the Intelligences. Man would serve them both as breeding ground, and relay control, subjected utterly to the unseen will of beings whose smallness put them beyond the greatest microscope.

An understanding that swept up and through Young's mind in that last instant of consciousness, before his mind fell before their final comprehension of the intricate network of nerve cells that long study, since first they entered his body on the dead world, had brought.

And Young understood, too, the suicides, the preservation that Ross had puzzled at. The red-flask poison the Intelligences knew, and hated. A lesser, swifter enzyme protein that shook down the proteins of man, or any proteinous material to its own form. One that destroyed equally the protein molecule that had gained intelligence. The injected stuff, a simple chemical poison, that, like formaldehyde, precipitated and hardened any protein, rendering the dead flesh forever useless to the Intelligences.

His body surged up from its chair as a last fierce urge

161

whipped through him before the rising tide of molecules destroyed his last conscious will. The familiar control room, the lab bench, reeled and faded behind red mist in the same instant that he rose. His mind had fallen to the planned attack of a billion unseen enemies, seeking through him to gain control of all space, for all time—

The dark mist faded very slowly from his eyes. Before he could see, even, he knew where he would find himself. His eyes opened on the metal walls of his own cabin, familiar things seen through a slow growing haze. A warm lethargy that had crept into legs and arms, was creeping inward to this last core that was himself. Fading memory and knowledge gained from the attackers made it clear; their greater, more complex molecules fell easier prey to the enzyme poison of the Planet of Death. For this last, brief second of time before it finally overcame him, too, in its warm lethargy, he understood.

Already the warm paralysis had reached, and stopped his motor nerves; he could not speak, or write, or signal now, just as before him Hall and then Ross had been helpless to warn, or explain.

The last brief flash of action though had gone unstayed, for the yet more complex paths of his subconscious mind had not so easily been traced. Unhampered, it had carried out his last strong will. The last drop of poison Ross had taken, but the egg— Dimly he saw it, half eaten beyond the growing haze of warm grey before his closing eyes.

And memory satisfied him of other things. The log, with a scrawled warning 'Intelligent molecules—' that he had thrust in self-hypnosis in the prepared, heat-proof cylinder. The synchronous motor turning slow before the drive of a humming tuning fork that molecules could not halt.

The circuit would close, the automatic controls would bring the ship to Earth's system, and halt it as the speed-fields collapsed. And slowly, because of that closed circuit, the atomics would labor and build up a temperature of 700 degrees absolute, where metal glowed dull and warning red—

And destroyed any molecule save only the very simplest, even those that might be partly sheltered in the asbestos cylinder, where even paper would be somewhat scorched—

Elimination

John Grantland looked across at his old friend's son intently and unhappily. Finally he sighed heavily and leaned back in his swivel chair. He lighted his pipe thoughtfully. Two slow puffs of smoke rose before he spoke.

'I'm a patent attorney, Dwight Edwards, and I'm at your disposal, as such, to do your bidding and help you to secure that patent you want. As you know, I'm also a civil-and-commercial-law expert of some standing in connection with that work. I can get that patent; I know it is patentable and unpatented as yet. But before I start proceedings, I have to tell you something, Dwight.

'You have enough to live on the rest of your life, a brilliant mind to increase it, a scientific ability to keep you occupied and useful to the world. This invention is not useful to the world. If you were a poor man, I would not hesitate in making the patent applications, because some wiser men, with more money, would buy it up and destroy the thing. But you aren't poor, and you would hold out till the thing was developed and going.'

'But – but Mr. Grantland, it's a thing the world needs! We have a fast-vanishing gasoline reserve – a coal supply being drawn on endlessly and recklessly. We need a new source of power, something to make the immense water-power supplies in inaccessible regions available. The system would do that, and conserve those vanishing resources, run automobiles, planes, even small factories and homes—'

'It would destroy our greatest resource, the financial structure of the nation. A resource is not a resource unless it is available, and only the system makes it available. The system is more valuable, more important to human happiness than any other resource, because it makes all others available.

'I know your natural desire, to develop and spread that system for canning and distributing electricity. It's a great invention. But—'

'But,' the younger man said somewhat bitterly, 'you feel that any really great, any important invention should be destroyed. There must be, you are saying, no real improvement, only little gadgets. There must be no Faradays who discover principles, only Sam Browns who invent new can openers and better mousetraps.'

Grantland laid down his pipe and leaned back in his chair silently.

Bitterly, the younger man was gathering his papers.

'Dwight,' said Grantland at length, 'I think I'll do best if I tell you of one invention that I have in my files here. I have shown these papers to just one other man than the men who made them. Curiously, he was your father. He—'

'My father? But he was not an inventor – he was a psychiatrist, utterly uninterested—'

'He was vitally interested in this. He saw the apparatus they made, and he helped me dismantle it, secretly, and destroy the tube Hugh Kerry and Robert Darnell made. That was twenty-two years ago, and it was something of a miracle I had, at the age of thirty-six, the sense to do that.

'I'm going to tell you mighty vague things and mighty vague principles, because you're too keen. It isn't very safe to tell you this, but I believe you will keep a promise. You must swear two things before I tell you the story: First, that you will not put that surprisingly acute mind of yours to work on what I say, because I cannot tell what clues I may give. I understand too little to know how much I understood; second, of course, that you will not spread this unpleasant story.'

The young man put down his papers, looked curiously at John Grantland. 'I agree to that, Mr. Grantland.'

Grantland stuffed his pipe thoughtfully in silence. 'Hugh Kerry and Bob Darnell were one of those fortuitous miracles, where the right combination came together. Hugh Kerry was the greatest mathematician the world has seen, at thirty-two.'

'I have heard of him; I've used his analytical methods. He died at thirty-three, didn't he?'

'I know,' said Grantland. 'The point is – so did Bob Darnell. Bob Darnell was something like Edison, on a higher level. Edison could translate theory into metal and glass and matter. Darnell could do that, but he didn't work with steel and copper and glass. He worked with atoms and electrons and radiation as familiarly as Edison worked with metal. And Darnell didn't work from theory; he worked from mathematics that no theory could be defined for.

'That was the pair the shifting probabilities of space time brought together – and separated. You've never heard of Darnell, because he did only one thing, and that one thing is on paper there, in that steel vault. In the first place, it is in a code that is burned into my memory, and not on paper. In the second place, it is safe because every equation in it is wrong, because we couldn't code equations easily, and the book that gave them right is out of print, forgotten.

'They came into my office first because they lived nearby,

and I'd gone to the same school. I hadn't much of a reputation then, of course. That was when you were just about getting into the sixth grade, Dwight – a good number of years ago.

'They had the tube then. They called it the PTW tube – Probability Time Wave. They'd been trying to make a television set that would see through walls – a device that would send out its own signals and receive them back as images.

'They went wrong, something about trying for the fourth-dimensional approach and slipping into a higher dimension. They said that Einstein's curved space theory was wrong, and it was the ten-dimensional multiple theory that was right.

'But you said something about Faradays and Sam Browns. That invention I suppressed was something so enormous, Dwight, that anything that ever has or ever will be invented is picayunish squabbling beside it. It was the greatest tower looming on the road of progress. It loomed above all other things as the sun looms greater than earth. It was the greatest thing that ever was or will be, because it necessarily incorporated the discovery of everything that ever will be or can be.'

'What – what could be so great? The power of the atom—'

'That was one of the lesser things it incorporated, Dwight. It would have meant that, in a year or so, and the secret of gravity, of interplanetary, interstellar flight, the conquest of age, and eternal life. Everything you can dream of, John, and all the things that any man ever will dream of.

'They knew all that when they came to me. They explained it all, and because I couldn't believe – they showed me. You cannot conceive of such a thing – anything – so inconceivably far-reaching in scope? I'm not surprised. They told me what I have told you, and but that they said it all in such quiet, assured voices, with such perfect and absolute confidence, I'd have called them liars and put it down to the vain boasting of the Sam Brown you mentioned, with his mighty new mousetrap and his miraculous can opener – the invention of the ages.

'It's simple when you know the answer, to see how true was their every claim. Their television slipped. It slipped aside, into some higher dimension, they guessed, and instead of penetrating the walls and the buildings through that fourth dimension they sought, they decided it had slipped out and beyond space and time, and looked back to review it, a mighty pageant of incredible history – the history that was to be.

'You see, in that was the incredible and infinite scope of the thing, because it showed, in the past, all that had been, the infinite sweep and march of all time from the creation to the present.

'But then the ordered ranks broke, for, from the present to the other end of infinity, no single thing or any circumstance is immutably fixed. Their PTW tube caught and displayed every possibility that was ever to exist. And somewhere in that vast sweep of probability, every possible thing existed. Somewhere, the wildest dream of the wildest optimist was, and became fact.

'On that screen tube I saw the sun born, and on it I saw the sun die a million deaths. I saw them move planets, and I saw the planets moving in birth. I saw life created, and I saw it created again in test tubes and laboratories. I saw man arise – and I saw men and women more perfect in body and mind than the dream of Praxiteles created from acetylene and ammonia. Because somewhere in the realms of possibility, remote or so near as to be probable, those dreams of every scientist came true, and with them, the unguessed dreams of unguessable intellects.

'Hugh Kerry and Bob Darnell came to me when the thing was new, and they faintly conceived of its possibilities. That was in 1950. And in five days the world would have known and been at their feet – but for two things – three, really. First, because the thing, they knew, was imperfect, and, what they didn't know, was severely limited. Second, because they had begun to trace their own life tracks, and were worried, even then. I caught some of that worry from them and held back. I never let them cast for my life tracks. Today I do not know what will come tomorrow. Third, and what was perhaps the determining reason, they were still poor, but growing rich rapidly by the information that machine brought them of the little, everyday things that were to be two days ahead.

'You could pile up an enormous fortune, Dwight, if you just knew with a probability of eighty-five on their scale of a hundred, what tomorrow and tomorrow would bring. They did, and first the number pool hated them and refused their business, then the betting rings refused their bets, and finally, even the stock market began to act unfavorably. Because they won, of course.

'But before then, they had begun to forget that, and concentrated on the life tracks the machine showed them.

'I said the machine was limited. It was limited by two factors: one was the obvious difficulty of seeing the forest and the shape of the forest when in the middle of it. They were in the middle of the parade, and there they must stay. They could not see the near future clearly, for the near forest was hidden by the trees. The far future they could see like a vast marching column that split and diverged slowly. They saw no individual figure, only the blended mass of the march to infinity.

'At a year, the parade began to blend, and the features were lost by the establishment of the trend. But, at two days, two weeks, their screen showed a figure blurred and broken by the splitting images that broke away, each following its own line of possible development.

'Look. A vision of me in the future by only ten minutes will show me in a thousand lifecourses. Primarily, there are two; I may live, or die. But even those two instantly became a thousand, for I may die now, or at any later instant. I may die by the falling of the building or the stoppage of my heart, by an assassin's bullet, by the knife of a disgruntled inventor. They are improbable, and their future images would, on Bob Darnell's screen, have been dim, and ghostly. The world might end in that ten minutes, so destroy me. That must be there, for it is possible, a very faint image, so shadowy it is scarcely visible.

'If I live, a thousand courses are open: I may sit here, smoking peacefully; the telephone may ring; a fire may break out. Probably I shall continue to sit, and smoke – so strong and solid on the screen is an image of myself sitting, smoking. But shading from it ever lighter, black and gray to faintest haziness, is each of those other possibilities.

'That confused them, made exact work difficult. To get their reports of the markets, they had to determine with an absolute rigor that the next day's paper should be put on a certain stand, spread to the page they wanted, and, come hell or high water, they would yet put that paper there, and not move it so much as a hairbreadth. The image became probable, highly probable. Its ghost images faded. They read it.

'And there's one other fault. I know the reason I'd rather not give it. Just take this for one of the facts of that invention that by the very stuff of space, time shall never be overcome. The place they might determine, or the time, with absolute exactitude, but never would they ever know both for any given event.

'And the third day they cast for their future tracks. The near future was a confused haze, but I was with them when they sought in the future far enough for the haze to go. Laughing, elated, they cast a hundred years ahead, when, Bob Darnell said, 'I'll be a man with my long white beard looped through my trousers and over my shoulders for suspenders!'

'They started their machine, and set the control for probabilities in a very low range, for the chance of Bob Darnell's living to one hundred and thirty-three years of age was remote. They had a device on their machine that would automatically sweep the future, till it found a lane that was occupied, a track that was not dead, in which Bob Darnell still lived. It was limited in speed – but not greatly, for each second it looked down five hundred thousand tracks.'

'Reaction speed of a photocell,' said the young man slowly. 'I know.'

'Dwight, try not to know,' pleaded Grantland. 'I mean to give no such hints – but only what is needed to understand.'

'If you say two times two – can you expect me to omit a mental four?' asked the young man. 'Five hundred thousand a second is the reaction of a photocell. What is there in this invention that demands its suppression?'

'That is part of it. Five hundred thousand tracks a second

it swept, and an hour passed, and another, and Darnell laughed at it.

'"I guess I'm not due for a long, full life,"' he said.

'And just then the machine clicked his answer. When we saw the image on the screen, we thought the range was wrong, for the Bob Darnell on the screen was a healthier, stronger, sounder man than the Bob Darnell beside me.

'He was tanned and lean and muscular; his hair was black as night, and his hands were muscular and firm-fleshed. He looked thirty, not a hundred and thirty. But his eyes were old, they were old as the hills, and keen with a burning vigor as they seemed to concentrate on us. Slowly he smiled, and firm, even teeth appeared between his lips.

'Darnell whistled softly. "They've licked old age," he almost whispered.

'Evidently they had. Hugh spoke. "They probably found it in some future age with this machine," he whispered tensely. "You're one keen old gentleman, Bob."

'"But that's not a good chance for life apparently," Darnell said. "I wonder how I can choose the course that leads me there?"

'"Live a clean life, drink nothing but water," Kerry said. "Turn on, O time, in your flight. Let's see what else we have."

'Darnell started the machine again – and it stopped almost instantly. One of Darnell's other tracks appeared. He'd gotten there that time with no outside aid, and he was horrible. "Ah-h-h—" said Bob distastefully. "I like the other way better. That face – turn it along, Hugh."

'The mean, rheumy-eyed, incredibly seamed face disappeared; the screen went blank. And it stayed blank. Those were Bob's only tracks at that age. "Not too bad," he said, though. "I didn't think I had a chance in the world."

'"Let's see what we get at ten years," Hugh suggested. "That's more to the point."

'"We'll wait all night getting through them," objected Bob. "But we'll take a few. Better start with about seventy probability. Ten years is long enough for me to die in, perhaps, so that ought to be fairly high."

'They started again. And it ran for an hour – two hours. Bob Darnell had stopped laughing now, because he didn't like that blank and stubborn assurance that he had a mighty slim chance of living ten years more. Two hours and a half and it was beginning to tell on Darnell. "Looks like I guessed too high," was all he said.

'Then we got a track. It was Bob Darnell, all right, but his face was round and soft and flatulent, and he lay on a soft rubber floor on his back, with a little pair of trunks on, and he was grinning senselessly with a blank, stupid face at a male nurse who was feeding him some kind of gruel that he slobbered and spilled down his fat, soft cheeks. There wasn't any mind at all behind the full, round eyes.

'It took us about ten seconds to take in that scene that was something like ten years in the future. Then Bob spoke, and his voice was flat and strained. "I'd say that was *dementia praecox*, and I'd say that damned machine was wrong, because I'm not going to be that way. I'm going to be dead first. It's the nastiest form of insanity I can think of offhand. Start that thing up, Hugh."

'The trails got closer together there. We got another one in half an hour, and all that half hour we stood in absolute silence in the dim laboratory, while the machine clicked and hummed, and the screen writhed and flickered with blankness, because neither of us could think of anything to say to Bob, and Bob was too busy thinking to say anything.

'Then the machine stopped again. It didn't take so long to understand that scene. Hugh started it on again. It found seven trails like that in the next hour. Then it found a sane trail, more or less, but it was a Bob Darnell who had gone through insanity. He wasn't actually insane, but his nervous system was broken.

'"Evidently you recover," I said, trying to be hopeful.

'Bob grinned – unpleasantly. He shook his head. "You don't recover. If you do – it wasn't *dementia praecox. Praecox* is an insanity that is simply a slow disintegration of the mind; it gets tired of worry and trouble, and decides the easiest way out is to go back to childhood, when there weren't any worries or troubles. But it goes back and discovers again the worries children have, and keeps going back and back, seeking the time when there were no troubles – and generally is stopped by pneumonia or tuberculosis or hemorrhage of the atrophied brain.

'"But it never recovers, and it's the most ghastly form of insanity there is, because it is hopeless. It turns a strong, sound man into a helpless, mindless infant. It's not like idiocy, because an idiot never grew up. This grows up, all right – and then grows down, lower than anything normal could be.

'"That's just one path where I had a nervous breakdown and got over it. That one – why it might lead to the one-hundred-and-thirty-four-year-old track. But just – go on, Hugh."

'Hugh went on – on and on, and we found three sound, sane tracks.

'I don't have to go into more detail. I think you can understand Darnell's feelings. We tried at five years, and a few more tracks showed up. At two years, that first night, we found eighteen tracks, and eleven of them were insane, and seven sane. We named the two-year tracks with the Greek alphabet.

'The track Bob wanted, the long track that took him to a hundred and thirty-four, and beyond, clear out to a point where he merged in the march of the infinite future, was his tau track. The alpha, beta, gamma, delta – all those were quite insane, and quite horrible. That meant that, by far, the greater probability led to the unpleasant tracks.

'"Hugh, I guess, it's your turn, if you want to try," said Bob finally. "We'll have to check these more carefully later."

'"I think I do want to know," Hugh said. "But maybe Grantland would like to go now. He can't be here all the time."

'"No, thank Heaven," I said, "I can't, and I don't want to know my tracks. Bob, I think one of the best ways to strike that tau track is to destroy this machine now."

'Bob stared at me, then grinned lopsidedly. "I can't now, John. For one thing, I have no right to; it means too much to the world. For another, I've got to find what decisions will put me on that long track. I made this thing because I knew I couldn't live to see that long march we've already seen, leading on to the infinity even this can't reach. Now, by all that is to be, I've got to find how I can reach that time!"

'"By all that is to be, Bob, I know in my bones you won't, if this machine endures."

'Bob grinned and shook his head at me.

'"I can't, John," he said.

'And Hugh started the machine down his trails. He'd set it for a hundred years, like Darnell, at a slightly higher figure than had disclosed the far end of Bob's tau track. We picked up Hugh's pretty quickly, and he too looked sound and healthy. But he had no second trail – one chance to live to be a hundred and thirty-three.

'"I'm about as good on long life as you, Bob," he said, "if somebody helps me, but I guess I can't make it alone."

'"Well, I'm not interested in going it alone myself," Bob replied. "It's not a hell of a lot better than some of those other things we've seen. Let's get closer home."

'They tried the ten-year track. And on Hugh Kerry's trails, the machine clicked and hummed for a long, long time, and Kerry began to look paler and paler in the light from that wavering screen, because he didn't even have a chance of insane life.

'"Let's leave it for the night," said Hugh finally. "It's eight o'clock, and I'm hungry as a wolf. We can leave it running on the recorder, and come back after supper, maybe."

'We came back after supper. It was ten, then. And the machine was still clicking and humming.

'We went home for the night. You see, reasonably enough, Hugh had assumed that he had a fair chance of living ten years, but he didn't, of course. The machine was examining nearly two billion chances every hour it ran – and finding them blank.

'Hugh was down at seven the next morning. I got there at ten and found Bob and Hugh sitting very quiet, trying to smoke. The machine was still humming and clicking, and there wasn't a thing at all on the recorder.

'"Looks like I'm not slated for a long life," Hugh greeted me unhappily, trying to grin. "It hasn't found – thank Heaven!" The machine stopped suddenly.

'It was Hugh, quite hale and sound, his hair a bit gray, his eyes a bit sunken, his face a bit lined, but sane – and sound.

'"That's what we called the tau track," said Bob after a

minute of examination. You make a hundred-year mark on the first try."

"'In other words," said Kerry softly, "I've got about as much chance of living ten years as I have of living a hundred. Yes. That's a good way to put it. A hell of a chance. What does it say at two years?"

'It took a long time, because we didn't want to start on the low probabilities, of course, and there just weren't any good ones. We didn't find anything very quickly. Eventually we knew he had three sane and one insane at ten years, and eleven altogether at two years – three insane. And they were all of them so far down in probability, they started working right away.

'But the thing that brought home the need of haste was that when we looked, just for a moment, at Bob's two-year trails – two of the sane, and five insane trails had vanished! They had been eliminated by decisions made since the previous evening. I knew, Bob and Hugh knew, what the decision was, but we didn't say anything. He had decided to look at Hugh's trails in that time, and found those few trails. They cut off at one year, we found, so they had to work on them. That, you see, reduced Bob Darnell's chances of finding the right trail – the tau trail that wasn't in tau position anymore, but, thank Heaven, still existed.

"'It's not so hard, though," said Kerry. "We need only look to see what developments we make tomorrow, and tomorrow's tomorrow, to find how to perfect this machine, to eliminate the near-future images. We'll get it."

'I had my business that I was trying to build up, so I had to leave them. I couldn't see them for five days, because I had to appear out in St. Louis, and stop over in Washington.

'When I got back I went around to see them, though it was nearly eleven o'clock. They were at it.

'"We've made some progress," Hugh said. "We've both mapped our trails carefully till they vanish in the near-future mists. We'll be able to hit that long trail for Bob fairly easily, but – I'm afraid I'll have to give mine up," he said, his face twitching just a little.

'"H-Has your long trail been eliminated by a decision?" I asked.

'"Hm-m-m – in a sense. I located one of its decision points by luck. It's only about a month away, apparently. It is less, I believe, but we can't tell. I took a snap view of the trail, and hit what is evidently a decision point on it. What you didn't know is that twenty-seven years of that long trail is hopeless paralysis in pain. I apply for euthanasia four times unsuccessfully. Since I know where that trail leads, and still apply for that – why, I think I don't want it, anyway. But the trouble is, really, that the decision point I snapped, by sheer luck, is an automobile accident.

'"We've been trying to take instantaneous exposures of the trails, in the near future, to eliminate the blurring. We can do it by using a blurred image to get space coordinates and snapping the controls into lock position. The time register is automatically thrown out of gear, so we have only a vague idea of time. We know it's this year – but whether it's late this month, or early next, I don't know. We can't know."

'"But the accident—"

'"I'd go through with it, perhaps – if I had some control. But Tom Phillips is driving. If I drive, of course, that's a different track altogether. He has my fate in his hands – and I can't bring myself to take it."

'"Have you told Tom?" I asked.

'"Not yet, but I'm expecting him over. I sent a note around that he ought to get today or tomorrow, I—"

'The telephone rang, Hugh answered it. Tom Phillips was on the other end. He had the note, luckily, as he was packing then to drive up to Boston. He wanted Hugh to come over and tell him the story, or whatever it was Hugh wanted him for. Naturally, it would do no good if Tom couldn't see the machine; so, by dint of nearly fifteen minutes' arguing, Hugh got him to come over.

'"Whew – if I hadn't been so afraid of riding with Tom, I would have gone over, at that," said Hugh, mopping his head. "He's a stubborn cuss when he gets an idea. I hope I can – eh? What, Bob?"

'Bob Darnell, in the laboratory, had called something.

'"What is it, Bob?" Hugh asked, going over.

'I went over, too. "Oh, hello, John. I didn't know you were back. Patent go through all OK?"

'"Fine,' I answered, "Everything's in order. What was it you wanted to tell Hugh?"

'"Yes – just told me. He had just finished calling Tom Phillips when you called him."

'"What! God! I called him – because his long track vanished while I was looking at it then! That was a decision point!"

'We looked eagerly. It was gone, all right. And suddenly Hugh stiffened. "Bob," he said, "I'm afraid; I'm scared as hell – because maybe that was a decision point, because I didn't go over for Tom. I'm going to—"

'He went, too – to call up Tom Phillips. But he was too late then, and he never got him. Tom hadn't seen a gravel truck smashing down a side street, hidden from him by a stopped trolley car.

'"I was supposed to go over for him," was all Hugh could say. "But how was I to know? We didn't know the time accurately. We couldn't, could we, Bob? I didn't know – I didn't know—"

'But to the day of his death, he could not shake the feeling that he had brought Tom Phillips out to be killed, almost deliberately. It meant nothing that he had called him to warn him. He had called him out to death. He had been slow in his warning.

'A week later they had mapped their future trails; they had every decision point mapped, and noted; they knew every move that they must make to take them down those trails that led to that maximum of life each was granted. Every decision, every turn and branch of the road that led to happiness, success – except those they must make in the next ten months.

'From a high peak they could see the road that led off across the broad fields of the open country to the distant city of life they sought. But the tangled, snarled traffic of the nearby city where they were, obscured the little alleys and twisting, crooked streets of the near future in an inextricable maze.

'"We'll get it, though," Hugh said confidently. "We're getting it better and better now. We've found a system that will work, we think. You see, if today we can see what we will develop tomorrow, we will be a day ahead, and then if we see what comes the day after, we'll be two days. In a week we should have the thing solved. It is only that it becomes so annoying to remember – this may be the decision day, and I do not know it. And Bob is working hard to find my decisions, because I have so few lines beyond this December, apparently. He has plenty of sound lines leading on through next year.

'"That seems to make my case the more imperative, for I do not want to die when life is so near. Yet we cannot know even this, for the paths twine and twist, and it may be that my decision point to the long trail I seek is in December. And, similarly, it may be that the decision point Bob seeks – is tomorrow. We cannot guess, we cannot know, who is in the more desperate position, the more immediately threatened state.

'"But tomorrow we will advance faster, because we have determined as inflexibly as our determination to place that newspaper on the stand, that we shall hereafter, invariably, put on the blackboard there the discoveries of the day, and the progress made. That, we think, will clear up the images."

'"Will clear up the images?" I asked in some surprise. Because, you remember, Dwight, that it instantly cleared up the newspaper images.

'Hugh looked a little worried.

'"Will," he replied. "You see, it didn't so very much at first, for some reason. I can't quite – but at any rate, by watching our progress that we are to make, we will make swift advance to the discovery of the secret, and long life."

'It seemed so clear, so true, so logical. If they could steal the inventions of a million years in the future, could they not spy on their own progress of the next day and the next? So simple, so logical an advance.

'But they missed one thing. There were many, many things they could try, and though they inflexibly determined that they would write on the blackboard the progress of the day, and did, the blackboard was blurred white and gray on the screen. For each of the thousand things they might try

181

was there, you see, and from the first day two probabilities entered: that they deciphered, and tried one of those courses, and that they did not decipher the next day's work, and had to develop it directly.

'Three times they read that blackboard. Each time the next day's blackboard read: "Did work shown by future image yesterday." So, when they did read it, remember, they saw only a day's work done, and the day's work was yet to be done, though they knew what it must be. If you are a repairman and know that tomorrow you must change the clutch plates and put in new transmission gears, that knowledge does not eliminate the operation.

'They thought it might spare them the blind alleys. But one of those days' work was a blind alley that they were forced to rip out the next.

'I was called over one day, the third time they read that blackboard, and they showed it to me. There were many, many images on it, and only one was legible, because it was very, very brief, and written very large.

'Hugh smiled lopsidedly at me when I came in. "Well, John, I think we've found one of my decision points," he said.

'"What! Got those near futures cleared up?" I was immensely pleased. They'd advanced a lot, you know, since I first saw the instrument. Their near-future images were sometimes quite readable; their selectivity had been increased a thousandfold. But there was still a mistiness, a sort of basic mistiness.

'"No,' Darnell interrupted. We read the blackboard. Come – you can see it."

'I did. It was quite easy to read, because Hugh had always been the one to write on the board, and his writing was cramped and neat. On many of those images the writing was cramped and neat. But on many others it was a broad, looping scrawl – Darnell's hand. It said simply: "Hugh Kerry killed today. May God have mercy on me."

'I swallowed hard before I spoke. "There's a lot of images there, Hugh."

'"Yes, but it's a decision point. Bob has sworn, and determined by all that's holy, he'll write the full facts on the case tomorrow, and not that message. The message still sticks, and none other has appeared. It's a decision point – and may God have mercy on me, too, for I don't know what that decision must be. It won't even tell me whether to stay indoors here or stay out of here."

'Dwight, that is the thing that pressed and pressed on them. It was like the old Chinese water torture, and each day was a drop of water that fell, and they were bound to the wheel of time that cannot stop or be stopped. They had now the vision to see across that wheel to another day and another age – but they could not slow that progress through time, nor speed it by a whit.

'The days must come, and they must go, for all their knowledge of time. And the sun that day sank, as it had a thousand thousand thousand times before, and would a thousand thousand thousand times again, and it rose on a new day. No force, nor will, nor wish could stay that progress; the day must come. And Hugh could not know, because the message was so stubborn, whether his decision lay in that laboratory or out in the open.

'I could not leave them. Yet I had to, because time still went on, and the courts went on. I left, on a case I know not the faintest detail of, save that I fought it with a bitter determination to win, and somehow won it.

'It was four thirty when I got back to the laboratory. Bob Darnell met me, and his face was white and tense. "Hugh?" I asked.

'"He's gone over to Teckno Products for some apparatus," said Darnell quietly. "He wouldn't let me go. He ought to be back. Come into the laboratory. I've been watching his trails."

'I went with him into the laboratory where the rustle and hum of the machine, and the flickering, greenish light of the screen made it seem a sorcerer's lair of necromancy. Bob looked at the screen, then he turned to me with an unpleasant grin. "It's blank, John. Those are Hugh Kerry's trails one year from today," he said. He walked over to the blackboard very slowly, like an automaton, and picked up a piece of chalk. Slowly he erased the words on the slate, and in a round, broad scrawl he wrote: "Hugh Kerry killed today. May God have mercy on me."

'"Bob," I said, "Bob – that's the message you swore you wouldn't write. Erase it – wait till we know, till we know what happened to him so we can write the details. That may—"

'"Save him?" asked Bob bitterly. "What matter now? He's dead now. But if you like, we can find the details. But nothing will do any good at all, because he's dead now, anyway. What good will it do to change that message? He's already taken the wrong trail, and reached the end, John. But I'll find out—"

'He called up the police. He asked if they knew what had happened to Hugh Kerry, how he had been killed.

'The telephone was a noisy one, always had been, and I heard the answer where I stood. "Hugh Kerry, eh? I have no report on anyone by that name. What makes you think he's been killed, and how?"

'"He must be dead by this time," said Bob. "Ask your men, please. I – what?"

'"The other desk man," said the man on the telephone, "just got a call, and he says if you're looking for a guy named Hugh Kerry, he was just killed by a girl driver at Fourteenth and Seventh. He stepped out from behind a parked car right— Say, who's calling?"

'"Thanks, officer. Robert Darnell calling, from One Forty-three East Eighty-seventh. I'm going right over to the scene—"

'We went over in my car, got there pretty quickly, but the ambulance had already taken Hugh Kerry and the girl driver away. We heard from her later. Hugh had simply walked right into the side of her car, practically tripped over her running board. She was in the hospital with hysterics then. She kept saying he looked so surprised – as though somebody had suddenly explained something to him. Somebody had, you see – a surprisingly easy answer to a complex problem.

'Bob Darnell tried to get his car, that Hugh had driven over to Teckno Products in, but the police picked him up. I wasn't a criminal lawyer, and I had to go downtown and get Bill Poole, a classmate of mine, to come and help him out.

'It was a bad problem, too, we found out. Three weeks before, Hugh Kerry had taken out a one-year term insurance policy for a hundred thousand dollars. And it had a double-indemnity clause in case of accidental death. The insurance company was fighting for their two hundred thousand dollars, and the police were fighting for a murder charge. Because, you remember, Bob Darnell had said over the telephone: "He must be dead by this time."

'The time machine was too wild. We couldn't get any

clear images to show them anything to speak of. But, finally, they had to let Bob go, because it's awfully difficult to prove murder when a man is killed in an automobile accident at one end of town, and a man you're accusing is calling the police station from the other. And they never tried to involve the poor girl who was the direct instrument of death.

'I went back with Bob Darnell, when they released him. I was with him when he started up the machine, and looked at his trails. There were only five left, because Hugh Kerry's trails were gone, now, and they had crossed and intertwined with Bob Darnell's, of course. The long trail was there, and one other sane trail – that ended in three years. The other three were all insane trails.

'Bob went to work harder than ever, and because I'd gotten behind in my work while Bob was tied up, I, too, had to go to work harder than ever. It was three weeks before I could even get around to the laboratory.

'Bob Darnell greeted me at the door when I came. He had one of those slip chains on the door, and opened it only a crack when he let me in. "Those insurance people kept bothering me," he explained. "They want to see what I'm doing all the time. They aren't going to, though."

'I looked at him, and his eyes and forehead were screwed up in worry and concentration.

'"John," he said finally, "you know it's too bad Hugh went after that apparatus Teckno was making. I got it and put it in, and they didn't make it right at all. I think maybe they're trying to make me order more so they can see how this works. I shouldn't have told the police about my chronoscope. But I put the apparatus in, and I think I got it in right, and, John, it makes the near-future images better, but what

186

do you think – it cuts out some of the long-range tracks. It won't show them all now."

'His voice seemed quite annoyed, and rather petulant, I thought.

'"It won't?" I said, quite softly, I think. "Let me see."

'"No. It won't show them right. There are five. I saw 'em myself. But this thing won't work right. It cuts out four of them, and only shows one little short one. There's something wrong with it. I figured out what once, but I can't seem to remember any more. But I don't like Teckno any more, and I won't buy anything from 'em any more. I'm going to make 'em take this back.

'"Help me disconnect it, John? You remember how the chronoscope works; I can't seem to find the connections since I put in the wrong stuff Teckno made. I've been so worried, John, with the insurance company bothering me, and this not working right."

'"It isn't working right, eh?" I asked. "There's only one trail left? Well, you know, Bob, they change."

'"No. There ought to be five trails. I know, cause I saw 'em," he said decisively.

'So I went into the laboratory with him, and I looked at the screen, and there was only one trail, as he had said. It was as I had expected since I entered the house that day. I told Bob then that I couldn't help him any more, but that I had a friend who might be able to, though I wasn't sure. So I went away and brought your father, Dwight, who was, as I told you, the only other man who ever saw the chronoscope or the drawings of it.

'He helped me take it apart and break up the parts that might have been revealing.'

John Grantland paused a long minute, his head sunk

forward on his chest. He raised it slowly and added, as though an afterthought: 'We were glad it was a very short track. It could have been so long—'

Dwight Edwards rose slowly, dropping his papers on Grantland's desk. He sighed as he turned away. 'The world doesn't need all its Faradays, does it?' And as he walked through the door, 'You'll take care of those papers for me—'

Twilight

'Speaking of hitch-hikers,' said Jim Bendell in a rather bewildered way, 'I picked up a man the other day that certainly was a queer cuss.' He laughed, but it wasn't a real laugh. 'He told me the queerest yarn I ever heard. Most of them tell you how they lost their good jobs and tried to find work out here in the wide spaces of the West. They don't seem to realize how many people we have out here. They think all this great beautiful country is uninhabited.'

Jim Bendell's a real estate man, and I knew how he could go on. That's his favorite line, you know. He's real worried because there's a lot of homesteading plots still open out in our state. He talks about the beautiful country, but he never went further into the desert than the edge of town. 'Fraid of it actually. So I sort of steered him back on the track.

'What did he claim, Jim? Prospector who couldn't find land to prospect?'

'That's not very funny, Baut. No; it wasn't only what he claimed. He didn't even claim it, just said it. You know, he didn't say it was true, he just said it. That's what gets me. I know it ain't true, but the way he said it – Oh, I don't know.'

By which I knew he didn't. Jim Bendell's usually pretty careful about his English – real proud of it. When he slips, that means he's disturbed. Like the time he thought the rattlesnake was a stick of wood and wanted to put it on the fire.

Jim went on: And he had funny clothes, too. They looked like silver, but they were soft as silk. And at night they glowed just a little.

I picked him up about dusk. Really picked him up. He was lying off about ten feet from the South Road. I thought, at first, somebody had hit him, and then hadn't stopped. Didn't see him very clearly, you know. I picked him up, put him in the car, and started on. I had about three hundred miles to go, but I thought I could drop him at Warren Spring with Doc Vance. But he came to in about five minutes, and opened his eyes. He looked straight off, and he looked first at the car, then at the Moon. 'Thank God!' he says, and then looks at me. It gave me a shock. He was beautiful. No; he was handsome.

He wasn't either one. He was magnificent. He was about six feet two, I think, and his hair was brown, with a touch of red-gold. It seemed like fine copper wire that's turned brown. It was crisp and curly. His forehead was wide, twice as wide as mine. His features were delicate, but tremendously impressive; his eyes were gray, like etched iron, and bigger than mine – a lot.

That suit he wore – it was more like a bathing suit with pajama trousers. His arms were long and muscled smoothly as an Indian's. He was white, though, tanned lightly with a golden, rather than a brown, tan.

But he was magnificent. Most beautiful man I ever saw. I don't know, damn it!

'Hello!' I said. 'Have an accident?'

'No; not this time, at least.'

And his voice was magnificent, too. It wasn't an ordinary voice. It sounded like an organ talking, only it was human.

'But maybe my mind isn't quite steady yet. I tried an

experiment. Tell me what the date is, year and all, and let me see,' he went on.

'Why – December 9, 1932,' I said.

And it didn't please him. He didn't like it a bit. But the wry grin that came over his face gave way to a chuckle.

'Over a thousand—' he says reminiscently. 'Not as bad as seven million. I shouldn't complain.'

'Seven million what?'

'Years,' he said; steadily enough. Like he meant it. 'I tried an experiment once. Or I will try it. Now I'll have to try again. The experiment was – in 3059. I'd just finished the release experiment. Testing space then. Time – it wasn't that, I still believe. It was space. I felt myself caught in that field, but I couldn't pull away. Field gamma-H 481, intensity 935 in the Pellman range. It sucked me in, and I went out.

'I think it took a short cut through space to the position the solar system will occupy. Through a higher dimension, effecting a speed exceeding light and throwing me into the future plane.'

He wasn't telling me, you know. He was just thinking out loud. Then he began to realize I was there.

'I couldn't read their instruments, seven million years of evolution changed everything. So I overshot my mark a little coming back. I belong in 3059.'

'But tell me, what's the latest scientific invention of this year?'

He startled me so, I answered almost before I thought.

'Why, television, I guess. And radio and airplanes.'

'Radio – good. They will have instruments.'

'But see here – who are you?'

'Ah – I'm sorry. I forgot,' he replied in that organ voice of his. 'I am Ares Sen Kenlin. And you?'

191

'James Waters Bendell.'

'Waters – what does that mean? I do not recognize it.'

'Why – it's a name, of course. Why should you recognize it?'

'I see – you have not the classification, then. 'Sen' stands for science.'

'Where did you come from, Mr Kenlin?

'Come from?' He smiled, and his voice was slow and soft. 'I came out of space across seven million years or more. They had lost count – the men had. The machines had eliminated the unneeded service. They didn't know what year it was. But before that – my home is in Neva'th City in the year 3059.'

That's when I began to think he was a nut.

'I was an experimenter,' he went on. 'Science, as I have said. My father was a scientist, too, but in human genetics. I myself am an experiment. He proved his point, and all the world followed suit. I was the first of the new race.'

'The new race – oh, holy destiny – what has – what will—"

'What is its end? I have seen it – almost. I saw them – the little men – bewildered – lost. And the machines. Must it be – can't anything sway it?'

'Listen – I heard this song.'

He sang the song. Then he didn't have to tell me about the people. I knew them. I could hear their voices, in the queer, crackling, un-English words. I could read their bewildered longings. It was in a minor key, I think. It called, it called and asked, and hunted hopelessly. And over it all the steady rumble and whine of the unknown, forgotten machines.

The machines that couldn't stop, because they had been started, and the little men had forgotten how to stop them, or even what they were for, looking at them and listening

– and wondering. They couldn't read or write any more, and the language had changed, you see, so that the phonic records of their ancestors meant nothing to them.

But that song went on, and they wondered. And they looked out across space and they saw the warm, friendly stars – too far away. Nine planets they knew and inhabited. And locked by infinite distance, they couldn't see another race, a new life.

And through it all – two things. The machines. Bewildered forgetfulness. And maybe one more. Why?

That was the song, and it made me cold. It shouldn't be sung around people of today. It almost killed something. It seemed to kill hope. After that song – I – well, I believed him.

When he finished the song, he didn't talk for a while. Then he sort of shook himself.

You won't understand (he continued). Not yet – but I have seen them. They stand about, like misshapen men with huge heads. But their heads contain only brains. They had machines that could think – but somebody turned them off a long time ago, and no one knew how to start them again. That was the trouble with them. They had wonderful brains. Far better than yours or mine. But it must have been millions of years ago when they were turned off, too, and they just haven't thought since then. Kindly little people. That was all they knew.

When I slipped into that field it grabbed me like a gravitational field whirling a space transport down to a planet. It sucked me in – and through. Only the other side must have been seven million years in the future. That's where I was. It must have been in exactly the same spot on Earth's surface, but I never knew why.

It was night then, and I saw the city a little way off. The Moon was shining on it, and the whole scene looked wrong. You see, in seven million years, men had done a lot with the positions of the planetary bodies, what with moving space liners, clearing lanes through the asteroids, and such. And seven million years is long enough for natural things to change positions a little. The Moon must have been fifty thousand miles farther out And it was rotating on its axis. I lay there a while and watched it. Even the stars were different.

There were ships going out of the city. Back and forth, like things sliding along a wire, but there was only a wire of force, of course. Part of the city, the lower part, was brightly lighted with what must have been mercury vapor glow, I decided. Blue-green. I felt sure men didn't live there – the light was wrong for eyes. But the top of the city was so sparsely lighted.

Then I saw something coming down out of the sky. It was brightly lighted. A huge globe, and it sank straight to the center of the great black-and-silver mass of the city.

I don't know what it was, but even then I knew the city was deserted. Strange that I could even imagine that, I who had never seen a deserted city before. But I walked the fifteen miles over to it and entered it. There were machines going about the streets, repair machines, you know. They couldn't understand that the city didn't need to go on functioning, so they were still working. I found a taxi machine that seemed fairly familiar. It had a manual control that I could work.

I don't know how long that city had been deserted. Some of the men from the other cities said it was a hundred and fifty thousand years. Some went as high as three hundred thousand years. Three hundred thousand years since human foot had been in that city. The taxi machine was in perfect condition, functioned at once. It was clean, and the city was clean and orderly. I saw a restaurant and I was hungry. Hungry for humans to speak to. There were none, of course, but I didn't know.

The restaurant had the food displayed directly, and I made a choice. The food was three hundred thousand years old, I suppose, I didn't know, and the machines that served it to me didn't care, for they made things synthetically, you see, and perfectly. When the builders made those cities, they forgot one thing. They didn't realize that things shouldn't go on forever.

It took me six months to make my apparatus. And near the end I was ready to go; and, from seeing those machines go blindly, perfectly, on in orbits of their duties with the tireless, ceaseless perfection their designers had incorporated in them, long after those designers and their sons, and their sons' sons had no use for them—

When Earth is cold, and the Sun has died out, those machines will go on. When Earth begins to crack and break, those perfect, ceaseless machines will try to repair her—

I left the restaurant and cruised about the city in the taxi. The machine had a little, electric-power motor, I believe, but it gained its power from the great central power radiator. I knew before long that I was far in the future. The city was divided into two sections, a section of many strata where machines functioned smoothly, save for a deep humming beat that echoed through the whole city like a vast unending song of power. The entire metal framework of the place echoed with it, transmitted it, hummed with it. But it was soft and restful, a reassuring beat.

There must have been thirty levels above ground, and

twenty more below, a solid block of metal walls and metal floors and metal and glass and force machines. The only light was the blue-green glow of the mercury vapor arcs. The light of mercury vapor is rich in high-energy quanta, which stimulate the alkali metal atoms to photo-electric activity. Or perhaps that is beyond the science of your day? I have forgotten.

But they had used that light because many of their worker machines needed sight. The machines were marvelous. For five hours I wandered through the vast power plant on the very lowest level, watching them, and because there was motion, and that pseudo-mechanical life, I felt less alone.

The generators I saw were a development of the release I had discovered – when? The release of the energy of matter, I mean, and I knew when I saw that for what countless ages they could continue.

The entire lower block of the city was given over to the machines. Thousands. But most of them seemed idle, or, at most, running under light load. I recognized a telephone apparatus, and not a single signal came through. There was no life in the city. Yet when I pressed a little stud beside the screen on one side of the room, the machine began working instantly. It was ready. Only no one needed it any more. The men knew how to die, and be dead, but the machines didn't.

Finally I went up to the top of the city, the upper level. It was a paradise.

There were shrubs and trees and parks, glowing in the soft light that they had learned to make in the very air. They had learned it five million years or more before. Two million years ago they forgot. But the machines didn't, and they were still making it. It hung in the air, soft, silvery light, slightly rosy, and the gardens were shadowy with it. There were no machines here now, but I knew that in daylight they must come out and work on those gardens, keeping them a paradise for masters who had died, and stopped moving, as they could not.

In the desert outside the city it had been cool, and very dry. Here the air was soft, warm and sweet with the scent of blooms that men had spent several hundreds of thousands of years perfecting.

Then somewhere music began. It began in the air, and spread softly through it. The Moon was just setting now, and as it set, the rosy-silver glow waned and the music grew stronger.

It came from everywhere and from nowhere. It was within me. I do not know how they did it. And I do not know how such music could be written.

Savages make music too simple to be beautiful, but it is stirring. Semi-savages write music beautifully simple, and simply beautiful. Your Negro music was your best. They knew music when they heard it and sang it as they felt it. Semi-civilized peoples write great music. They are proud of their music, and make sure it is known for great music. They make it so great it is top-heavy.

I had always thought our music good. But that which came through the air was the song of triumph, sung by a mature race, the race of man in its full triumph! It was man singing his triumph in majestic sound that swept me up; it showed me what lay before me; it carried me on.

And it died in the air as I looked at the deserted city. The machines should have forgotten that song. Their masters had, long before.

I came to what must have been one of their homes; it was a dimly-seen doorway in the dusky light, but as I stepped up to it, the lights which had not functioned in three hundred thousand years illuminated it for me with a green-white glow, like a firefly, and I stepped into the room beyond. Instantly something happened to the air in the doorway behind me; it was as opaque as milk. The room in which I stood was a room of metal and stone. The stone was some jet-black substance with the finish of velvet, and the metals were silver and gold. There was a rug on the floor, a rug of just such material as I am wearing now, but thicker and softer. There were divans about the room, low and covered with these soft metallic materials. They were black and gold and silver, too.

I had never seen anything like that. I never shall again, I suppose, and my language and yours were not made to describe it.

The builders of that city had right and reason to sing that song of sweeping triumph, triumph that swept them over the nine planets and the fifteen habitable moons.

But they weren't there any more, and I wanted to leave. I thought of a plan and went to a sub-telephone office to examine a map I had seen. The old World looked much the same. Seven or even seventy million years don't mean much to old Mother Earth. She may even succeed in wearing down those marvelous machine cities. She can wait a hundred million or a thousand million years before she is beaten.

I tried calling different city centers shown on the map. I had quickly learned the system when I examined the central apparatus.

I tried once – twice – thrice – a round dozen times. Yawk City, Lunon City, Paree, Shkago, Singpor, others. I was beginning to feel that there were no more men on all Earth. And I felt crushed, as at each city the machines replied and did my bidding. The machines were there in each of those far vaster cities, for I was in the Neva City of their time. A small city. Yawk City was more than eight hundred kilometers in diameter.

In each city I tried several numbers. Then I tried San Frisco. There was someone there, and a voice answered and the picture of a human appeared on the little glowing screen. I could see him start and stare in surprise at me. Then he started speaking to me. I couldn't understand, of course. I can understand your speech, and you mine, because your speech of this day is largely recorded on records of various types and has influenced our pronunciation.

Some things are changed; names of cities, particularly, because names of cities are apt to be polysyllabic, and used a great deal. People tend to elide them, shorten them. I am in – Nee-vah-dah – as you would say? We say only Neva. And Yawk State. But it is Ohio and Iowa still. Over a thousand years, effects were small on words, because they were recorded.

But seven million years had passed, and the men had forgotten the old records, used them less as time went on, and their speech varied till the time came when they could no longer understand the records. They were not written any more, of course.

Some men must have arisen occasionally among that last of the race and sought for knowledge, but it was denied them. An ancient writing can be translated if some basic rule is found. An ancient voice though – and when the race has forgotten the laws of science and the labor of mind.

So his speech was strange to me as he answered over that circuit. His voice was high in pitch, his words liquid, his tones sweet. It was almost a song as he spoke. He was excited and called others. I could not understand them, but I knew where they were. I could go to them.

So I went down from the paradise gardens, and as I prepared to leave, I saw dawn in the sky. The strange-bright stars winked and twinkled and faded. Only one bright rising star was familiar – Venus. She shone golden now. Finally, as I stood watching for the first time that strange heaven, I began to understand what had first impressed me with the wrongness of the view. The stars, you see, were all different.

In my time – and yours, the solar system is a lone wanderer that by chance is passing across an intersection point of Galactic traffic. The stars we see at night are the stars of moving clusters, you know. In fact our system is passing through the heart of the Ursa Major group. Half a dozen other groups center within five hundred light-years of us.

But during those seven millions of years, the Sun had moved out of the group. The heavens were almost empty to the eye. Only here and there shone a single faint star. And across the vast sweep of black sky swung the band of the Milky Way. The sky was empty.

That must have been another thing those men meant in their songs – felt in their hearts. Loneliness – not even the close, friendly stars. We have, stars within half a dozen light-years. They told me that their instruments, which gave directly the distance to any star, showed that the nearest was one hundred and fifty light-years away. It was enormously bright. Brighter even than Sirius of our heavens. And that made it even less friendly, because it was a blue-white supergiant. Our sun would have served as a satellite for that star.

I stood there and watched the lingering rose-silver glow die as the powerful blood-red light of the Sun swept over the horizon. I knew by the stars now, that it must have been several millions of years since my day; since I had last seen the Sun sweep up. And that blood-red light made me wonder if the Sun itself was dying.

An edge of it appeared, blood-red and huge. It swung up, and the color faded, till in half an hour it was the familiar yellow-gold disk.

It hadn't changed in all that time.

I had been foolish to think that it would. Seven million years – that is nothing to Earth, how much less to the Sun? Some two thousand thousand thousand times it had risen since I last saw it rise. Two thousand thousand thousand days. If it had been that many years – I might have noticed a change.

The universe moves slowly. Only life is not enduring; only life changes swiftly. Eight short millions of years. Eight days in the life of Earth – and the race was dying. It had left something: machines. But they would die, too, even though they could not understand. So I felt. I – may have changed that. I will tell you. Later.

For when the Sun was up, I looked again at the sky and the ground, some fifty floors below. I had come to the edge of the city.

Machines were moving on that ground, leveling it, perhaps. A great wide line of gray stretched off across the level desert straight to the east. I had seen it glowing faintly before the Sun rose – a roadway for ground machines. There was no traffic on it.

I saw an airship slip in from the east. It came with a soft, muttering whine of air, like a child complaining in sleep; it grew to my eyes like an expanding balloon. It was huge when it settled in a great port-slip in the city below. I could hear now the clang and mutter of machines, working on the materials brought in, no doubt. The machines had ordered raw materials. The machines in other cities had supplied. The freight machines had carried them here.

San Frisco and Jacksville were the only two cities on North America still used. But the machines went on in all the others; because they couldn't stop. They hadn't been ordered to.

Then high above, something appeared, and from the city beneath me, from a center section, three small spheres rose. They, like the freight ship, had no visible driving mechanisms. The point in the sky above, like a black star in a blue space, had grown to a moon. The three spheres met it high above. Then together they descended and lowered into the center of the city, where I could not see them.

It was a freight transport from Venus. The one I had seen land the night before had come from Mars, I learned.

I moved after that and looked for some sort of a taxiplane. They had none that I recognized in scouting about the city. I searched the higher levels, and here and there saw deserted ships, but far too large for me, and without controls.

It was nearly noon – and I ate again. The food was good.

I knew then that this was a city of the dead ashes of human hopes. The hopes not of *a* race, not the whites, nor the yellow, nor the blacks, but the human race. I was mad to leave the city. I was afraid to try the ground road to the west, for the taxi I drove was powered from some source in the city, and I knew it would fail before many miles.

It was afternoon when I found a small hangar near the outer wall of the vast city. It contained three ships. I had been searching through the lower strata of the human section – the upper part. There were restaurants and shops and theatres there. I entered one place where, at my entrance, soft music began, and colors and forms began to rise on a screen before me.

They were the triumph songs in form and sound and color of a mature race, a race that had marched steadily upward through five millions of years – and didn't see the path that faded out ahead, when they were dead and stopped, and the city itself was dead – but hadn't stopped. I hastened out of there – and the song that had not been sung in three hundred thousand years died behind me.

But I found the hangar. It was a private one, likely. Three ships. One must have been fifty feet long and fifteen in diameter. It was a yacht, a space yacht, probably. One was some fifteen feet long and five feet in diameter. That must have been the family air machine. The third was a tiny thing, little more than ten feet long and two in diameter. I had to lie down within it, evidently.

There was a periscope device that gave me a view ahead and almost directly above. A window that permitted me to see what lay below – and a device that moved a map under a frosted-glass screen and projected it onto the screen in such a way that the cross-hairs of the screen always marked my position.

I spent half an hour attempting to understand what the makers of that ship had made. But the men who made that were men who held behind them the science and knowledge of five millions of years and the perfect machines of those ages. I saw the release mechanism that powered it. I understood the principles of that and, vaguely, the mechanics. But there were no conductors, only pale beams that pulsed so swiftly you could hardly catch the pulsations from the corner of the eye. They had been glowing and pulsating, some half dozen of them, for three hundred thousand years at least; probably more.

I entered the machine, and instantly half a dozen more beams sprang into being; there was a slight suggestion of a quiver, and a queer strain ran through my body. I understood in an instant, for the machine was resting on gravity nullifiers. That had been my hope when I worked on the space fields I discovered after the release.

But they had had it for millions of years before they built that perfect deathless machine. My weight entering it had forced it to readjust itself and simultaneously to prepare for operation. Within, an artificial gravity equal to that of Earth had gripped me, and the neutral zone between the outside and the interior had caused the strain.

The machine was ready. It was fully fueled. You see they were equipped to tell automatically their wants and needs. They were almost living things, every one. A caretaker machine kept them supplied, adjusted, even repaired them when need be, and when possible. If it was not, I learned later, they were carried away in a service truck that came automatically; replaced by an exactly similar machine; and carried to the shops where they were made, and automatic machines made them over.

The machine waited patiently for me to start. The controls were simple, obvious. There was a lever at the left that you pushed forward to move forward, pulled back to go back. On the right a horizontal, pivoted bar. If you swung it left, the ship spun left; if right, the ship spun right. If tipped up, the Ship followed it, and likewise for all motions other than backward and forward. Raising it bodily raised the ship, as depressing it depressed the ship.

I lifted it slightly, a needle moved a bit on a gauge

comfortably before my eyes as I lay there, and the floor dropped beneath me. I pulled the other control back, and the ship gathered speed as it moved gently out into the open. Releasing both controls into neutral, the machine continued till it stopped at the same elevation, the motion absorbed by air friction. I turned it about, and another dial before my eyes moved, showing my position. I could not read it, though. The map did not move, as I had hoped it would. So I started toward what I felt was west.

I could feel no acceleration in that marvelous machine. The ground simply began leaping backward, and in a moment the city was gone. The map unrolled rapidly beneath me now, and I saw that I was moving south of west. I turned northward slightly, and watched the compass. Soon I understood that, too, and the ship sped on.

I had become too interested in the map and the compass, for suddenly there was a sharp buzz and, without my volition, the machine rose and swung to the north. There was a mountain ahead of me; I had not seen, but the ship had.

I noticed then what I should have seen before – two little knobs that could move the map. I started to move them and heard a sharp clicking, and the pace of the ship been decreasing. A moment and it had steadied at a considerably lower speed, the machine swinging to a new course. I tried to right it, but to my amazement the controls did not affect it.

It was the map, you see. It would either follow the course, or the course would follow it. I had moved it and the machine had taken over control of its own accord. There was a little button I could have pushed – but I didn't know. I couldn't control the ship until it finally came to rest and lowered itself to a stop six inches from the ground in the center of what must have been the ruins of a great city. Sacramento, probably.

I understood now, so I adjusted the map for San Frisco, and the ship went on at once. It steered itself around a mass of broken stone, turned back to its course, and headed on, a bullet-shaped, self-controlled dart.

It didn't descend when it reached San Frisco. It simply hung in the air and sounded a soft musical hum. Twice. Then I waited, too, and looked down.

There were people here. I saw the humans of that age for the first time. They were little men – bewildered – dwarfed, with heads disproportionately large. But not extremely so.

Their eyes impressed me most. They were huge, and when they looked at me there was a power in them that seemed sleeping, but too deeply to be roused.

I took the manual controls then and landed. And no sooner had I got out, than the ship rose automatically and started off by itself. They had automatic parking devices. The ship had gone to a public hangar, the nearest, where it would be automatically serviced and cared for. There was a little call set I should have taken with me when I got out. Then I could have pressed a button and called it to me – wherever I was in that city.

The people about me began talking – singing almost – among themselves. Others were coming up. Leisurely. Men and women – but there seemed no old and few young. What few young there were, were treated almost with respect, carefully taken care of lest a careless footstep on their toes or a careless step knock them down.

There was reason, you see. They lived a tremendous time. Some lived as long as three thousand years. Then – they simply died. They didn't grow old, and it never had been learned why people died as they did. The heart stopped, the brain ceased thought – and they died. But the young children, children not yet mature, were treated with the utmost care. But one child was born in the course of a month in that city of one hundred thousand people. The human race was growing sterile.

And I have told you that they were lonely? Their loneliness was beyond hope. For, you see, as man strode toward maturity, he destroyed all forms of life that menaced him. Disease. Insects. Then the last of the insects, and finally the last of the man-eating animals.

The balance of nature was destroyed then, so they had to go on. It was like the machines. They started them – and now they can't stop. They started destroying life – and now it wouldn't stop. So they had to destroy weeds of all sorts, then many formerly harmless plants. Then the herbivora, too, the deer and the antelope and the rabbit and the horse. They were a menace, they attacked man's machine-tended crops. Man was still eating natural foods.

You can understand. The thing was beyond their control. In the end they killed off the denizens of the sea, also, in self-defense. Without the many creatures that had kept them in check, they were swarming beyond bounds. And the time had come when synthetic foods replaced natural. The air was purified of all life about two and a half million years after our day, all microscopic life.

That meant that the water, too, must be purified. It was – and then came the end of life in the ocean. There were minute organisms that lived on bacterial forms, and tiny fish that lived on the minute organisms, and small fish that lived on the tiny fish, and big fish that lived on the small fish – and the beginning of the chain was gone. The sea was devoid of life in a generation. That meant about one thousand and five hundred years to them. Even the sea plants had gone.

And on all Earths there was only man and the organisms he had protected – the plants he wanted for decoration, and certain ultra-hygienic pets, as long-lived as their masters. Dogs. They must have been remarkable animals. Man was reaching his maturity then, and his animal friend, the friend that had followed him through a thousand millennia to your day and mine, and another four thousand millenniums to the day of man's early maturity, had grown in intelligence. In an ancient museum – a wonderful place, for they had, perfectly preserved, the body of a great leader of mankind who had died five and a half million years before I saw him – in that museum, deserted then, I saw one of those canines. His skull was nearly as large as mine. They had simple ground machines that dogs could be trained to drive, and they held races in which the dogs drove those machines.

Then man reached his full maturity. It extended over a period of a full million years. So tremendously did he stride ahead, the dog ceased to be a companion. Less and less were they wanted. When the million years had passed, and man's decline began, the dog was gone. It had died out.

And now this last dwindling group of men still in the system had no other life form to make its successor. Always before when one civilization toppled, on its ashes rose a new one. Now there was but one civilization, and all other races, even other species, were gone save in the plants. And man was too far along in his old age to bring intelligence and mobility from the plants. Perhaps he could have in his prime.

Other worlds were flooded with man during that million years – the million years. Every planet and every moon of the system had its quota of men. Now only the planets had their populations, the moons had been deserted. Pluto had been left before I landed, and men were coming from Neptune, moving in toward the Sun, and the home planet, while I was there. Strangely quiet men, viewing, most of them, for the first time, the planet that had given their race life.

But as I stepped from that ship and watched it rise away from me, I saw why the race of man was dying. I looked back at the faces of those men, and on there I read the answer. There was one single quality gone from the still-great minds – minds far greater than yours or mine. I had to have the help of one of them in solving some of my problems. In space, you know, there are twenty coordinates, ten of which are zero, six of which have fixed values, and the four others represent our changing, familiar dimensions in space-time. That means that integrations must proceed in not double, or triple, or quadruple – but ten integrations.

It must have taken me too long. I would never have solved all the problems I must work out. I could not use their mathematics machines; and mine, of course, were seven million years in the past. But one of those men was interested and helped me. He did quadruple and quintuple integration, even quadruple integration between varying exponential limits – in his head.

When I asked him to. For the one thing that had made man great had left him. As I looked in their faces and eyes on landing I knew it. They looked at me, interested at this rather unusual-looking stranger – and went on. They had come to see the arrival of a ship. A rare event, you see. But they were merely welcoming me in a friendly fashion. They were not curious! Man had lost the instinct of curiosity.

Oh, not entirely! They wondered at the machines, they

wondered at the stars. But they did nothing about it. It was not wholly lost to them yet, but nearly. It was dying. In the six short months I stayed with them, I learned more than they had learned in the two or even three thousand years they had lived among the machines.

Can you appreciate the crushing loneliness it brought to me? I, who love science, who see in it, or have seen in it, the salvation, the raising of mankind – to see those wondrous machines, of man's triumphant maturity, forgotten and misunderstood. The wondrous, perfect machines that tended, protected, and cared for those gentle, kindly people who had – forgotten.

They were lost among it. The city was a magnificent ruin to them, a thing that rose stupendous about them. Something not understood, a thing that was of the nature of the world. It was. It had not been made: it simply was. Just as the mountains and the deserts and the waters of the seas.

Do you understand – can you see that the time since those machines were new was longer than the time from our day to the birth of the race? Do we know the legends of our first ancestors? Do we remember their lore of forest and cave? The secret of chipping a flint till it had a sharp-cutting edge? The secret of trailing and killing a saber-toothed tiger without being killed oneself?

They were now in similar straits, though the time had been longer, because the languages had taken a long step toward perfection, and because the machines maintained everything for them through generation after generation.

Why, the entire planet of Pluto had been deserted – yet on Pluto the largest mines of one of their metals were located; the machines still functioned. A perfect unity existed throughout the system. A unified system of perfect machines.

And all those people knew was to do a certain thing to a certain lever produced certain results. Just as men in the Middle Ages knew that to take a certain material, wood, and place it in contact with other pieces of wood heated red, would cause the wood to disappear, and become heat. They did not understand that wood was being oxidized with the release of the heat of formation of carbon dioxide and water. So those people did not understand the things that fed and clothed and carried them.

I stayed with them there for three days. And then I went to Jacksville. Yawk City, too. That was enormous. It stretched over – well, from well north of where Boston is today to well south of Washington – that was what they called Yawk City.

I never believed that, when he said it, said Jim, interrupting himself. I knew he didn't. If he had I think he'd have bought land somewhere along there and held for a rise in value. I know Jim. He'd have the idea that seven million years was something like seven hundred, and maybe his great-grandchildren would be able to sell it.

Anyway, went on Jim, he said it was all because the cities had spread so. Boston spread south. Washington, north. And Yawk City spread all over. And the cities between grew into them.

And it was all one vast machine. It was perfectly ordered and perfectly neat They had a transportation system that took me from the North End to the South End in three minutes. I timed it. They had learned to neutralize acceleration.

Then I took one of the great space liners to Neptune.

There were still some running. Some people, you see, were coming the other way.

The ship was huge. Mostly it was a freight liner. It floated up from Earth, a great metal cylinder three quarters of a mile long, and a quarter of a mile in diameter. Outside the atmosphere it began to accelerate. I could see Earth dwindle. I have ridden one of our own liners to Mars, and it took me, in 3048, five days. In half an hour on this liner Earth was just a star, with a smaller, dimmer star near it. In an hour we passed Mars. Eight hours later we landed on Neptune. M'reen was the city. Large as the Yawk City of my day – and no one living there.

The planet was cold and dark – horribly cold. The sun was a tiny, pale disk, heatless and almost lightless. But the city was perfectly comfortable. The air was fresh and cool, moist with the scent of growing blossoms, perfumed with them. And the whole giant metal framework trembled just slightly with the humming, powerful beat of the mighty machines that had made and cared for it.

I learned from records I deciphered, because of my knowledge of the ancient tongue that their tongue was based on, and the tongue of that day when man was dying, that the city was built three million, seven hundred and thirty thousand, one hundred and fifty years after my birth. Not a machine had been touched by the hand of man since that day.

Yet the air was perfect for man. And the warm, rose-silver glow hung in the air here and supplied the only illumination.

I visited some of their other cities where there were men. And there, on the retreating outskirts of man's domain, I first heard the Song of Longings, as I called it.

And another, The Song of Forgotten Memories. Listen:

He sang another of those songs. There's one thing I know, declared Jim. That bewildered note was stronger in his voice, and by that time I guess I pretty well understood his feelings. Because, you have to remember, I heard it only secondhand from an ordinary man, and Jim had heard it from an eye-and-ear witness that was not ordinary, and heard it in that organ voice. Anyway, I guess Jim was right when he said: 'He wasn't any ordinary man.' No ordinary man could think of those songs. They weren't right. When he sang that song, it was full of more of those plaintive minors. I could feel him searching his mind for something he had forgotten, something he desperately wanted to remember – something he knew he should have known – and I felt it eternally elude him. I felt it get further away from him as he sang. I heard that lonely, frantic searcher attempting to recall that thing – that thing that would save him.

And I heard him give a little sob of defeat – and the song ended. Jim tried a few notes. He hasn't a good ear for music – but that was too powerful to forget. Just a few hummed notes. Jim hasn't much imagination, I guess, or when that man of the future sang to him he would have gone mad. It shouldn't be sung to modern men; it isn't meant for them. You've heard those heart-rending cries some animals give, like human cries, almost? A loon, now – he sounds like a lunatic being murdered horribly.

That's just unpleasant. That song made you feel just exactly what the singer meant – because it didn't just sound human – it was human. It was the essence of humanity's last defeat, I guess. You always feel sorry for the chap who loses after trying hard. Well, you could feel the whole of humanity trying hard – and losing. And you knew they couldn't afford to lose, because they couldn't try again.

He said he'd been interested before. And still not wholly upset by these machines that couldn't stop. But that was too much for him.

I knew after that, he said, that these weren't men I could live among. They were dying men, and I was alive with the youth of the race. They looked at me with the same longing, hopeless wonder with which they looked at the stars and the machines. They knew what I was, but couldn't understand.

I began to work on leaving.

It took six months. It was hard because my instruments were gone, of course, and theirs didn't read in the same units. And there were few instruments, anyway. The machines didn't read instruments; they acted on them. They were sensory organs to them.

But Reo Lantal helped where he could. And I came back.

I did just one thing before I left that may help. I may even try to get back there sometime. To see, you know.

I said they had machines that could really think? But that someone had stopped them a long time ago, and no one knew how to start them?

I found some records and deciphered them. I started one of the last and best of them and started it on a great problem. It is only fitting it should be done. The machine can work on it, not for a thousand years, but for a million, if it must.

I started five of them actually, and connected them together as the records directed.

They are trying to make a machine with something that man had lost. It sounds rather comical. But stop to think before you laugh. And remember that Earth as I saw it from the ground level of Neva City just before Reo Lantal threw the switch.

Twilight – the suns has set. The desert out beyond, in its

mystic, changing colors. The great, metal city rising straight-walled to the human city above, broken by spires and towers and great trees with scented blossoms. The silvery-rose glow in the paradise of gardens above.

And all the great city-structure throbbing and humming to the steady gentle beat of perfect, deathless machines built more than three million years before – and never touched since that time by human hands. And they go on. The dead city. The men that have lived, and hoped, and built – and died to leave behind them those little men who can only wonder and look and long for a forgotten kind of compan-ionship. They wander through the vast cities their ancestors built, knowing less of them than the machines themselves.

And the songs. Those tell the Story best, I think. Little, hopeless, wondering men amid vast unknowing, blind machines that started three million years before – and just never know how to stop. They are dead – and can't die and be still.

So I brought another machine to life, and set it to a task which, in time to come, it will perform.

I ordered it to make a machine which would have what man had lost. A curious machine.

And then I wanted to leave quickly and go back. I had been born in the first full light of man's day. I did not belong in the lingering, dying glow of man's twilight.

So I came back. A little too far back. But it will not take me long to return – accurately this time.

'Well, that was his story,' Jim said. 'He didn't *tell* me it was true – didn't say anything about it. And he had me thinking so hard I didn't even see him get off in Reno when we stopped for gas.

'But – he wasn't an ordinary man,' repeated Jim, in a rather belligerent tone.

Jim claims he doesn't believe the yarn, you know. But he does; that's why he always acts so determined about it when he says the stranger wasn't an ordinary man.

No, he wasn't, I guess. I think he lived and died, too, probably, sometime in the thirty-first century. And I think he saw the twilight of the race, too.

Night

Condon was staring through the glasses with a face tense and drawn, all his attention utterly concentrated on that one almost invisible speck infinitely far up in the blue sky, and saying over and over again in the most horribly absent-minded way, 'My Lord, my Lord—'

Suddenly he shivered and looked down at me, sheer agony in his face. 'He's never coming down. Don, he's never coming down—'

I knew it, too – knew it as solidly as I knew the knowledge was impossible. But I smiled and said: 'Oh, I wouldn't say that. If anything, I'd fear his coming down. What goes up comes down.'

Major Condon trembled all over. His mouth worked horribly for a moment before he could speak. 'Talbot – I'm scared I – I'm horribly scared. You know – you're his assistant – you know he's trying to defeat gravity. Men aren't meant to – it's wrong – wrong—'

His eyes were glued on those binoculars again, with the same terrible tensity, and now he was saying over and over in that absent-minded way, 'Wrong – wrong – wrong—'

Simultaneously he stiffened, and stopped. The dozen or so other men standing on that lonely little emergency field stiffened; then the major crumpled to the ground. I've never before seen a man faint, let alone an army officer with a DS medal. I didn't stop to help him, because I knew something had happened. I grabbed the glasses.

Far, far up in the sky was that little orange speck – far, where there is almost no air, and he had been forced to wear a stratosphere suit with a little alcohol heater. The broad, orange wings were overlaid now with a faint-glowing, pearl-gray light. And it was falling. Slowly, at first, circling aimlessly downward. Then it dipped, rose, and somehow went into a tail spin.

It was horrible. I know I must have breathed, but it didn't seem so. It took minutes for it to fall those miles, despite the speed. Eventually it whipped out of that tail spin – through sheer speed, whipped out and into a power dive. It was a ghastly, flying coffin, hurtling at more than half a thousand miles an hour when it reached the Earth, some fifteen miles away.

The ground trembled, and the air shook with the crash of it. We were in the cars and roaring across the ground long before it hit. I was in Bob's car, with Jeff, his laboratory technician – Bob's little roadster he'd never need again. The engine picked up quickly, and we were going seventy before we left the field, jumped a shallow ditch and hit the road-the deserted, concrete road that led off toward where he must be. The engine roared as Jeff clamped down on the accelerator. Dimly, I heard the major's big car coming along behind us.

Jeff drove like a maniac, but I didn't notice. I knew the thing had done ninety-five but I think we must have done more. The wind whipped tears in my eyes so I couldn't be sure whether I saw mounting smoke and flame or not. With Diesel fuel there shouldn't be – but that plane had been doing things it shouldn't. It had been trying out Carter's antigravity coil.

We shot up the flat, straight road across wide, level country, the wind moaning a requiem about the car. Far ahead I saw the side road that must lead off toward where Bob should be, and lurched to the braking of the car, the whine and sing of violently shrieking tires, then to the skidding corner. It was a sand road; we slithered down it and for all the lightness and power, we slowed to sixty-five, clinging to the seat as the soft sand gripped and clung.

Violently Jeff twisted into a branching cow path, and somehow the springs took it. We braked to a stop a quarter of a mile from the plane.

It was in a fenced field of pasture and wood lot. We leaped the fence, and raced toward it: Jeff got there first, just as the major's car shrieked to a stop behind ours.

The major was cold and pale when he reached us. 'Dead,' he stated.

And I was very much colder and probably several times as pale. 'I don't know!' I moaned. 'He isn't there!'

'Not there!' The major almost screamed it. 'He must be – he has to be. He has no parachute – wouldn't take one. They say he didn't jump—'

I pointed to the plane, and wiped a little cold sweat from my forehead. I felt clammy all over, and my spine prickled. The solid steel of the huge Diesel engine was driven through the stump of a tree, down into the ground perhaps eight or nine feet, and the dirt and rock had splashed under that blow like wet mud.

The wings were on the other side of the field, flattened, twisted straws of dural alloy. The fuselage of the ship was a perfect silhouette – a longitudinal projection that had flattened in on itself, each separate section stopping only as it hit the ground.

The great torus coil with its strangely twined wrappings of hair-fine bismuth wire was intact! And bent over it, twisted, utterly wrecked by the impact, was the main-wing stringer – the great dural-alloy beam that supported most of the ship's weight in the air. It was battered, crushed on those hair-fine, fragile bismuth wires – and not one of them was twisted or misplaced or so much as skinned. The back frame of the ponderous Diesel engine – the heavy supercharger was the anvil of that combination – was cracked and splintered. And not one wire of the hellish bismuth coil was strained or skinned or displaced.

And the red pulp that should have been there – the red pulp that had been a man – wasn't. It simply wasn't there at all. He hadn't left the plane. In the clear, cloudless air, we could see that. He was gone.

We examined it, of course. A farmer came, and another, and looked, and talked. Then several farmers came in old, dilapidated cars with their wives and families, and watched.

We set the owner of the property on watch and went away – went back to the city for workmen and a truck with a derrick. Dusk was falling. It would be morning before we could do anything, so we went away.

Five of us – the major of the army air force, Jeff Rodney, the two Douglass Co. men whose names I never remembered and I – sat in my – our – room. Bob's and Jeff's and mine. We'd been sitting there for hours trying to talk, trying to think, trying to remember every little detail, and trying to forget every ghastly detail. We couldn't remember the detail that explained it, nor forget the details that rode and harried us.

And the telephone rang. I started. Then slowly got up and answered. A strange voice, flat and rather unpleasant, said: 'Mr. Talbot?'

'Yes.'

It was Sam Gantry, the farmer we'd left on watch. 'There's a man here.'

'Yes? What does he want?'

'I dunno. I dunno where he came from. He's either dead or out cold. Gotta funny kind of an aviator suit on, with a glass face on it. He looks all blue, so I guess he's dead.'

'Lord! Bob! Did you take the helmet off?' I roared.

'No, sir, no – no, sir. We just left him the way he was.'

'His tanks have run out. Listen. Take a hammer, a wrench, anything, and break that glass faceplate! Quick! We'll be there.'

Jeff was moving. The major was, too, and the others. I made a grab for the half-empty bottle of Scotch, started out, and ducked back into the closet. With the oxygen bottle under my arm I jumped into the crowded little roadster just as Jeff started it moving. He turned on the horn, and left it that way.

We dodged, twisted, jumped and stopped with jerks in traffic, then leaped into smooth, roaring speed out toward the farmer's field. The turns were familiar now; we scarcely slowed for them, sluing around them. This time Jeff charged through the wire fence. A headlight popped; there was a shrill scream of wire, the wicked *zing* of wire scratching across the hood and mud guards, and we were bouncing across the field.

There were two lanterns on the ground; three men carried others; more men squatted down beside a still figure garbed in a fantastic, bulging, airproof stratosphere suit.

They looked at us, open-mouthed as we skidded to a halt, moving aside as the major leaped out and dashed over with the Scotch. I followed close behind with the oxygen bottle.

Bob's faceplate was shattered, his face blue, his lips blue and flecked with froth. A long gash across his cheek from the shattered glass bled slowly. The major lifted his head without a word, and glass tinkled inside the helmet as he tried to force a little whisky down his throat.

'Wait!' I called. 'Major, give him artificial respiration, and this will bring him around quicker – better.' The major nodded, and rose, rubbing his arm with a peculiar expression.

'That's cold!' he said, as he flipped Bob over, and straddled his back. I held the oxygen bottle under Bob's nose as the major swung back in his arc, and let the raw, cold oxygen gas flow into his nostrils.

In ten seconds Bob coughed, gurgled, coughed violently, and took a deep shuddering breath. His face turned pink almost instantly under that lungful of oxygen, and I noticed with some surprise that he seemed to exhale almost nothing, his body absorbing the oxygen rapidly.

He coughed again; then: 'I could breathe a heck of a sight better if you'd get off my back,' he said. The major jumped up, and Bob turned over and sat up. He waved me aside, and spat. 'I'm – all right,' he said softly.

'Lord, man, what happened?' demanded the major.

Bob sat silent for a minute. His eyes had the strangest look – a hungry look – as he gazed about him. He looked at the trees beyond and at the silent, watching men in the light of the lanterns; then up, up to where a myriad stars gleamed and danced and flickered in the clear night sky.

'I'm back,' he said softly. Then suddenly he shivered, and looked horribly afraid. 'But – I'll have to be – then – too.'

He looked at the major for a minute, and smiled faintly. And at the two Douglass Co. men. 'Your plane was all right. I started up on the wings, as arranged, went way up, till I thought surely I was at a safe height, where the air wasn't too dense and the field surely wouldn't reach to Earth. Lord! – reach to Earth! I didn't guess how far that field extended. It touched Earth – twice.

'I was at forty-five thousand when I decided it was safe, and cut the engine. It died, and the stillness shocked me. It was so quiet. So quiet.

'I turned on the coil circuit, and the dynamotor began to hum as the tubes warmed up. And then – the field hit me. It paralyzed me in an instant. I never had a chance to break the circuit, though I knew instantly something was wrong – terribly wrong. But the very first thing it did was to paralyze me, and I had to sit there and watch the instruments climb to positions and meanings they were never meant for.

'I realized I alone was being affected by that coil – I alone, sitting directly over it. I stared at the meters and they began to fade, began to seem transparent, unreal. And as they faded into blankness I saw clear sky beyond them; then for a hundredth of a second, like some effect of persistence of vision, I thought I saw the plane falling, twisting down at incredible speed, and the light faded as the Sun seemed to rocket suddenly across the sky and vanish.

'I don't know how long I was in that paralyzed condition, where there was only blankness – neither dark nor light, nor time nor any form – but I breathed many times. Finally, form crawled and writhed into the blankness, and seemed to solidify beneath me as, abruptly, the blankness gave way to a dull red light. I was falling.

'I thought instantly of the forty-five thousand feet that lay between me and the solid Earth, and stiffened automatically in terror. And in the same instant I landed in a deep blanket of white snow, stained by the red light that lighted the world.

'Cold. Cold – it tore into me like the fang of a savage animal. What cold! The cold of ultimate death. It ripped through that thick, insulated suit and slashed at me viciously, as though there were no insulation there. I shivered so violently I could scarcely turn up the alcohol valves. You know I carried alcohol tanks and catalyst grids for heating, because the only electric fields I wanted were those of the apparatus. Even used a Diesel instead of gas engine.

'I thanked the Lord for that then. I realized that whatever had happened I was in a spot indescribably cold and desolate. And in the same instant, realized that the sky was black. Blacker than the blackest night, and yet before me the snow field stretched to infinity, tainted by the blood-red light, and my shadow crawled in darker red at my feet.

'I turned around. As far as the eye could see in three directions the land swept off in very low, very slightly rolling hills, almost plains – red plains of snow dyed with the dripping light of sunset, I thought.

'In the fourth direction, a wall – a wall that put the Great Wall of China to shame – loomed up half a mile – a blood-red wall that had the luster of metal. It stretched across the horizon, and looked a scant hundred yards away, for the air was utterly clear. I turned up my alcohol burners a bit more and felt a little better.

'Something jerked my head around like a giant hand – a sudden thought. I stared at the Sun and gulped. It was four times – six times – the size of the Sun I knew. And it wasn't setting. It was forty-five degrees from the horizon. It was red. Blood-red. And there wasn't the slightest bit of radiant heat reaching my face from it. That Sun was cold.

'I'd just automatically assumed I was still on Earth, whatever else might have happened, but now I knew I couldn't be. It must be another planet of another sun – a frozen planet – for that snow was frozen air. I knew it absolutely. A frozen planet of a dead sun.

'And then I changed even that. I looked up at the black sky above me, and in all the vast black bowl of the heavens, not three-score stars were visible. Dim, red stars, with one single sun that stood out for its brilliance – a yellowish-red sun perhaps a tenth as bright as our Sun, but a monster here. It was another – a dead – space. For if that snow was frozen air, the only atmosphere must have been neon and helium. There wasn't any hazy air to stop the light of the stars, and that dim, red sun didn't obscure them with its light. The stars were gone.

'In that glimpse, my mind began working by itself; I was scared.

'Scared? I was so scared I was afraid I was going to be sick. Because right then I knew I was never coming back. When I felt that cold, I'd wondered when my oxygen bottles would give out, if I'd get back before they did. Now it was not a worry. It was simply the limiting factor on an already-determined thing, the setting on the time bomb. I had just so much more time before I died right there.

'My mind was working out things, working them out all by itself, and giving answers I didn't want, didn't want to know about. For some reason it persisted in considering this was Earth, and the conviction became more and more fixed. It was right. That was Earth. And it was old Sol. Old – old Sol. It was the time axis that coil distorted – not gravity at all. My mind worked that out with a logic as cold as that planet.

'If it was time it had distorted, and this was Earth, then it had distorted time beyond imagining to an extent as meaningless to our minds as the distance a hundred million light years is. It was simply vast – incalculable. The Sun was dead. The Earth was dead. And Earth was already, in our time, two billion years old, and in all that geological time, the Sun had not changed measurably. Then how long was it since my time? The Sun was dead. The very stars were dead. It must have been, I thought even then, billions on billions of years. And I grossly underestimated it.

'The world was old – old – old. The very rocks and ground radiated a crushing aura of incredible age. It was old, older than – but what is there? Older than the hills? Hills? Gosh, they'd been born and died and been born and worn away again, a million, a score of million times! Old as the stars? No, that wouldn't do. The stars were dead – then.

'I looked again at the metal wall, and set out for it, and the aura of age washed up at me, and dragged at me, and tried to stop this motion when all motion should have ceased. And the thin, unutterably cold wind whined in dead protest at me, and pulled at me with the ghost hands of the million million million that had been born and lived and died in the countless ages before I was born.

'I wondered as I went. I didn't think clearly; for the dead aura of the dead planet pulled at me. Age. The stars were dying, dead. They were huddled there in space, like decrepit old men, huddling for warmth. The galaxy was shrunk. So tiny, it wasn't a thousand light years across; the stars were separated by miles where there had been light years. The magnificent, proudly sprawling universe I had known, that flung itself across a million million light years, that flung radiant energy through space by the millions of millions of tons was – gone.

'It was dying – a dying miser that hoarded its last broken dregs of energy in a tiny cramped space. It was broken and shattered. A thousand billion years before the cosmical constant had been dropped from that broken universe. The cosmical constant that flung giant galaxies whirling apart with ever greater speed had no place here. It had hurled the universe in broken fragments, till each spattered bit felt the chill of loneliness, and wrapped space about itself, to become a universe in itself while the flaming galaxies vanished.

'That had happened so long ago that the writing it had left in the fabric of space itself had worn away. Only the gravity constant remained, the hoarding constant, that drew things together, and slowly the galaxy collapsed, shrunken and old, a withered mummy.

'The very atoms were dead. The light was cold; even the red light made things look older, colder. There was no youth in the universe. I didn't belong, and the faint protesting rustle of the infinitely cold wind about me moved the snow in muted, futile protest, resenting my intrusion from a time when things were young. It whinnied at me feebly, and chilled the youth of me.

'I plodded on and on, and always the metal wall retreated, like one of those desert mirages. I was too stupefied by the age of the thing to wonder; I just walked on.

'I was getting nearer, though. The wall was real; it was fixed. As I drew slowly nearer, the polished sheen of the wall died and the last dregs of hope died. I'd thought there might be some one still living behind that wall. Beings who could build such a thing might be able to live even here. But

I couldn't stop then; I just went on. The wall was broken and cracked. It wasn't a wall I'd seen; it was a series of broken walls, knitted by distance to a smooth front.

'There was no weather to age them, only the faintest stirring of faint, dead winds – winds of neon and helium, inert and uncorroding – as dead and inert as the universe. The city had been dead a score of billions of years. That city was dead for a time ten times longer than the age of our planet to-day. But nothing destroyed it. Earth was dead – too dead to suffer the racking pains of life. The air was dead, too dead to scrape away metal.

'But the universe itself was dead. There was no cosmic radiation then to finally level the walls by atomic disintegration. There had been a wall – a single metal wall. Something – perhaps a last wandering meteor – had chanced on it in a time incalculably remote, and broken it. I entered through the great gap. Snow covered the city – soft, white snow. The great red sun stood still just where it was. Earth's restless rotation had long since been stilled – long, long since.

'There were dead gardens above, and I wandered up to them. That was really what convinced me it was a human city, on Earth. There were frozen, huddled heaps that might once have been men. Little fellows with fear forever frozen on their faces huddled helplessly over something that must once have been a heating device. Dead perhaps, since the last storm old Earth had known, tens of billions of years before.

'I went down. There were vastnesses in that city. It was huge. It stretched forever, it seemed, on and on, in its deadness. Machines, machines everywhere. And the machines were dead, too. I went down, down where I thought a bit of light and heat might linger. I didn't know then how long death had been there; those corpses looked so fresh, preserved by the eternal cold.

'It grew dark down below, and only through rents and breaks did that bloody light seep in. Down and down, till I was below the level of the dead surface. The white snow persisted, and then I came to the cause of that final, sudden death. I could understand then. More and more I had puzzled, for those machines I'd seen I knew were far and beyond anything we ever conceived – machines of perfection, self-repairing, and self-energizing, self-perpetuating. They could make duplicates of themselves, and duplicate other, needed machines; they were intended to be eternal, everlasting.

'But the designers couldn't cope with some things that were beyond even their majestic imaginations – the imaginations that conceived these cities that had lived beyond – a million times beyond – what they had dreamed. They must have conceived some vague future. But not a future when the Earth died, and the Sun died, and even the universe itself died.

'Cold had killed them. They had heating arrangements, devices intended to maintain forever the normal temperature despite the wildest variations of the weather. But in every electrical machine, resistances, balance resistances, and induction coils, balance condensers, and other inductances. And cold, stark, spatial cold, through ages, threw them off. Despite the heaters, cold crept in colder – cold that made their resistance balances and their induction coils superconductors! That destroyed the city. Superconduction – like the elimination of friction, on which all things must rest. It is a drag and a thing engineers fight forever. Resistance and friction must finally be the rest and the base of all things, the force that holds the great bed bolts firm and the brakes that stop the machines when needed.

'Electrical resistance died in the cold and the wonderful machines stopped for the replacement of defective parts. And when they were replaced, they, too, were defective. For what months must that constant stop – replacement – start – stop – replacement have gone on before, at last defeated forever, those vast machines must bow in surrender to the inevitable? Cold had defeated them by defeating and removing the greatest obstacle of the engineers that built them – resistance.

'They must have struggled forever – as we would say – through a hundred billion years against encroaching harshness of nature, forever replacing worn, defective parts. At last, defeated forever, the great power plants, fed by dying atoms, had been forced into eternal idleness and cold. Cold conquered them at last.

'They didn't blow up. Nowhere did I see a wrecked machine; always they had stopped automatically when the defective resistances made it impossible to continue. The stored energy that was meant to re-start those machines after repairs had been made had long since leaked out. Never again could they move, I knew.

'I wondered how long they had been, how long they had gone on and on, long after the human need of them had vanished. For that vast city contained only a very few humans at the end. What untold ages of lonely functioning perfection had stretched behind those at-last-defeated mechanisms?

'I wandered out, to see perhaps more, before the necessary end came to me, too. Through the city of death. Everywhere little self-contained machines, cleaning machines that had kept that perfect city orderly and neat stood helpless and crushed by eternity and cold. They must have continued functioning for years after the great central power stations failed, for each contained its own store of energy, needing only occasional recharge from the central stations.

'I could see where breaks had occurred in the city, and, clustered about those breaks were motionless repair machines, their mechanisms in positions of work, the debris cleared away and carefully stacked on motionless trucks. The new beams and plates were partly attached, partly fixed and left, as the last dregs of their energy were fruitlessly expended in the last, dying attempts of that great body to repair itself. The death wounds lay unmended.

'I started back up. Up to the top of the city. It was a long climb, an infinite, weary climb, up half a mile of winding ramps, past deserted, dead homes; past, here; and there, shops and restaurants; past motionless little automative passenger cars.

'Up and up, to the crowning gardens that lay stiff and brittle and frozen. The breaking of the roof must have caused a sudden chill, for their leaves lay green in sheaths of white, frozen air. Brittle glass, green and perfect to the touch. Flowers, blooming in wonderful perfection showed still; they didn't seem dead, but it didn't seem they could be otherwise under the blanket of cold.

'Did you ever sit up with a corpse?' Bob looked up at us – through us. 'I had to once, in my little home town where they always did that. I sat with a few neighbors while the man died before my eyes. I knew he must die when I came there. He died – and I sat there all night while the neighbors filed out, one by one, and the quiet settled. The quiet of the dead.

'I had to again. I was sitting with a corpse then. The corpse of a dead world in a dead universe, and the quiet didn't have to settle there; it had settled a billion years ago, and only my coming had stirred those feeble, protesting ghosts of eon-dead hopes of that planet to softly whining protest – protest the wind tried to sob to me, the dead wind of the dead gases. I'll never be able to call them inert gases again. I know. I know they are dead gases, the dead gases of dead worlds.

'And above, through the cracked crystal of the roof, the dying suns looked down on the dead city. I couldn't stay there. I went down. Down under layer after layer of buildings, buildings of gleaming metal that reflected the dim, blood light of the Sun outside in carmine stains. I went down and down, down to the machines again. But even there hopelessness seemed more intense. Again I saw that agonizing struggle of the eternally faithful machines trying to repair themselves once more to serve the masters who were dead a million million years. I could see it again in the frozen, exhausted postures of the repair machines, still forever in their hopeless endeavors, the last poor dregs of energy spilled in fruitless conflict with time.

'It mattered little. Time himself was dying now, dying with the city and the planet and the universe he had killed.

'But those machines had tried to hard to serve again – and failed. Now they could never try again. Even they – the deathless machines – were dead.

'I went out again, away from those machines, out into the illimitable corridors, on the edge of the city. I could not penetrate far before the darkness became as absolute as the cold. I passed the shops where goods, untouched by time in this cold, still beckoned those strange humans, but humans for all that; beckoned the masters of the machines that were

232

no more. I vaguely entered one to see what manner of things they used in that time.

'I nearly screamed at the motion of the thing in there, heard dimly through my suit the strangely softened sounds it made in the thin air. I watched it stagger twice – and topple. I cannot guess what manner of storage cells they had – save that they were marvelous beyond imagination. That stored energy that somehow I had released by entering was some last dreg that had remained through a time as old as our planet now. Its voice was stilled forever. But it drove me out – on.

'It had died while I watched. But somehow it made me more curious. I wondered again, less oppressed by utter death. Still, some untapped energy remained in this place, stored unimaginably. I looked more keenly, watched more closely. And when I saw a screen in one office, I wondered. It was a screen. I could see readily it was television of some type. Exploratively, I touched a stud. Sound! A humming, soft sound!

'To my mind leaped a picture of a system of these. There must be – interconnected – a vast central office somewhere with vaster accumulator cells, so huge, so tremendous in their power once, that even the little microfraction that remained was great. A storage system untouchable to the repair machines – the helpless, hopeless power machines.

'In an instant I was alive again with hope. There was a strange series of studs and dials, unknown devices. I pulled back on the stud I had pressed, and stood trembling, wondering. Was there hope?

'Then the thought died. What hope? The city was dead. Not merely that. It had been dead, dead for untold time. Then the whole planet was dead. With whom might

233

I connect? There were none on the whole planet, so what mattered it that there was a communication system?

'I looked at the thing more blankly. Had there been – how could I interpret its multitudinous devices? There was a thing on one side that made me think of a telephone dial for some reason. A pointer over a metal sheet engraved with nine symbols in a circle under the arrow of the pointer. Now the pointer was over what was either the first or the last of these.

'Clumsily, in these gloves, I fingered one of the little symbol buttons inlaid in the metal. There was an unexpected click, a light glowed on the screen, a lighted image! It was a simple projection – but what a projection! A three-dimensional sphere floated, turning slowly before my eyes, turning majestically. And I nearly fell as understanding flooded me abruptly. The pointer was a selector! The studs beneath the pointer I understood! Nine of them. One after the other I pressed, and nine spheres – each different – swam before me.

'And right there I stopped and did some hard thinking. Nine spheres. Nine planets. Earth was shown first – a strange planet to me, but one I knew from the relative size and the position of the pointer must be Earth – then, in order, the other eight.

'Now – might there be life? Yes. In those nine worlds there might be, somewhere.

'Where? Mercury – nearest the Sun? No, the Sun was too dead, too cold, even for warmth there. And Mercury was too small. I knew, even as I thought, that I'd have one good chance because whatever means they had for communication wouldn't work without tremendous power. If those incredible storage cells had the power for even one shot, they had no more. Somehow I guessed that this apparatus might incorporate no resistance whatever. Here would be only very high frequency alternating current, and only condensers and inductances would be used in it. Super-cooling didn't bother them any. It improved them. Not like the immense direct-current power machinery.

'But where to try? Jupiter? That was big. And then I saw what the solution must be. Cold had ruined these machines, thrown them off by making them too-perfect conductors. Because they weren't designed to defend themselves against spatial cold. But the machines – if there were any – on Pluto for instance, must originally have been designed for just such conditions! There it had always been cold. There it always would be cold.

'I looked at that thing with an intensity that should have driven my bare eyesight to Pluto. It was a hope. My only hope. But – how to signal Pluto? They could not understand! If there were any "they."

'So I had to guess – and hope. Somehow, I knew, there must be some means of calling the intelligent attendant, that the user might get aid. There was a bank of little studs – twelve of them – with twelve symbols, each different, in the center of the panel, grouped in four rows of three. I guessed. Duodecimal system.

'Talk of the problems of interplanetary communication! Was there ever such a one? The problem of an anachronism in the city of the dead on a dead planet, seeking life somewhere, somehow.

'There were two studs, off by themselves, separate from the twelve – one green, one red. Again I guessed. Each of these had a complex series of symbols on it, so I turned the pointer on the right to Pluto, wavered, and turned it to

Neptune. Pluto was farther. Neptune had been cold enough; the machines would still be working there, and it would be, perhaps, less of a strain on the dregs of energy that might remain.

'I depressed the green symbol hoping I had guessed truly, that red still meant danger, trouble and wrongness to men when that was built – that it meant release and cancellation for a wrongly pressed key. That left green to be an operative call signal.

'Nothing happened. The green key alone was not enough. I looked again, pressed the green key and that stud I had first pressed.

'The thing hummed again. But it was a deeper note now, an entirely different sound, and there was a frenzied clicking inside. Then the green stud kicked back at me. The Neptune key under the pointer glowed softly; the screen began to shimmer with a grayish light. And, abruptly, the humming groaned as though at a terrific overload; the screen turned dull; the little signal light under Neptune's key grew dim. The signal was being sent – hurled out.

'Minute after minute I stood there, staring. The screen grew very slowly, very gently duller, duller. The energy was fading. The last stored driblet was being hurled away – away into space. "Oh," I groaned, "it's hopeless – hopeless to—"

'I'd realized the thing would take hours to get to that distant planet, traveling at the speed of light, even if it had been correctly aligned. But the machinery that should have done that through the years probably had long since failed for lack of power.

'But I stood there till the groaning motors ceased altogether, and the screen was as dark as I'd found it, the signal light black. I released the stud then, and backed away, dazed by the utter collapse of an insane hope. Experimentally I pressed the Neptune symbol again. So little power was left now, that only the faintest wash of murky light projected the Neptune image, little energy as that would have consumed.

'I went out. Bitter. Hopeless. Earth's last picture was long, long since painted – and mine had been the hand that spent Earth's last poor resource. To its utter exhaustion, the eternal city had strived to serve the race that created it, and I, from the dawn of time had, at the end of time, drained its last poor atom of life. The thing was a thing done.

'Slowly I went back to the roof and the dying suns. Up the miles of winding ramp that climbed a half mile straight up. I went slowly – only life knows haste – and I was of the dead.

'I found a bench up there – a carved bench of metal in the midst of a riot of colorful, frozen flowers. I sat down, and looked out across the frozen city to the frozen world beyond, and the freezing red Sun.

'I do not know how long I sat there. And then something whispered in my mind.

'"We sought you at the television machine."

'I leaped from the bench and stared wildly about me.

'It was floating in the air – a shining dirigible of metal, ruby-red in that light, twenty feet long, perhaps ten in diameter, bright, warm orange light gleaming from its ports. I stared at it in amazement.

'"It – it worked!" I gasped.

'"The beam carried barely enough energy to energize the amplifiers when it reached Neptune, however," replied the creature in the machine.

'I couldn't see him – I knew I wasn't hearing him, but somehow that didn't surprise me.

'"Your oxygen has almost entirely given out, and I believe

your mind is suffering from lack of oxygen. I would suggest you enter the lock; there is air in here."

'I don't know how he knew, but the gauges confirmed his statement. The oxygen was pretty nearly gone. I had perhaps another hour's supply if I opened the valves wide – but it was a most uncomfortably near thing, even so.

'I got in. I was beaming, joyous. There was life. This universe was not so dead as I had supposed. Not on Earth, perhaps, but only because they did not choose! They had space ships! Eagerly I climbed in, a strange thrill running through my body as I crossed the threshold of the lock. The door closed behind me with a soft *shush* on its soft gaskets, locked, and a pump whined somewhere for a moment; then the inner door opened. I stepped in – and instantly turned off my alcohol burners. There was heat – heat and light and air!

'In a moment I had the outer lacings loose, and the inner zipper down. Thirty seconds later I stepped out of the suit, and took a deep breath. The air was clean and sweet and warm, invigorating, fresh-smelling, as though it had blown over miles of green, Sun-warmed fields. It smelled alive, and young.

'Then I looked for the man who had come for me. There was none. In the nose of the ship, by the controls, floated a four-foot globe of metal, softly glowing with a warm, golden light. The light pulsed slowly or swiftly with the rhythm of his thoughts, and I knew that this was the one who had spoken to me.

'"You had expected a human?" he thought to me. "There are no more. There have been none for a time I cannot express in your mind. Ah, yes, you have a mathematical means of expression, but no understanding of that time, so it is useless. But the last of humanity was allowed to end before the Sun changed from the original G-O stage – a very, very long time ago."

'I looked at him and wondered. Where was he from? Who – what – what manner of thing? Was it an armor-encased living creature or another of the perfect machines?

'I felt him watching my mind operate, pulsing softly in his golden light. And suddenly I thought to look out of the ports. The dim red suns were wheeling across those ports at an unbelievable rate. Earth was long since gone. As I looked, a dim, incredibly dim, red disk suddenly appeared, expanded – and I looked in awe at Neptune.

'The planet was scarcely visible when we were already within a dozen millions of miles. It was a jeweled world. Cities – the great, perfect cities – still glowed. They glowed in soft, golden light above, and below, the harsher, brighter blue of mercury vapor lighted them.

'He was speaking again. "We are machines – the ultimate development of man's machines. Man was almost gone when we came.

'"With what we have learned in the uncounted dusty megayears since, we might have been able to save him. We could not then. It was better, wiser, that man end than that he sink down so low as he must, eventually. Evolution is the rise under pressure. Devolution is the gradual sinking that comes when there is no pressure – and there is no end to it. Life vanished from this system – a dusty infinity I cannot sort in my memory – my type memory, truly, for I have complete all the memories of those that went before me that I replace. But my memory cannot stretch back to that time you think of – a time when the constellations—

'"It is useless to try. Those memories are buried under

others, and those still buried under the weight of a billion centuries.

'"We enter" – he named a city; I cannot reproduce that name – "now. You must return to Earth though in some seven and a quarter of your days, for the magnetic axis stretches back in collapsing field strains. I will be able to inject you into it, I believe."

'So I entered that city, the living city of machines, that had been when time and the universe were young.

'I did not know then that, when all this universe had dissolved away, when the last sun was black and cold, scattered dust in a fragment of a scattered universe, this planet with its machine cities would go on – a last speck of warm light in a long-dead universe. I did not know then.

'"You still wonder that we let man die out?" asked the machine. "It was best. In another brief million years he would have lost his high estate. It was best.'

'"Now we go on. We cannot end, as he did. It is automatic with us."

'I felt it then, somehow. The blind, purposeless continuance of the machine cities I could understand. They had no intelligence, only functions. These machines – these living, thinking, reasoning investigators – had only one function, too. Their function was slightly different – they were designed to be eternally curious, eternally investigating. And their striving was the more purposeless of the two, for theirs could reach no end. The cities fought eternally only the blind destructiveness of nature; wear, decay, erosion.

'But their struggle had an opponent forever, so long as they existed. The intelligent – no, not quite intelligent, but something else – curious machines were without opponents. They had to be curious. They had to go on investigating.

And they had been going on in just this way for such incomprehensible ages that there was no longer anything to be curious about. Whoever, whatever designed them gave them function and forgot purpose. Their only curiosity was the wonder if there might, somewhere, be one more thing to learn.

'That – and the problem they did not want to solve, but must try to solve, because of the blind functioning of their very structure.

'Those eternal cities were limited. The machines saw now the limit, and saw the hope of final surcease in it. They worked on the energy of the atom. But the masses of the suns were yet tremendous. They were dead for want of energy. The masses of the planets were still enormous. But they, too, were dead for want of energy.

'The machines there on Neptune gave me food and drink – strange, synthetic foods and drinks. There had been none on all the planet. They, perforce, started a machine, unused in a billion years and more, that I might eat. Perhaps they were glad to do so. It brought the end appreciably nearer, that vast consumption of mine.

'They used so very, very little, for they were so perfectly efficient. The only possible fuel in all the universe is one – hydrogen. From hydrogen, the lightest of elements, the heaviest can be built up, and energy released. They knew how to destroy matter utterly to energy, and could do it.

'But while the energy release of hydrogen compounding to the heavy elements is controllable, the destruction of matter to energy is a self-regenerative process. Started once, it spreads while matter lies within its direct, contiguous reach. It is wild, uncontrollable. It is impossible to utilize the full energy of matter.

'The suns had found that. They had burned their hydrogen until it was a remnant so small the action could not go on.

'On all Earth there was not an atom of hydrogen – nor was there on any planet, save Neptune. And there the store was not great. I used an appreciable fraction while I was there. That is their last hope. They can see the end now.

'I stayed those few days, and the machine is came and went. Always investigating, always curious. But there is in all that universe nothing to investigate save the one problem they do not want to solve – the problem they are sure they cannot solve.

'The machine took me back to Earth, set up something near me that glowed with a peculiar, steady, gray light. It would fix the magnetic axis on me, on my location, within a few hours. He could not stay near when the axis touched again. He went back to Neptune, but a few millions of miles distant, in this shrunken mummy of the solar system.

'I stood alone on the roof of the city, in the frozen garden with its deceptive look of life.

'And I thought of that night I had spent, sitting up with the dead man. I had come and watched him die. And I sat up with him in the quiet. I had wanted some one, any one to talk to.

'I did then. Overpoweringly it came to me I was sitting up in the night of the universe, in the night and quiet of the universe, with a dead planet's body, with the dead, ashen hopes of countless, nameless generations of men and women. The universe was dead, and I sat up alone – alone in the dead hush.

'Out beyond, a last flicker of life was dying on the planet

Neptune – a last, false flicker of aimless life, but not life. Life was dead. The world was dead.

'I knew there would never be another sound here. For all the little remainder of time. For this was the dark and the night of time and the universe. It was inevitable, the inevitable end that had been simply more distant in my day – in the long, long-gone time when the stars were mighty lighthouses of a mighty space, not the dying, flickering candles at the head of a dead planet.

'It had been inevitable then; the candles must burn out for all their brave show. But now I could see them guttering low, the last, fruitless dregs of energy expiring as the machines below had spent their last dregs of energy in that hopeless, utterly faithful gesture – to attempt the repair of the city already dead.

'The universe had been dead a billion years. It had been. This, I saw, was the last radiation of the heat of life from an already-dead body – the feel of life and warmth, imitation of life by a corpse. Those suns had long and long since ceased to generate energy. They were dead, and their corpses were giving off the last, lingering life-heat before they cooled.

'I ran. I think I ran – down away from the flickering, red suns in the sky. Down to the shrouding blackness of the dead city below, where neither light, nor heat, nor life, nor imitation of life bothered me.

'The utter blackness quieted me somewhat. So I turned off my oxygen valves, because I wanted to die sane, even here, and I knew I'd never come back.

'The impossible happened! I came to with that raw oxygen in my face. I don't know how I came – only that here is warmth and life.

'Somewhere, on the far side of that bismuth coil, inevitable still, is the dead planet and the flickering, guttering candles that light the death watch I must keep at the end of time.'